BuZz MonKeY

BuZz MonKeY

SAM HILL

An Otto Penzler Book

————

CARROLL & GRAF PUBLISHERS
NEW YORK

BUZZ MONKEY

An Otto Penzler Book
Carroll & Graf Publishers
An Imprint of Avalon Publishing Group Inc.
161 William St., 16th Floor
New York, NY 10038

First Carroll & Graf edition 2003

Library of Congress Cataloging-in-Publication Data is available.

ISBN: 0-7867-1261-9

Interior design by Simon M. Sullivan
Printed in the United States of America
Distributed by Publishers Group West

Dedicated to my friends
Phil, Guy, and Bill

BuZz MonKeY

CHAPTER 1

As usual, I woke early. That's the problem with having a bedroom that used to be the basketball court of an elementary school. A row of large frosted windows perches all around the top of high cinder-block walls. On this winter morning, soft gray light oozed through the glass and spilled down the walls, where it had puddled and leaked onto me. I could of course have had the windows replaced or put in some sort of curtain, but the truth is I like the room as is.

I have not even had the floor refinished where the shiny shellac had yellowed, making the pine underneath a dark brown and turning what had once been brightly painted red lines into a roan brown. Above the bed in the rafters hang two old satin banners proclaiming Winterville the regional basketball champ. Bleachers stand folded against the wall, a Nautilus machine and Stairmaster sit on a mat in one corner, and the large bed is stuck right in the center of the tip-off circle. Beside the bed is a small table with a stack of books, a remote control for the lights, and a cordless phone.

Once a week or so, a few old friends from the university drive

1

out for a game of half-court three on three, and we just carry the bed and the table down to the end that houses the exercise equipment and park it there until we are done. We move it carefully so as not to scratch the floor. Being able to play half-court basketball in your bedroom is one of the perks of owning your own school.

On this morning, I opened one eye and squinted through the half-light at the large clock hung over the door. Through the wire mesh, the face read 7:31. In an hour or so, Polymath, Inc. would start waking up. I would hear cars rolling up in the gravel lot outside, and the big doors would begin slamming just as they had fifty years ago when the school had been home to four hundred children. Phones would start ringing. And I would spend another boring day with thirty boring librarians, who insisted on being called researchers, doing boring searches for boring companies. Please God, let us get a tough one today, I had prayed silently. Let us get a real stinker that takes more than a grade-six education and five minutes on the Internet. I rolled over and pulled the pillow over my head.

Gently I felt the bed sag beside me as someone sat down. With the pillow over my head, I didn't hear Gillie coming. This straight life is making me dull, I thought. I have to get back out soon. Gillie is my office manager, one hundred and eighty pounds, five ten, gorgeous. I pulled the pillow down so I could see her bright blue eyes, dark brown shoulder-length curls and a complexion appropriate to a maiden name of Marcianello. This morning she wore orange from lips to toes.

"Morning, boss," she said.

Just as I did every morning, dressed or undressed, I said, "Good morning, Gillie. How are George and the kids?"

"Good," she said, "Robbie got a valentine from a little heartbreaker named Linda Parrington and is walking around in a fog.

The baby's tooth is still coming in. We were up all night with her. George's George." They were an odd pair, make-up-for-lost-time Gillie and laid-back George. She said she loved him, and was loyal in her own way.

I knew she would not have come in this early without a reason. "What's up?" I asked.

"I stopped by the office and saw a message from Shaw's on the E-mail," she said.

I yawned. "Oh, look at that," she teased. "He's too cool to admit he's excited."

I rolled over and closed my eyes and suddenly knew I'd had the dream again, without remembering, just knowing. Behind me she laughed and I felt the bed rise as she stood. Her heels clicked on my precious hardwood. I had been taught in gym class to never, ever walk on a court in street shoes. But when I said that to Gillie, she just laughed and dared me to find a scuff from her shoes. And she was right—I never had. I heard her stop and the clicks came closer. She knelt on the bed and placed one hand on my shoulder. In a soft singsong, she whispered in my ear, "Can't fool me."

The heels clicked again, this time without interruption. As soon as I heard the metal door close, I swung quickly to my feet. Slipping my underwear on, I padded to the door labeled "Boy's Locker Room." Inside I saw Benny, the other member of my management team.

Benny and his two-man crew, EJ and Dice, take care of the place, from patching the old roof and bush-hogging the lawn to fixing computers and pulling new T-3 lines when we convert a classroom into another research station. T-3s are the highest-speed data lines available today. A site that takes a minute to download on the Gateway at home, we can pull down in one-tenth of a second. He is a small black man, as scrawny as a distance runner and has an uneven wispy mustache and goatee. All he wore on this morning was a white towel around his waist and a pair of shower thongs.

"'Ood 'orning, 'op," he said around the toothbrush. Since it used to be an elementary school, the sinks come up to about midthigh. We brushed in comfortable companionship for a moment. It always makes me feel a bit odd to realize that Gillie and Benny and the thirty-five employees of Polymath depend on me for their livelihood. Plus the network of freelancers spread from Key West to Anchorage. And the part-time accountant, and the travel agent. It feels sometimes like I feed half of Athens, Georgia.

But of course it's just an illusion that comes when the payroll is tight. The university feeds Athens, Georgia, and most of my staff are moonlighters from the huge research libraries there. But not Gillie and Benny. For them, Polymath pays the bills. Like me, Benny lives at the school, but in the old band wing. My friends come to play ball, his to practice brass instruments.

I started Polymath because people who do what I do need a way to show income. You can't just live well and pay cash in today's world. The quickest way to show up on the radar screen of the IRS is not to show up. A routine check on a traffic ticket can end up causing an audit. It's happened.

Some of us own bars or laundromats or record stores. Me, I own Polymath, although Gillie is the legal president and Benny the board secretary. Polymath, Gillie, and Benny are all squeaky legit. Surprisingly the business has done pretty well—certainly far better than I ever intended.

The name "Polymath" means someone who knows everything, is an expert in a number of fields. That's what we do. I started it in college completing footnotes for dissertations and term papers, then found out that corporate downsizing had created a need on a far larger scale. The big publishing houses no longer have real editors and fact checkers. Now they have only what are known as acquiring editors—that is, staffers who spend their day on the phone trying to convince Madonna to let them have some hack ghostwrite a diet book with her name on it. The publishing houses—even the good ones—send letters to authors telling them that it is their responsibility to check the facts, so the authors call us. As do the big consulting firms, the law firms, newspapers, and just about anyone who cares about being right.

Each day the researchers at Polymath answer an average of two hundred questions. Most of these are pretty simple: Mark Twain never said, "if I had more time I would have written a shorter letter," Blaise Pascal did. American authors invariably attribute all quotes to Twain just as all British writers do to Wilde. Most of the time the inquiries are relatively mundane, correcting, attributing, and dating the same hundred quotes over and over and over again. A few are difficult and fun. But dull or interesting, together they pay the mortgage on the school and allow me to show a forty thousand-dollar salary each year to the IRS. And it pays Gillie, EJ, Dice, and Benny nice salaries.

On the shelf in front of Benny sat a straight razor, white pearl with inlaid garnets and rubies, a gaudy thing that he claimed once belonged to Huddie Ledbetter, better known as Leadbelly, the convicted murderer with the voice so sweet that the governor of Mississippi pardoned him. It would not surprise me if Benny put a bit more blood on it during his years on the Atlanta streets as what he called a "co and pro" guy. That stands for "collection and protection." Benny had worked for the drug dealers as a bodyguard cum tough guy, all hundred thirty-five pounds of him.

I heard a door open and out of the corner of my eye saw a brown coat. "Harlan," I said quietly. I needn't have bothered. Benny smoothly dropped a washcloth over the razor in a movement so fast you weren't sure you'd seen his hands move. One minute there had been a straight razor on the shelf. The next minute there was a white cloth with the faintest of ridges down the center.

"Good morning, gentlemen," Harlan said in that oily voice of his.

I grunted. Benny shot me a look and replied in his usual polite way. Harlan was one of those academics who thinks dressing in faux English makes you smarter. Today he wore a tan turtleneck, brown corduroy slacks, and a Harris tweed jacket with elbow patches. The clothes were off the rack, but Dr. Harlan Q. Winslow was tall and thin, with a mass of blond hair and a thin golden beard, and wore his clothes well. I didn't like him, but it seemed most of the faculty wives did and he had a formidable reputation as the campus lothario. He dropped a magazine and a book on the edge of one of the sinks and stepped up to a urinal. The book spine identified it as *Vanderbilt, Morgan and Gates: Secrets of the Great Wealthbuilders*.

"Whatcha readin' now, Harlan?" Benny asked. Harlan was passionate about becoming rich and read every magazine and book he could find on the topic. He was convinced that he had the right stuff to be a CEO/entrepreneur. The magazine, I could see now, was *Fortune Small Business*.

"Bill Gates, Benny. Do you know who he is?" smarmed the academic.

"No, who is he?" Benny lied in a deadpan tone.

"He's the world's richest man. And in this book he says the secret to building a great fortune is disintermediation. Do you know what that is?" Harlan said.

This conversation was taking on the tone of a visit to Mister Rogers' Neighborhood. "Can you say disintermediation, children?" I wondered how long this would go on before Benny snapped and shoved his head in a toilet. But Benny showed no signs of breaking. He smiled warmly at Harlan. "Disintermutation?"

"Disintermediation," corrected Harlan. He radiated patience. "It means cutting out the middleman. Going direct from the people who create the value to those who pay for it." He gave me a sidelong glance as he zipped up. "Well, time to dig my ton of coal. Ta-ta, gents." He left through the same door he'd entered. The door made a noisy clang that reverberated through the locker room.

"How do you put up with that?" I asked.

"It's an old school. We keep reworking the closing arms, but they leak too much air, so the door slams. Don't make them anymore, so we can't replace them. Anyway, the noise isn't so bad, except in a couple of the rooms," he said.

I knew he had misunderstood me deliberately. "I meant how do you put up with Harlan?"

Benny shrugged. "He's a supercilious fool. You can't kill fools— you know that. Harlan's a feeb, an educated feeb, but a feeb. This town is full of learned feebs. If you want me to kill them all, I'm going to have to talk to Gillie about some overtime."

Supercilious? I didn't show that I was proud of him, but I was. In the three years Benny had been here he'd steadily been working his way through our rather large library. A few weeks ago, he'd floated the idea of going to college. I was waiting for him to raise it again, afraid if I brought it up it might scare him away. "Well, he annoys the hell out of me," I said.

"When you go this long between trips, *everything* annoys the hell out of you."

"Thanks!"

"Don't be so touchy, Top. Anyway, looks to me like something is up and you'll be heading out soon anyway," he said equitably.

"You been talking to Gillie?" In every office in the world, the boss as a topic of conversation is the one constant.

"Nope, I can see the spring in your step and the gray fire in your eyes," he said.

I looked in the mirror and saw the same impassive stone face I always displayed. Nerves of steel. Unreadable sphinx. He must have been talking to Gillie. I rinsed the shaving foam from the razor and replaced it in the kit bag. I popped the kit in the first locker and headed for the showers. The second locker in the row held my two canes, which I still needed from time to time. A stack of white towels lay on one of the wooden benches, and I grabbed a couple as I walked by.

In the shower, I closed my eyes and leaned my head against the green tile wall, and let the water pour down over my back. One of the few changes I'd made was to raise one of the showerheads a foot and install a high-volume nozzle. Now hot, hot water flooded down my back and ran around to sluice off my chin. Gillie and Benny were right. I couldn't wait to get to the computer and see if Shaw's had a job for me. It was time for a trip.

CHAPTER 2

B Y THE TIME I FINISHED MY SHOWER, BENNY WAS GONE. He and Gillie would be powering up workstations and sorting the overnight inquiry stream by priority and research requirements in anticipation of the morning prep meeting.

From a locker, I selected the first elements of my normal work wear: a pair of Lee blue jeans and a clean T-shirt, pink, which bore a design with a hot pepper and the words "Chuey's, Austin, Texas." Chuey's serves what is arguably the best Tex-Mex food on the planet. On the back of the shirt was a picture of a dachshund and the slogan, "Beg all you want, you ain't getting any." A long-ago girlfriend had brought it over to sleep in. Since the Georgia sun had not yet begun to heat the old building, I added a red-and-gray plaid flannel shirt and a green Patagonia vest. A set of blue old-school Converse All Stars and I was ready to run the Polymath empire, such as it was.

I grabbed a cup of coffee and headed to my office, where Gillie and Benny were waiting with the inquiry list. The office used to belong to the principal, and is still much the same as it was in the late thirties. There are fourteen-foot ceilings and three large white globe lights that hang down on long cords. Waist-high dark brown tongue-and-groove wood runs all the way around the room. Above the wood, the inside wall is a long pane of frosted glass.

Gillie and Benny sat at a small round conference table in what was the nurse's office before I had the wall removed. Above their heads flickered four television screens, tuned permanently to CNN, BBC World News, CNBC, and the Cartoon Network. The light from the six outside windows, each of which starts about a foot above my waist and climbs almost to the ceiling, brightened the room. In the casements of the windows is a small rain forest of plants that I am not allowed to touch because they belong to Gillie. Bookcases fill the other wall; their middle shelves are devoted to my collection of tops.

Gillie frowned, "Do you dress with your eyes closed?"

"What's the stream look like?" I ignored the sarcasm and moved over to my desk to check E-mail. There were a dozen or so, two of which looked interesting. One was from Shaw's. The other was from Bob John Wynn.

"Busy day. Three hundred and eighty-four, but nothing that looks too hard," Gillie answered to my back. I only half-registered her answer.

As always, Shaw's was terse. A time, a place, and a name. The time was tomorrow, the place a bar in Atlanta, and the name was Soames. I stood quietly and reread the note carefully.

Soames did the sticky ones. For a moment, my excitement was tainted with a little shadow of apprehension, but only for a moment. I was going on a trip. A little riff of the buzz drifted across my consciousness, and I felt my tongue thicken.

"What's it look like?" I asked.

"You just asked me that, and I just answered you."

I pivoted and blinked at her. "Sorry. Just one more minute." She smiled indulgently. I turned back to the screen to check Bob John's E-mail. His E-mail was even more clipped than Shaw's—just a subject line that read "Urgent. Have you seen Dee Lane?"

I closed the mail window and clicked on the voice mail log, a program which automatically lists the number of everyone who calls my direct line, whether they leave a message or not. There were seven calls today, all from Bob John. After an internal debate, I decided not to call him back until I had a chance to call Dee Lane, and calling Dee Lane before noon was useless.

I walked over to the table and plopped down in an empty chair. Gillie refilled my cup from a thermos and we settled down to work through the inquiry stream. There was a bit of white dust on the handle of the thermos where she'd poured. There is often dust around. We are in a perpetual state of remodeling. She grimaced and pulled out a Kleenex from the box on the table and wiped the handle, and then her hands.

As usual, most were "I-read's" and quotes. An "I-read" is where someone says, "Last week I read a statistic that said blah blah blah, but I don't remember where. I think it was in *USA Today*." "I-reads" are tricky because the line or the source can be a hundred and eighty degrees off. *USA Today* can be the *Financial Times*. Last week can be last year. A statistic on the growth in aluminum can be about steel. Even if they are correct, it can be difficult to find them, especially if they are small points buried in larger articles or from obscure, poorly referenced sources. We have learned to keep a hard copy of the major airline magazines on hand just to source "I-reads." After a while, you develop a pretty good sixth sense for which ones are likely to be the most difficult, and we divide them among the staff appropriately.

Most of the rest were quote checks. Very few quotes are ever worded and sourced correctly the first time around. A few of the misattributions were funny. An up-and-coming young televangelist with the unlikely name of Munion Grubbs wanted to use the biblical quote, "The road to Hell is paved with good intentions," but couldn't find it in his *Thurman's Bible Encyclopedia*. With good reason—it was said by Karl Marx in 1867 in *Das Kapital*. It was tempting to let it go, but we resisted. Though not before Gillie got a case of the giggles so bad that she shook the table and my coffee spilled.

There were also a few apocryphals, including a request for the citation for the Everett Dirksen quote, "A billion here, a billion there, pretty soon you're talking about real money." Except he never said it—at least, according to the head of the Dirksen Library. We'd send them the standard page with the earliest attribution, which usually sufficed.

There were a dozen or so that were more difficult, and those we split between Harlan and Maggie Peterson. As we worked, out of habit, I wrapped a string around the blue peg top and sailed it over the rug and onto the worn oak flooring, where it thudded softly, then danced across the uneven surface. Every time it hit one of the ridges between the boards, it gave a little hop in the air.

About ten, they rose to leave. Gillie folded her hands together and interlacing her fingers, stretched to the ceiling. "Mmmm," she grunted, then dropped her hands and gave a little shake.

"Hey, Top," Benny said, "I have one."

"Tough?" I asked.

"Intractable," he said with a shadow of a smile.

"Put your money on the table," I said, pulling a wrinkled ten out of my jeans pocket.

Benny covered the bet. "Shoot," I said.

"This American system of ours, call it Americanism, call it Capitalism, call it what you like, gives each and every one of us a great opportunity if we only seize it with both hands and make the most of it," he said softly.

"Gillie, you want a shot?" I asked. Benny smiled, gaining confidence.

She pursed her lips. "Mikhael Gorbachev," she guessed.

"Not bad," I said, "Not bad." I waited a few seconds to give Benny the impression I was struggling. "But it was Al Capone."

"Really?" She looked at Benny.

He nodded, then dropped another ten on top of the two on the table. "Full cite?"

"He said it in 1929, but it first appeared in print in 1956, in an interview by Claud-without-an-e Cockburn," I put my hand over the pile of bills and raised my eyebrows.

Benny said to Gillie, "He's good." I stuffed the money in my shirt pocket.

"Yeah, but for God's sake don't tell him, it will just make him harder to live with." Gillie turned, picked up her stack of papers, and left with a finger wave. Benny stayed behind a moment.

"I heard a noise last night. Checked it out this morning. It looks like someone tried a couple of the doors last night," Benny said.

"Kids?"

"Probably," he answered. "You want me to turn on the klaxon?"

"Nah, if they set it off, it will wake up the neighborhood. I'll get up tonight and chase them off," I said.

"OK," he answered, and turned and left. I spent most of the morning drinking coffee and spinning the different tops, waiting for noon so I could call Dee Lane. And pacing, wondering what Shaw's had that required Soames to come to Atlanta.

Bob John called four more times, but I didn't pick up.

CHAPTER 3

A LITTLE BEFORE NOON, I CALLED DEE LANE, ON ALL SIX of the numbers I knew; office line, home line, fax line, car cell, personal cell, and answering service. There was no answer except at the service, and they were noncommittal on whether he was calling in to pick up messages or not. I left a page. While I was punching in my number, I saw a red flag come up on the corner of the screen, and with it an insistent ping. I hung up the phone, keyed an acknowledgment to Gillie, sighed, and moved over to the door, pulling it open before the knock came.

"Good morning, Top," Bob John Wynn said easily. He stood there with a stenographer's notebook and black two-way radio in one hand. The other hand held a lightweight, deep blue wind-breaker, and hung casually on his right side, where I could see the butt of his standard-issue nine-millimeter pistol sticking out of his belt holster. His DEA badge hung around his neck.

"Hey, Bob John, what's happening?" I stood in the doorway, blocking it. This was not the Bob John who came out to the gym to play ball, but the official Bob John, and I didn't want him in here. Along the Mississippi, the Army Corps of Engineers hires people to walk the levee, looking for damp spots on the side away from the river, places that will turn into leaks during floods. Bob John's presence, here in my office with a gun on his hip, was seepage between my two worlds.

"Ought to get your answering machine fixed," he said. I grunted. He looked over my shoulder casually. "You with someone? Mind if I come in?"

"Any chance it can wait until tonight?"

"No, not really, Top. Only take a few minutes—I promise."

"I'm right in the middle of sorting out the day's inquiry stream, and I've got a dozen or so people waiting on me to finish."

"Top, I need to talk to you now. It's important."

I sighed and swung open the door. If Bob John Wynn really wanted to come in, I was sure he could find a way to do it, probably by using that black radio to call a judge. Better not force the issue. He entered, looking around curiously, and raised an eyebrow toward the round table. I nodded. He walked over, pausing to take a long look at the big safe, and then sat down, only to spring straight up immediately.

"Shoot!" he barked. That was as profane as I'd ever heard Bob John become in the twenty-plus years we'd known each other.

"What?"

"I sat on something sharp." Rubbing his backside with one hand, he fished in the cushion with the other, pulling out a small red plastic Wham-O top with a sharp steel point.

"Are you all right?" I held my face straight.

"Go ahead and laugh. I would." He smiled. "Yeah, I'm OK. I won't sue you this time."

"You wouldn't get much if you did. Coffee?" I asked.

"Sure."

I poured a mug from the thermos left by Gillie. I left an inch of space at the top for his milk and sugar, then added both.

"That's it." He smiled. "Hasn't changed since we were Boy Scouts."

"'There is nothing in this world constant.' Jonathan Swift," I said and passed the cup across the desk. He sipped loudly.

"So what can I do for you, Bob John?"

He didn't answer, but crossed his legs and surveyed the room. "I'm always amazed by all these tops."

"One of those things," I answered and stopped.

"How many do you have in all?" he said.

"Never counted." My leg gave a jiggle, but I caught myself and stopped it.

Bob John swung his head from the tops to face me, "You seen Dee Lane lately?" DeWayne Lane, better known as Dee Lane, a semiregular at our weekly basketball games, and our friend since we three were in General Jackson Grade School.

"Two weeks ago at the game—same time you saw him." I said. "Why?" Strictly speaking, true, but I didn't mention that Dee Lane had left me a message late Friday. The message had been brief: "Top, brother. Need a little help. See you tomorrow." Benny and I had gone into town to watch the Lady Dogs play Tennessee, and Dee Lane had never shown.

"He's missing. Nobody's seen him since Saturday last. Athens PD drove by his house this morning, and his carport is empty."

I phrased my answer carefully, "Bob John, it's not real unusual for Dee Lane to disappear for a while, you know."

"You and I both know what Dee Lane does for a living, Top," he said. I did not react.

"He smuggles dope," Bob John said stubbornly.

17

"I'm out of all that."

"But now you're into something else," he said. I did not answer.

He watched me closely. "This time he may have gone too far. Lots of rumors on the street."

I couldn't picture Bob John on the street. To me, Bob John would always be the earnest and energetic president of the prom committee, last seen scurrying down lockered walls with stacks of posters under his arm and his hands filled with rolls of masking tape. But he was promoted quickly in the agency, and perhaps there was a Bob John I didn't know. All of us think of our friends as frozen in a time of our own choosing.

"What sorts of rumors?" I asked

"Are you all right? Do you need to take care of something?" Bob asked helpfully, "I can wait." He eyed the computers casually.

"No, that's OK," I said.

"You sure?"

"What sort of rumors?" I repeated.

He turned the top in his hand, not looking at me now. "You know Raoul Menes?"

"No. Should I?"

He looked at me quizzically, skepticism shining in his wide-open, friendly eyes. "I just figured you would have heard of him. He lives in Atlanta, runs all the coke in this part of the country. His father was one of the original five Colombian drug lords in the sixties, but he grew up in the States."

"Bob John, I'm out of that now. Have been for a long time. And I have to get back to work," I looked at my watch ostentatiously. I had nothing else to do, but I did not want to discuss Dee Lane with the DEA. Rule one is never talk to the police, ever. If you do, no matter how smart or careful you are, sooner or later you will tell them something that they can put together with something else and use against you.

Bob John ignored my impatience and continued. "Word is Dee Lane was moving a shipment for Raoul out of West Palm. Now the shipment is missing, duffel bag with a million and change is missing, and Dee Lane is missing."

"I never heard of Dee Lane shorting anyone in anything."

"There are witnesses that saw Dee Lane get onboard a small Falcon jet at Jax three days ago. That jet went about sixty miles offshore then dropped off radar. Coast Guard's been out looking, found some debris. So some people figure Dee Lane tried to cash out, ran for it, and something happened to the plane and now he's dead."

"Do you believe it?" I said.

"There's another story out there," he said evasively.

"What's that?" I said.

"That he booked for the Caribbean, flew low and slow, and shoved a load of garbage out the door, and is retired now," he answered.

"Why not? He's been talking about doing just that since we were sophomores in high school."

"Because he's not a rip-off artist, never has been. You said it. Because that mysterious duffel bag is missing. Because some folks say he gave Top Keirnan, his old high-school chum and smuggling buddy, the bag to hold for him, and that it's stashed in this old dump, and as big a sucker as you can be for your friends, I can't believe even you would be dumb enough to bring that sort of action down on your own doorstep." He watched me closely to see my reaction.

I started. "Does anybody really believe that?"

"Yeah, I think it's safe to say some do."

"Who?" I asked.

"Who do you think? Top, be careful. Get out of town for a while if you can. Things might get crazy around here."

CHAPTER 4

AFTER BOB JOHN LEFT, I WENT LOOKING FOR BENNY. I found him in a classroom we were converting to house research stations. He was on his back on the floor under a desk, screwing something onto the underside of the surface. His crew, two young African-American men named EJ and Dice, held the desktop while he worked.

"Hey, Top," Dice said. "What's up?"

"Morning, guys. Looking for the boss," I said. I gingerly knelt on the floor and peered under the desk. "Benny, when you get some time, could you come see me?"

"How about now?" he said, rolling out from under the desk and standing up. He meticulously brushed off his pants. He spoke to EJ, "Do every desk just like this one. Don't forget to put lock washers on every single bolt, OK?"

"Got it." EJ grinned.

"I mean it!" Benny warned.

"I said 'I got it.' Trust me, I got it. Lock washer on every bolt, put together just like this one," EJ answered.

Benny gave him a look, and turned back to me. We left the

classroom, and Benny said, "He will, too. EJ's turning into a good worker. Dice, though, I have to watch every minute. You want to go to your office?"

"Why don't we just walk the school?" I said. We have a standard weekly circuit, inside then out, an hour-long ramble that takes us to every nook and cranny of the old building. Usually when we walk it, Benny carries a clipboard and we make a list of what needs to be repaired next. We both enjoy the circuit, watching the school slowly come back to life as we work it. But, the to-do list never seems to shrink, despite the four of us working almost full time on it. Some days more than others, I also enjoy just the feeling of the place, the long shiny halls, the only light coming from the windows and doors at the end of the corridors. I almost expect a bell to ring at any moment, the doors to pop open, and hundreds of kids to swarm out into the halls, engulfing us.

I explained Bob John's visit.

"It sounds like you need to get out of town," he said.

"I've got a job offer. Might be good for a few weeks. But I'm worried about leaving with this Dee Lane stuff going on," I answered.

He shrugged. "I think we'll be OK."

"The system is designed to prevent break-ins. I'm more worried about somebody coming through the front door with a gun."

"Our ability to handle that is pretty good, too," he said.

"You know Menes. Ever work for him?" I asked.

Benny shook his head. "I worked mostly for Elbert Day. He and Menes are competitors. If you work for one, you don't work for the other. It's like Coke and Pepsi or Chevy and Ford. You're either an Elbert man or a Raoul man."

"What can you tell me about him?" I asked.

"What do you want to know? Number-one thing is that he is genuinely dangerous. He's Colombian and looks like a drug boss, but doesn't sound like it," Benny answered.

"Why not?"

"Went to some private school right near Atlanta. Top, Menes is no TV bad guy. Dude's completely off the wall. Very violent and totally unpredictable."

"Unpredictable as in using too much of his own product?" I asked.

"No, unpredictable as in psychotic."

"You think the thing with the doors last night might have been him?"

"Personally? Not likely. Raoul very seldom leaves Atlanta. He's paranoid, so he likes to stay close to home. Possible he sent someone."

"I wonder if we're in the middle of this thing, or just on the edges?"

"That was a rhetorical question, right?"

"Pretty much. This could all be some DEA game to catch Menes or Dee Lane, and we could just be part of the furniture."

"Or it could be genuine."

"Yup," I agreed.

We walked quietly for a few minutes. I stopped and pointed. "Look at that, there's a bubble on the plaster up near the trim. Same place as last time. That damn roof is leaking again, same spot. I think it's the seal around the standpipe."

"Too much tar on that seal for it to be leaking. I think we have a leak somewhere else, and it's running down the rafter and ending up here. Maybe it's still damp." He pulled a Nextel cell phone and radio off his belt and asked EJ to come down and bring a ladder and a flashlight. "Top, do what you think is best. We can take care of ourselves here."

"Thanks, Benny."

"Hey, Top," Benny said. "What do you want me to do about Harlan and this disintermediation stuff? You know he's trying to figure out how to steal a few clients and some researchers and go out on his own. He thinks you're making a mint here."

"Can he crack the codes?" When I set up Polymath, I'd anticipated just such a possibility and set up a software program that scrambled all the inquiries and all the answers. The same system distributed the inquiries so that no one client and researcher ever had too much contact.

"Harlan? He can't do the Monday puzzle in the *New York Times* without cheating," Benny snorted. Monday is the easiest. They get harder every day after that.

"What's his Ph.D. in?"

Benny answered, "Harlan doesn't have one. It's a doctorate of education, and it's in something like teaching the philosophy of art. No he's just being a pain in the butt, sneaking around the mail basket and trying to slip messages into his outbounds."

I thought a minute. "Let him find out the identity of 102."

Benny grinned. "Kenzie-Hamlin?"

"The one and only. We lose money on them anyway because they ask so many follow-ups. They're also cheap. If he offers them a twenty percent price cut, they'll drop us like a stone despite their contract. Let him have them," I said.

"So you figure he'll steal them, cut his price, and go broke. Disintermutate his own silly self. Then when they come crawling back, you can renegotiate the contract." Benny smiled.

"That's it."

Benny shook his head. "You're a trip, Top. Anybody else in the world would just fire the guy. You take this loyalty thing pretty far sometimes, don't you think?"

"That's rhetorical, right?"

CHAPTER 5

I LEFT BENNY AND RETURNED TO THE OFFICE, WHERE I opened the old safe, and pulled out a nine-millimeter SIG Sauer, legal, and put it into a shoulder holster which I put on over my T-shirt. Then I covered it with my flannel shirt and vest, making it a concealed weapon, and thus illegal. I slipped an additional clip in my back pocket. As I closed the safe and stood, my left leg, the weaker one, buckled, and I fell sideways, landing on my butt. The legs hated the morning cold, but loosened up as the day warmed up. I pulled myself up on the safe, and grabbed a walnut walking stick from the umbrella stand that stood by the door. Gingerly I made my way out to the shed and got in the truck.

Dee Lane's house is exactly 13.6 miles from the school, door to door. When I first moved here, the area between Winterville and Athens was mostly soybean fields and third-generation piney woods. Now, as soon as I crossed the railroad tracks, I found myself in suburbia, with stoplights every quarter mile and shopping centers on every corner. I don't know if it was the buzz or Bob John's warning but I drove erratically, varying speeds and making lots of turns with not a lot of signaling, and keeping a close eye on the rearview mirror. If I was being followed, they were too good for me to spot. Still, I took the most circuitous route I could think of to get to the other side of the city.

Dee Lane lives just inside the city limits of Athens proper, in a small brick home on Biscayne Drive in the neighborhood behind the new mall. Like most of the houses on the street, it was a split-level, three bedrooms, built back in the early seventies when 1500 square feet was a good-sized living space. The neighborhood felt empty, as it probably was. This was a working-class subdivision, mostly assistant professors and administrators at the university with teenagers who would be at school by now. Except for one brown older-model Oldsmobile two doors down, there were no cars parked anywhere on the drive. I drove by slowly. The carport was empty, and the house had a quiet, empty look about it. At the end of the street I turned around, drove back slowly, and parked in the driveway, with the front of the truck pointing toward the street.

I pulled my duplicate key off the ring as I walked up to the kitchen door. From about six feet away, though, I saw it was unnecessary. Someone had already punched out the lowest pane of glass, and the door stood slightly ajar. I took a step backward, quietly laid the walking stick on the cement floor of the carport and eased the SIG out of the holster, holding it against the side of my leg and away from the road.

There was no movement on the street, no curtains opening or flashes of movement at any of the windows. I moved carefully, keeping most of my weight on my stronger leg. With my left foot I poked at the door, it swung open. Just inside the door I could see the alarm panel, its wiry guts hanging halfway down the wall.

There was no sound in the house. Whoever did this had pulled the curtains. Beyond the kitchen, down in the little sunken area that was the TV room, burned a single bulb in a floor lamp from which the shade had been removed. It cast a stark yellow light over the room.

I pushed the door open slowly and stepped inside. My feet crunched on cereal, dumped in the center of the kitchen floor along with rice, flour, and lentils, the packages discarded against the railing that bordered the kitchen. My heart hammered against my eardrums, and I could feel the hairs on my arms standing on end feeling every breeze, acting as primeval sensory supplements. I caught a glimpse of a face out of the corner of my eye and swung the gun around, only to see my own grinning reflection in the glass of a cabinet front.

The searchers were long gone. The items from the freezer were piled in the sink, a soggy melted mess that was starting to smell. The searchers must have been here all night. Every cabinet had been emptied, cushions were sliced, books riffled and piled in a heap. In the center of every room was a small pyramid of broken and discarded items. If Bob John's cruiser had driven by this morning, they must have been in a hurry to get to the Krispy Kreme.

They'd used a hammer to punch holes in the wallboard, every twelve inches across the entire walls, giving it a strangely neat and planned appearance. Carpet was peeled up, and in a couple of places someone had used a crowbar to pry up the flooring. In the hall upstairs, the ladder was pulled down, and up top the six-inch pink insulation had been pulled up and shoved in a corner.

In Dee Lane's bedroom, the floor of the closet was ripped apart. Dee Lane kept a tiny safe there, which never held anything more than a twenty-five-year-old bottle of Macallan single malt. Someone had pulled it from the floor, using a chain saw to cut out the floor joists it was bolted to. The chain-saw, a small green electric Poulan Dee Lane kept to trim limbs, was discarded on the box springs.

I worked the house systematically, even getting a flashlight from the truck, going into the backyard and kneeling to peer into the crawl space. It was empty. Dee Lane's usual travel bags and black leather coats were gone. Whoever had searched the house hadn't bothered to take the chain saw or the television. All in all, I was in the house for just over an hour. When I came out, the Oldsmobile was gone and the street was completely empty.

CHAPTER 6

I HAD ONE MORE STOP TO MAKE. ONE DAY IN NOVEMBER, I'D been driving down Milledge, spotted red taillights ahead and decided to cut through the backstreets. And a few minutes later, out of the corner of my eye, I'd seen Dee Lane letting himself into a small downstairs apartment in a four-unit block usually rented out by students. I hadn't stopped. If Dee Lane had any idea anyone knew about his bolt-hole—even me—he'd feel compelled to move, and I didn't want to put him through the hassle. It was the merest of chances that I'd even seen it, since Dee Lane would not have visited his hole more than once a month, if that, and then just to check on things.

Again, I drove erratically, zigzagging across town, crossing my own trail and keeping one eye on my mirrors. Once I thought I saw a familiar brown car three cars back, remembered the empty Oldsmobile, and took a few extra turns, but didn't see it again. I parked on Milledge in a Subway parking lot. Opening the toolbox on the driver's side with a key, I pulled out a twelve-inch flat steel pry bar, which I slipped up my sleeve, cupping the dull end in my palm. I walked the three blocks to the apartments, moving slowly and using the stick, but the balky leg still ached by the time I got there.

Taking one last look around, I walked up to the front door and rang the doorbell. There was no answer. Gently I tapped on the cheap-looking front door. Instead of a hollow wooden thud, a deep metallic tink came back. Steel door. That felt like Dee Lane. Making a big show of it, I patted my pockets, looked under the doormat, then turned and walked across the thin lawn and around the building. If this was Dee Lane's bolt-hole, odds were good that his neighbors had no idea what he looked like, or if he had a roommate. I took one last glance around, popped open a window, quickly pried the security bars loose from the jamb, and boosted myself inside.

The place was empty, but clearly Dee Lane had been here. Three pairs of sunglasses sat on the cheap bureau. In the closet, I could see two long scuffed, black leather jackets. The furniture looked worn, suggesting that the place came furnished. Beside the bed was a stack of books and videotapes, and several suitcases of different styles and sizes were piled in the closet. I moved through the small place quickly. The bed was made with a sheet and blankets. In the bathroom, the towel racks were empty, but the seat of the toilet was down and on it sat a stack of white and green towels, still in their Target wrappers. The front room held a sofa, armchair, and a new stereo system, still in the box, but no Dee Lane. And no duffel bag. There were two massive dead bolts on the front door.

I peered out the front curtain to see if perhaps some neighbor had spotted me and called the cops. There was no cop car out there, but there was a dirty brown Oldsmobile. It was empty. Without hesitation, I reached for the SIG and spun. As I turned, my leg gave out and I crumpled, just as someone hit me in the back of the head with a soft heavy object. The sap bounced off my skull, just above the base of the spine, a good spot, but a glancing blow.

Blue fire exploded across my field of vision. To my scrambled senses, it seemed the floor was floating up to meet me. I stayed awake just long enough to feel my face hit the cheap carpeting and bounce slightly.

I woke up in the late afternoon, the sun already down behind the pines. I could hear someone still in the apartment with me and froze. Voices, one or two male, and one high-pitched. Probably female. Under me I could feel the hard lump of the SIG, my fingers still wrapped around the butt. Someone was confident in their work, hadn't even disarmed me. I rolled to one side and eased the gun out, but my lower arm was asleep, and the gun dropped from my lifeless fingers onto the carpet. A wave of nausea rose in my throat. I closed my eyes and fought it, and passed out again.

I woke again, just in time to hear the sound of a door, and a car starting. I pulled myself to the wall and using the back of the sofa for leverage, peeked over the edge of the windowsill. The brake lights of the Oldsmobile flashed briefly at the corner, then moved away.

It took a couple of attempts, but I finally focused on my watch, 5:47. I'd been out two hours. Not bad for a tap. A sap is a professional's weapon, and this had been applied professionally. If I had not been falling already, I'd still be out, and have more than a dull, thudding headache. I probed carefully with my fingertips. Nothing felt broken. Slowly I raised myself to a three-quarters stand and collapsed onto what was left of the sofa. An hour or so, and I'd be OK.

I looked around at the gutted furniture and piles of debris, and shook my head, disgusted at myself for leading them right to it. Closing my eyes, I massaged my temples.

CHAPTER 7

GILLIE LAY NAKED UNDER THE SHEET BESIDE ME, HER head propped up on one arm. On her hip was perched a half-empty Starbucks cup. The big clock over the door read 6:35. She had arrived a half hour ago.

"Oh, really. Don't worry about George," she said softly. "He gets all he wants and more."

"I'm not worrying about George," I lied.

"Yes, you are," she said, "but you shouldn't. Consider yourself an exercise machine, sort of horizontal aerobics."

"I feel so cheap," I answered. I lay on my back, looking up at the two banners, my hands behind my head.

"Oh, poor boy. You'll get over it." She smiled, then leaned over and kissed me gently on the forehead, holding the sheet pulled up over her large breasts. Through the whiteness of the cotton I could see two darker circles. I unlaced my hand, reached over and pulled the covering down. Sighing meaningfully, she tugged it back up, but I pulled it down again. She curled her lip and shook her head, but this time she left it bunched around her waist. A coffee brown ringlet fell across her face and she twisted her mouth to try to blow it back up. It flew up, and flopped right back down onto her cheek. Using the hand with the coffee cup, she hooked the renegade curl with her little finger and tucked it back behind an ear.

"You know," she said. "I hate to say it, but you're a lot of fun when you get ready for a trip. You get so cranked."

"I do not."

"Sure." She smiled and looked at me closely. "What's the matter?"

"The Dee Lane thing." I hadn't told her about Dee Lane's apartment. I levered myself up on one arm and touched the spot behind my left ear surreptitiously. A spike of pain shot into the base of my skull, and I locked my jaw to keep from grimacing.

"We're probably safer without you."

"Boy, you're full of ways to make a guy feel wanted this morning aren't you?" I feigned hurt.

"I thought I was, or weren't you paying attention?"

"Oh, that," I said.

"Yeah, that." She changed the subject. "So what do you think about you meeting the guy in Atlanta? You don't think it could involve Dee Lane, do you?"

"Shaw's doesn't ask you to work in your own backyard. Policy. I don't know what it means. Maybe nothing."

"The mysterious Shaw's." She injected a note of dramatic over-pronunciation into her voice, and smiled.

"They're unique—I'll give them that."

"You're unique." She took another hit of her latte.

"Thanks."

"It wasn't a compliment," she drawled.

"I know."

She didn't say anything else for a long time, just lay there, drinking the coffee. I watched her. "Gillie, what would you say if I hung it up?"

She looked at me closely and took a sip of coffee before answering. "I'd say fine, but you'd have to let me lay off people when work is slow, and you won't do that. And you'd have to find something to do so you didn't explode."

I nodded. The pain stabbed again and I closed my eyes. How could I explain the love of the buzz, that mix of adrenaline and the emotion when it all gets cooking. There's nothing like it. Even sex.

"Maybe we should think about it before too long, anyway," I said.

"Is that what's bothering you?"

"Nothing is bothering me!" I snapped.

"Sure."

"Bob John says no one has seen Dee Lane since Saturday. He usually calls."

"Maybe he just took off in a hurry. I was here Saturday working on invoices while you and Bennie went to the game. No calls," she said.

"Check the call logs when you get a chance, would you? See if maybe he called and hung up."

"Sure," she answered. I was half in love with Gillie, and I suspected, her with me. Or maybe not. She wanted more than a beat-up old school and refrigerator full of beer. Of course, there was more than that in our way. Like two kids and a hell of a nice guy named George. Sometimes after sex, it got awkward like this, all those other things wandering around the edge of the conversation, unsaid.

She finished her coffee, and just lay there smiling softly. A tear leaked out of a corner of her eye and began to roll over one of those prominent cheeks. She quickly caught it with the heel of her hand and wiped it away, and without hesitating stood up, gathered her clothes in her arms, then padded barefoot to the girls' locker room. She didn't look back. Her feet left faint steam prints on the cool shellacked floor that quickly faded. I watched her all the way.

I lay there for a few minutes with my eyes closed, trying to kill another fifteen minutes. But the buzz was too strong, so I got up and shaved and showered. A call from Shaw's usually meant you had to be there yesterday. Just in case, I packed my travel bag carefully and slowly, a process which took ten minutes and left me with an hour to kill. The legs felt better this morning. I balanced on my left leg and bounced softly. It held.

Too nervous to read, I peeled off my shirt and went over to the minigym in the corner, where I did squats with full weights for ten furious minutes until my thigh muscles began quivering and my breath shortened. Then, breaking the cardinal rule of weight lifting: one body part at a time, I worked pecs and abs for another fifteen minutes. Finally, I dragged myself back to the shower. My body was calmer, but my mind sang with the electrical buzz.

CHAPTER 8

TWO HOURS AFTER I'D RISEN, BENNY PULLED THE OFFICIAL Polymath truck, a white Ford F-150, around to the side door of the gym, and opened the passenger door. The rain came down in sheets. I stood just inside the door and watched it for a minute, waiting to see if it showed any signs of letting up. Finally I threw the bags across the gap and onto the seat. Benny wrestled them over into the cargo space of the extended cab. He motioned me to get in, and I dashed across the six feet and dove through the open door. I slammed the door, and leaned back, using my fingers as a towel to rake my face dry.

He slipped the truck into gear, turned us around, and we slowly splashed down the driveway. I saw Harlan stepping carefully around the puddles in the lot. Today he wore charcoal gray slacks, black shirt, with the top button buttoned, of course, and a dark sports coat. But the sartorial effect was spoiled by the Burberry plaid golf umbrella and black rubber shoe protectors, both of which seemed to me at odds with his reputation as a devil-may-care ladies' man. He didn't look up as we passed, too busy trying to stay dry.

Most of the ride was quiet. Benny was seldom chatty, nor did this early gray day encourage exuberance. The steady rain washed clay from the hillsides and filled the ditches with orange brown streams, their surface pockmarked with more raindrops. It would have been much redder in the old days, before the kudzu, the imported Chinese weed that now covered the entire state with its broad leaves. These days kudzu vines climbed every telephone pole and pine tree and smothered every unused building. The omnipresent growth threw a green blanket over abandoned cars rusting at the back of overgrown fields and sent ambitious tendrils creeping down into the ditches and toward the tarmac.

I bought the school just after Benny came to work at Polymath. Then the kudzu had completely covered the school. Most of the walls and part of the roof were completely overgrown, and it had taken us days of working shirtless in the hot sun to strip it off. Every time we scratched our arms on the ropy vines, we cursed the USDA bureaucrats who first brought it in seventy years ago. Overcultivation of cotton in the twenties left the South's topsoil depleted and naked from the Atlantic to the Gulf. The imported kudzu provided the ground some relief from the driving winter rains of north Georgia. Without it, this part of the country would be a wasteland.

Soon we turned from the two lanes of Voyles Road onto the four lanes of the Danielsville Highway, then on to 29. We skirted the northwest edge of Athens. Water sprayed up in twin wings as we glided along. The wipers beat a steady slow rhythm appropriate to the gray winter day. Benny drove carefully. Before the new highway that connected Athens to I-85, it could take two hours to reach Atlanta. Now it takes an hour.

An hour if you survive the ride. The four-lane is not a controlled-access highway, and many of the locals haven't yet come to terms with the improvements. Every so often we crested a hill to find an ancient pickup truck casually turning out into eighty-mile-an-hour traffic. On either side, through the tree line, we could see patches of cleared land where new Atlanta suburbs were beginning to spring up.

"What would you think if we buy this truck when the lease is up, and get a Lexus?"

Because he was so short, his half of the split-bench seat was pulled up four inches farther than mine and he turned his head half around to look at me, causing him to drop two wheels off onto the shoulder. But with his reflexes, he smoothly nudged us back up on the concrete almost as soon as we heard the sound of the tires on the grooved sideway.

"You OK?" I asked.

"Oh, I'm OK. The only thing you ever spend money on is that old falling-down pile of bricks. You don't even own a decent pair of jeans. Lexus sounds like sixth-floor talk." Athens General has a large psych ward, referred to by locals by number because of its former location on the top floor of the hospital.

The rain stopped, and he switched off the wipers. But the day remained dark, and funnel-shaped wisps of cloud hung from the low ceiling and floated like lost ghosts across the top of the endless pine forests on either side. Water droplets shown on every pine needle and roadside sign. I angled my head to look up at the sky and wondered if the flights were on time.

I returned my attention to Benny. "Gillie has been telling me we ought to push on the client-development front. Bring some prospects in, show them the operation, see if we can't grow a bit. Maybe she's right."

"Are you serious?" he asked. I looked away from him, eyeing the pine forest, now thinning out and giving way to the walls of subdivisions.

"Completely."

He thought about this for a while, then spoke again. "If we're going to get serious about Polymath, maybe I should postpone the school thing."

"No way."

"So you think it's still a good idea?"

"Go for it. Polymath will pick up the tab, give you time off, whatever it takes."

"I'm not asking you to pick up the bill."

"I know, but it's a good investment for us. You plan on leaving anytime soon?"

"No."

"Then it will help the firm for you to get a degree. Legitimate business expense," I hid my pleasure at the news. "Anything we can do to help you get started? GED classes? References for your application?"

"I've already done all that. Received my GED in September and was accepted in November for the spring." He did a poor job of concealing his pride.

I hoped I did a better job of hiding mine. "Well, you sneaky dog!"

He smiled shyly. "If it didn't go well, I didn't want you trying to console me."

"Any idea what you'll study? Music?"

"Composition, I think," he answered.

"You start in the spring?"

"Fall. Does that work for you?"

"Sure, can't think why not." I smiled out the window where he couldn't see it.

"Hey, Top, do you believe this Dee Lane thing is genuine?"

"No idea. Maybe. Probably. No. I don't know. Shit, who knows? Bob John's DEA, could be a big elaborate game to trap Menes or Dee Lane."

"Menes is not a man to trifle with."

"So you say."

Benny spoke carefully. "I hate to broach this, Top, but would Dee Lane set you up?"

"Same answer, Benny. Who knows? But I doubt it. We've been through some real stuff together."

On the dashboard was a pair of wraparound Sinatra-style shades left there by Dee Lane a few months ago. He probably didn't miss them, since he had countless pairs—more than I had tops. He always carried one or two extra in the pockets of the long black coat he wore rain or shine, night or day, summer or winter. Dee Lane worked out the "Lane look" in high school: black jeans, black T-shirt and black calf-length leather jacket. He never wore the same pair of shades two days in a row. With his extreme height and thinness, dark clothes, thatch of wild blond hair, and goggled eyes, he looked like an exotic crane.

I looked up at the gray sky again, and fidgeted in my seat, not sure if my restlessness was the usual nervous anticipation before a trip or something else. "You know Dee Lane's a smuggler, right?"

Benny nodded, "There are rumors."

"Anyway, Dee Lane is big-time. Two, maybe three guys, in his league," I continued.

"Drugs?" Benny asked.

"Anything. Guns into Mexico, dope into the U.S. and Europe, computer chips out of Japan, jewels, paintings—you name it. Even smuggled a jet engine into Iraq. He's handled way more than a measly mil and a half. It doesn't make sense to me why he'd decide to grab and run now, and why he'd point it to me. That's not Dee Lane's style."

"He certainly has style. No game, but style."

"You're just pissed because he dunked on you once."

"Took three steps."

"But he still did it."

"Top, you think somebody else might have taken him out and hung the chicken on you?"

"Where in the hell did you get that?" I said, my annoyance genuine and visible.

Benny turned to face me, and put on his most serious face. "Why the reminiscing, Top, unless you think it might not matter anymore?"

He had me there.

CHAPTER 9

W ELL, I'M GOING TO BE LATE. TELL THEM TO HOLD tight until I get there." Soames said into the mouthpiece, then snapped the small cell phone shut. He spoke in a soft, sweet South African accent, so the sentence came out "I'm geng ti bee late." "Sith Ifrica" was how he would have pronounced his birthplace. Soames is medium height, slightly overweight, and that day wore a nondescript gray suit with an open-necked white shirt. His red hair lay limply across his blotchy pink scalp. He has a long face defined by large, watery faded blue eyes and a narrow, straight nose. Between us, a battered black briefcase rested at our feet.

Like his suit, Soames himself blends in. Had I not known, I would have pegged him as a sales rep, maybe for a smallish industrial equipment firm, forty-five, two kids, his only excitement an occasional fiddle on his travel expense report. He looks just as he probably wants to look: unremarkable and uninteresting, the sort that should you find yourself sitting beside on the plane, would cause you to deliberately avoid eye contact and open the novel you'd bought at the newsstand. But Soames worked for Shaw's, the world's leading booking agency for mercenaries, bodyguards, and probably worse.

As always, he had a cigarette in his left hand. He held it in orange-stained fingertips about six inches from the thin slit that was his mouth. When that one went, he would light another off the butt. He smoked them quickly, deep drags that created a quarter-inch of glowing ash with each inhalation. Like most chain smokers, he timed his sentences to match his exhalations, and every word came out with a puff of smoke around it. The ashtray was full between us, suggesting he had been here awhile, and two packs of Benson & Hedges sat neatly stacked in front of him. The lighter that lay beside the packs was a battered steel Zippo, with the SAS wings and sword emblem on the side. It was hard to imagine Soames as an operative. Perhaps he bought the thing in a souvenir shop at Heathrow.

Danny's Bar and Grill is a T-shaped room. We sat at a round table in the center of the long part of the T, midway between the bar and the entrance way. Danny's is a neutral zone, a place that the intelligence agencies, police, and criminals have designated as a meeting place for those who in other circumstances would have been at each other's throats. Legend had it that CIA brokered the Noriega deal with the Cubans here, paying them a small fortune to sit by quietly.

The room was very dark. The only illumination came from the red neon strip that ran over the bar and a thin white glow that sliced down the middle of the heavy black curtains separating the entry vestibule from the main room. Once my eyes adjusted, I could make out maybe twenty-five tables in the place, and half were taken. The two feet of smoke that hung in a thick layer across the room burned my eyes. But asking Soames to put out his cigarette would not have done any good, since everyone else in the place also seemed to be smoking madly, and his was a relatively minor contribution to the overall fug.

Two waitresses leaned against the bar, talking. Occasionally, they would park their cigarettes and drinks, pick up a dirty rag and a round plastic tray and amble over in response to a signal from one of the customers. The smaller of the waitresses was a stick, junkie-thin, with dyed blond hair attached to inch-long black roots, and the other was large and dark, Gillie's size and coloration, but looked nothing like her. Frick and Frack. The tables were occupied mostly by men.

"How do you fly?" I leaned over to hear his answer over the dull din of the conversation and tape playing in the background.

"Patches," Soames said, "Give me bloody nightmares, but keeps me from throttling the flight attendants." It came out, "Thret-tleeng the flit ittendents."

"Nightmares?"

"Yeah, the doctors say to wear them the whole trip, even while you sleep, but most of us don't smoke while we sleep, now, do we? So you wake up with these crazy dreams, sweating like a mule," he grumbled. "You ever smoked?"

"No."

"Smart man. Terrible bloody habit." Then, changing the subject, he asked, "So how are you?"

"I'm fine, Soames. How's business?"

"Business is always good. No real quality conflicts going at the moment, except that mess in the Horn, but we're doing a good business in bodyguarding. High margins, but terrible loss rate of staff." He said all this in the same conversational tone he would have used had he been manager of a fruit stand. "Bananas moving well, avocados a bit scarce this year."

There are many flavors of adrenaline buzz, from the low level one I now enjoyed to the peak full-on rush that makes you nauseous and gives little old ladies Ripley-like powers to lift rail cars. The mild euphoria I felt now seemed too much just to be excitement over the trip, but the sharpness of my vision and the dry mouth were signs I recognized well. Studies at Michigan have shown that even low levels of adrenaline increase light sensitivity by up to half, making it possible to see in the dark and extending your peripheral vision by up to 38 percent. Without shifting my head I could watch about 220 degrees of the room.

Out of the corner of my right eye I could see a table that held an older man, whose elegant European-cut suit, white cuffed shirt and silver tie looked out of place in the seedy atmosphere of Danny's. He was locked in earnest conversation with a thirty-something fellow who looked like a consultant or an investment banker: blue suit, white shirt and red tie, along with horn-rimmed glasses. The older man had a sharp, vulpine face with a sloping forehead and a chin that fell away below his small mouth. He wore his white hair slicked straight back. As I watched, this older man shook his head emphatically, shot his cuffs, and turned sideways at the table, crossing his legs as he turned. I shifted my eyes back smoothly to Soames, but he noticed the quick peek.

"The fellow with the pointy face is Gerald Morton. He's the CIA liason officer for the DEA. I wonder what he's doing here." said Soames.

"And the yuppie?" I asked.

"Not American. Russian, I'd suspect. The young ones all dress like that now. I don't know him, but the table nearest them has bodyguards. Those lads belong to him. Must be a heavy hitter for Danny to let him bring that sort in here." I didn't ask how he knew this, but I believed him.

Soames nodded toward the end of the bar, where a very large bouncer with slabs of muscle stood still, his hands out of sight beneath the bar. Standing beside him, a small, heavy red-faced man with wispy white hair surveyed the room. Danny looked a lot like the older Mickey Rooney, but with more chiseled features. His short snow-white hair stood on end around his head, where it caught the dim red light above the bar and gave him an odd scarlet halo. He smiled benignly as he gazed out on the room.

Soames said, "You know Danny's story, eh?"

I didn't answer. He continued anyway. "Bloodiest gunman of them all in the old IRA, lasted right up through the seventies. Imagine that if you're a young trooper in Belfast, getting your bloody face blown away by a wee old man who looks like Santa Claus."

"Soames, can we get to the assignment? I know Danny."

He pursed his lips to acknowledge my request, then said, "Ah, well, that's the thing, then. Settle down, Top, will you? I can feel you vibrating from here."

"What?"

"I've got a bit of bad news I'm afraid. Wanted to talk to you about it, face-to-face," he said. You couldn't hurry a Soames. He finished his beer and licked the foam off his upper lip. With an automatic motion, he lit another cigarette and stubbed out the old one in the overcrowded ashtray. I sat still, waiting for him to finish. Over the years I had learned more and more about the agency, snippets gathered in loose conversations in bars and in the back of trucks in Central American jungles and pieced together in the long recovery times after particularly painful outings. Soames was more than just another desk at Shaw's, he was the boss—or close to it. I held my breath and waited for the details of the assignment, which from his buildup, I could expect to be very dangerous. A little shiver of expectation tingled up the base of my scalp.

"There is no assignment," he said.

My heart lurched against the inside of my rib cage as if I'd stood on the brakes in the fast lane. I stared at him puzzled. "What do you mean, there's no assignment?" I asked. "It's been four months since Peru."

"It has taken us four months to clean that one up, Top. Eight people died and the corpse of one of our clients showed up on the front page of the *International Herald Tribune*."

"So you think that was my fault?"

"We think it was," he said without blinking. "Not on purpose, you know, but we think it was your fault in a way."

I held his stare. "That idiot husband promised me twenty-four hours. He waited four. We were walking out the front door free and clear when half the Peruvian police force showed up and started shooting. One of *them* shot the woman, not the guerrillas."

"An armored vehicle was on the way—surely you might have expected that. Perhaps you could have waited."

"She was dying, had minutes left, at most. It was only forty meters, and we had surprise on our side," I argued.

"She died, Top, and the girl was hit."

"What would you have done, Soames? Tell me that."

"I don't know. I really don't know. These things are never very clear. Something happened," he answered. His tone was expressionless and his face unreadable behind its smoky curtain. But his right hand shuffled the two packs of cigarettes now, rhythmically pulling the bottom one out, and when the upper one dropped onto the table, putting the lower one on top. His fish eyes watched me to see my reaction.

"Just for argument's sake, and if I did the only thing I could?" I pushed.

"It doesn't really matter. You've crossed the line, Top."

"What line?"

"The line between an effective field operative and a reckless one. Or, said more clinically, we think that you have become an adrenaline addict, that you've started taking risks that you don't need to take."

His face remained impassive, but the blotches on his scalp glowed a beet red now. I stared at his Adam's apple bobbing up and down like a knobby cork, and measured the distance to it from my table hand. I could kill him right now, and considered doing so, not caring about his damned SAS lighter or the goon behind the bar. Waves of blood rippled through my veins and crested under the thin skin of my temples. A red curtain hung around the edges of my vision. I could hear my breath rasping in my throat. I fought to regain control before speaking.

"I went into a very heavily armed compound in Lima to bring out two kidnap victims. I lost the mother, but I got the little girl out. They would have killed them both and you know it. Ransom or no ransom."

"Because of Peru, and because of Porto Allegre and Culiacan." He named the two assignments that preceded the one in Lima.

"So you think I've lost it?"

"Yes." A flash of sympathy passed over his face, then disappeared. He pulled his chair into the table and leaned across. "Look at yourself man. Your leg is shaking and your eyes are flying around like pinballs. You're dancing around like you've got a three-gram coke habit, man."

"I don't touch the stuff and you know it."

"Top, man, for God's sake. You're telegraphing your thoughts. I can read your eyes. I saw you almost lose it a minute ago. It took everything you've got to get control back, and you've been resting for four months. Do you think that's the sort of operative who makes good decisions? No, it's the sort that turns a simple retrieval into a bloody Waco."

"What's going on here, Soames? I'm the same man I was when you hired me," I pushed.

"Yes and no, Top. You're like all good field agents, high-strung with a taste for danger. But for some people, the taste grows. It's like any other addiction. As the tolerance builds, you start going farther and farther out to get the rush, and the assignments get more and more out of control. And then you die. The Force Recon psychs at Parris Island have a phrase for it: from buzz monkey to buzz junkie." he said. "If we keep booking you, sooner or later you will get Shaw's into serious trouble, and you will get yourself killed."

I clenched and unclenched my hand. "I need an assignment."

"I know," he said.

"I need to get out of town for a while. Dee Lane's got me hooked into something nasty. I've been told to get clear by people who know."

"So we've heard. Take a cruise," he answered.

"Don't screw with me, Soames."

"I'm not screwing with you, Top. I'm saving your life. Take some time off."

"How much time? Six months? A year? Forever?"

He didn't answer, just sat there, staring at me unblinkingly through the smoke. My glass was empty. I raised it in the air and waggled it. The stick waitress nodded and pointed to Soames. It was my turn to nod. She brought the two dark brews over, and set them down on the table. He lifted a bill off the small stack on the table and dropped it on the tray. She didn't even pretend to make change, just smiled thanks and moved away. I waited until she was out of earshot.

"And if I decline?"

"Nothing." He shrugged.

"What do you mean, nothing?"

"I mean nothing, Top. Do what you want to do. Work freelance, go back to the smuggling racket, whatever."

"Soames . . ."

"It's done, Top." He rose, leaving his last beer barely touched on the table. "There's an envelope in the briefcase, parting gift, call it. Give me fifteen minutes, will you?" He stood, and I watched his back as he shuffled away awkwardly. The hem was out on one side of his cheap suit jacket, and a flap of silk peeked out as he extended his arm to part the heavy black curtain.

CHAPTER 10

FOR A MOMENT, I PLAYED WITH THE IDEA OF TOSSING THE damn briefcase in a Dumpster unopened. But I needed twenty grand to replace the curtains in the auditorium. I stared at the damn thing, hating it. I drained the Guinness and motioned the heavier waitress over. "Bring me two Heinekens—enough of this Irish piss." She raised an eyebrow, but didn't say anything.

When she brought them, I gave her a ten. "Which way is the john?"

She jutted her jaw toward a spot over my left shoulder, "Past the end of the bar where Sid and Danny are standing." That made Sid the big bouncer. I drained one of my two beers and stood up, picking up the briefcase. I left the full one on the table. An old field trick to make them think you were coming back. Habit—I didn't really have any reason to do it. The waitress didn't appear surprised that I chose to take the briefcase to the bathroom with me.

It was a small bathroom, just one urinal and a toilet. There was no lock on the door, so I closed myself inside the stall. On my key ring was a tiny black flashlight. Holding it between my teeth, I aimed the beam at the combination lock. When I tried to open it, as expected, the latch did not move. I tried using my birthdate as the combination, with no luck, then tried 8-9-4, the date of my first assignment with Shaw's. Sure enough, the latch popped open.

The case did not hold cash, as I'd expected. Instead, inside were two manila envelopes and a smaller white business envelope with no markings on it. I shook the contents of the first out onto the bottom of the case. To my surprise, none of the three contained money. The white envelope held a single white typed sheet, folded three times. The two manila envelopes held fat clips of documents and photographs. I read the note first. In Shaw's fashion it was not long.

To: TK
From: MMS
Subject: Assignment 304.14.378

On Tuesday, Feb 17, a call was received requesting asset recovery assistance. The caller, an intermediary with whom we are familiar, said he represented an Atlanta businessman, with no previous history with the firm, but whose referral sources are impeccable. The asset to be recovered was described as a large sum of money, allegedly being held by the confederate of an ex-employee of the businessman. Terms were the standard 30 percent plus a termination bonus. Timing was immediate.

Upon hearing the specifics of the engagement, Shaw's elected to decline the assignment, citing conflict of interest. It is to be expected the prospective client will continue to seek resolution of this problem, using alternative resources.

Good luck.

S.

So that was my severance, Shaw's turning down a half million to retrieve Menes' money. It was hard to think of the grimly businesslike Shaw's affectionately, but for a moment I did. Nice gesture, Soames.

From habit, I tore the note from Shaw's into pieces and dropped it into the toilet. The other two envelopes both held files, thick files, stacks of copies of surveillance photos, arrest records, field reports, wiretap transcripts and memorandums detailing movements. The first and larger envelope held two files, both apparently DEA, one for Menes and one for Dee Lane. The documents were clearly copies, but good quality and judging from the copy lines on the edges of the page, were made from physical files, not electronic downloads. I don't know which surprised me more, the thickness and thoroughness of the copies, or that Shaw's had them. On the outside of Dee Lane's file was written in pencil: "No contact recently."

But I was surprised even more when I turned over the next clipped stack, because there was a grainy photo of a muscular man, hairline retreating slightly, early thirties, squinty gray eyes, and standard-issue smirk on his face. Of course, the face was mine.

CHAPTER 11

"AIRPORT?" BENNY ASKED AS I OPENED THE TRUCK DOOR. I pulled the files out from where I'd stuffed them in my waistband, outside my shirt but underneath the jacket. The briefcase was back in the bathroom, locked and tucked behind a stall. I tossed the manila folders into the backseat.

"Nope. Home." He didn't say anything, just put the truck into gear and pulled smoothly out of the space he'd been backed into.

"Wait," I said. "You got any plans for the evening?"

He shook his head. "No."

"Then let's get on 285 and head north. Might as well see what we can learn about this duffel bag of money I'm supposed to be holding."

"You all right, Top?"

"I just got fired."

"For what?"

"For losing my edge, becoming a buzz junkie." Benny said nothing. "What do you think of that?" I pressed.

"I don't know enough to have an opinion," he said. I pondered that slim vote of confidence for a moment. He turned and watched my reaction. Then: "Are you hungry?"

"Yeah, I am. Want to get a burger?" I asked.

"Sure," and pulled us smoothly into a Burger King. Four kids in uniform stood around to the side under the drive-up window awning, smoking. Inside, it was early, between breakfast and lunch, and we were the only customers. A pretty light-skinned African-American girl with a name tag that said "Rowonda" took our order. Under the cap, her hair was woven into a pattern of intricate braids. She had a bright, fresh-looking tattoo of a red-and-green dragon on the left side of her neck. She ignored me, but couldn't help staring at Benny with undisguised curiosity. I gave her a twenty and she made change.

As she handed it back, she stared at Benny. "You name Benny?" she asked.

"No," Benny said. "My name is Charles. Why, do I look like a Benny?"

"Yeah, you look like a guy what used to live around here named Benny, badass motherfucker." As she said it, she swung her head, and the microphone caught part of the last word. "Ucker" boomed out across the empty restaurant. A middle-aged woman with a hair net popped her head up above the aluminum hamburger tray and scowled at Rowonda.

Rowonda made a face and said, "Sorry, Mama—I mean, Mrs. McPherson."

The older woman locked her jaw and shoved our burgers into their chutes. She looked at us hard, especially at Benny. "Get the customers their drinks, Rowonda," she said tightly. Benny stared back at her, a half-smile on his face.

"Should we get out of here?" I asked.

"No, it's cool."

Still, we sat at a booth in the corner, where we could face the door and feel the comfort of a wall behind us. As we worked on the burgers, fries, and onion rings, Benny asked, "What did you get fired from?"

I paused. I had never spoken about this to anyone, and it felt odd to discuss it now. "Shaw's is a booking agency for mercenaries. My specialty was retrieval. I stole stuff back from thieves, recovered kidnap victims, that sort of stuff."

"I'm glad you're going to be around. I don't like the feel of this Dee Lane thing," He showed no curiosity and slurped a bit of his strawberry shake. "My street antennae are tingling."

I grunted noncommittally. My Spidersense wasn't telling me a thing, except I was out of work—although I could still feel the lump behind my ear.

"So, how long before you hook up with another outfit?" Benny looked at my face. "Sorry, Top. Maybe you don't want to talk about it."

"Benny, there *is* no other outfit. Shaw's is it for freelance operatives. I could put an ad in one of those *Soldier of Fortune*–type magazines or message boards, but Foosball always claimed those were setups, traps set by the FBI to keep track of the loonies."

"Who's Foosball?" he asked. I shoved away my barely eaten burger. Rowonda came over and picked up our trays for us, then wiped the table. She flipped her cloth neatly as she cleared the edge of the table, and cradled the crumbs in her cupped hand. I lifted the little packet of fries off the top tray before she could move it.

"You-all want some coffee, or something?" she asked.

I smiled. "I didn't know Burger King had table service."

"No, well, it's just we empty and all, so I thought I'd ask," she muttered. She couldn't take her eyes off Benny. "Man, you look just like Benny Culpepper."

"Who?" I asked.

"Benny Culpepper. Everybody in Atlanta was scared of this guy, he'd cut your throat in a second, and nothing you could do about, either. Didn't matter if you had a shotgun pointed right at his face. He was like that guy in that movie, *The Matrix*—he could just step out the way of bullets."

"I don't look scary, do I?" Benny forced a smile. I didn't blame her suspicion. His smile was as natural as the work of a mortician's apprentice.

"You look like Benny Culpepper," she said stubbornly. "I seen him once when I was a kid. Somebody told me who he was."

"Two coffees. Could you do that?" I asked. Rowonda nodded, stared at Benny for another second or two, and left.

"I hate to see those neck tattoos. Gangs marking their property, like an inventory tag," Benny said softly. "I came up before tats became so fashionable. Good thing I live in a place where fashions are twenty years behind, isn't it?"

"You asked about Foos," I said.

"Yes."

"Edgar Hagenfuss. Ex-Special Forces turned mercenary. He was my mentor. Got me into this business. Introduced me to Shaw's." I nibbled a fry.

"Can't you just call him?"

"Nope He's dead. Slipped off a dock on Lake Conroe, in Texas where he lived. Boat swung back and cracked his skull. After all he'd done, it was a pretty anticlimactic way to finish up," I said. I fiddled with the packet of fries. Finally I said, "You want to hear about it?"

"If you are comfortable talking about it," Benny said softly.

"Does that mean yes?"

"Yes."

"Dee Lane and I were supposed to be moving a load of pot from Belize. His gig. I was muscle. Way it went was these guys in Chiapas over in Mexico wanted to get into the pot business. Idea was they were going to bring a truckload of high-grade stuff through Campeche and down to Belize City, and Dee Lane would take it up to Houston. But some of the Mexican Mafia up in Guadalajara found out about it. They tipped off the army."

"To get rid of the competition?" Benny asked.

"Exactly. The army raids the fields, paraquats the pot, and shoot the guys we were waiting for. Anyway, we didn't know any of that, so we were sitting in Belize City, drinking beer and waiting on this truckload of pot to show up."

"How long did you wait?"

"That was the problem. We were supposed to give them four days, but Dee Lane likes Belize, so we would scuba in the morning and go sit around every afternoon drinking beer and waiting on these poor bastards. We did this for about two weeks, and I was starting to go crazy when this big, beefy, red-haired guy comes up to Dee Lane in the bar. Dee Lane introduces him as Foosball. He asks if he can talk to Dee Lane a minute. They go over to another table, and every once in a while they both look up and look at me, then they go back to talking. Finally, after about ten minutes of this, they come back, and Dee Lane asks me if I want to do a job with Foosball."

"What sort of job?"

"Scaring off some banana poachers."

"Sounds like a bad joke," he said.

"Well, that's how it started. I did one job with him, then another, and after a while, I'd go stay with him and his wife in Texas from time to time and he'd teach me about guns and tradecraft. And after a while, he sort of retired and I just took over." Rowonda brought our coffees and set them on the table. She unloaded a fistful of sugar and creamers between us. I put a five on her tray, told her to keep the change, and we left. Before getting into the truck, I walked out to the highway and looked in both directions, making sure there were no brown Oldsmobiles in sight.

CHAPTER 12

I WAS TIRED OF TALKING AFTER THAT AND WE DROVE QUIETLY up the I-985 spur, past Dawsonville and Dahlonega and on to Arlene. As we left the interstate and wound our way along the smaller roads, the sophisticated billboards gave way to homemade signs that advertised services like "L.T.'s Stump Grinding" and "Hog Creek Primitive Baptist Church." In the top of one spindly pine, thirty feet or so up, was a worn yellow sign that simply said, "REPENT." A few miles down the road and around a curve, another sat in the top of an equally unsteady-looking pine and said, "NOW."

We neared Arlene, driving past the small family-run motels and trailer courts, a new Mobil station that hadn't been there the last time I'd come through, and a small used-car lot, its long strings of plastic triangles drooping in the cool, sodden air. A line of ten-year-old cars with prices written in soap on the inside of their windshields sat facing the highway, as guardedly hopeful as ugly kids at the eighth-grade dance.

We came to a T junction where the highway ended, and I pointed left with a finger. Benny peered curiously as we turned the corner, and rode slowly up Main Street. "What do you call this genre of architecture?"

"School," I said.

"School architecture?" Benny seemed genuinely puzzled.

"No, they talk about architecture as being of a school, not a genre," I said shortly. "This is fake Bavarian. There's a big Oktoberfest here every fall. Years and years ago the Chamber of Commerce talked all the merchants into redoing the fronts of their stores and the signage. Now the town gets twenty thousand people a day during two weeks in October."

"That's it? Does it have any industry or anything? I mean, no offense, but people live off selling beer for two weeks a year?"

"Not quite, but close. Arlene's the official festival town of the South. There's a festival every weekend. Cloggers one week, gospel singers the next, folk artists, you name it. See that park?"

"Sure," he answered.

"During the season, it's full of white tents and Winnebagos, and it takes you an hour to drive down this street. People everywhere," I said.

"You still come up?"

"Bob John and Dee Lane more than me. Dee Lane's mom and sister are still here. Bob John's father is the local attorney, so Bob John comes for the holidays. My parents used to own the hardware store, Keirnan's Building Supplies. "See it there?" I pointed.

"No urge to go into the family business?"

"I *did* go into the family business. My dad ran the store, but my mom was also the town librarian. Anyway, no, I never thought about running the store. I thought I was going to race bicycles, saw myself riding in the Tour de France." Benny glanced involuntarily at my knees, but didn't say anything. The town looked much the same as it had a year or so ago, the last time I'd come up, except for the new Mobil station.

"Nice place," he said. "You miss it?"

I'd never thought about Arlene as a nice place. His was an interesting perspective. "No, not really. Parents gone, Dee Lane and Bob John down in Athens—that's about it for me."

"Where are we going?" Benny asked. He stopped at a stop sign, and before we could pull away, a small, withered hand tapped gently on my window. I rolled it down.

"Honus, is that you?" said a tiny old lady carrying a red-flowered umbrella. She stood less than a foot from the truck window, her head extended toward me like a turtle's.

"Yes, Miss Crosby," I said. She broke out in a toothy smile. "Miss Crosby, this is Benny Culpepper. He works with me in my business down in Athens." She appraised him with friendly curiosity and started to say something else, but someone behind us leaned on their horn. I mumbled apologies and motioned Benny to move along. Behind us, Miss Crosby shook her finger at the driver who beeped.

Benny gave her a rare smile. I continued, "Stay on this road. In about a mile, we'll see a small sign on your side that says Daisy Trail Bed and Breakfast. We'll turn there," I answered. Benny drove carefully, well within the limit and saw the sign without me pointing it out. We slowed and waited for the oncoming traffic to pass, and turned across the highway.

As we drove up the long driveway lined by pine trees and white plank fences that looked like wood but were really aluminum, I explained to Benny, "Dee Lane's mom and sister run this place. It's sort of a bed-and-breakfast, but you can also bring your horse or rent one. Trails run through the property. It backs up on the state forest. Nice place to ride if you like that sort of thing."

"Are you thinking Dee Lane is here, or that they know where he is?" he asked.

"Probably neither. What we're really here for is to look in that big old barn out in the back. Let's park in the gravel lot." We climbed out of the truck.

Benny asked, "Do I lock it?"

"Doesn't matter. Lock it if you want to, but nobody's going to mess with it."

Up on the hill to our left sat the main house, and to our right sat the stables and the riding rings. I led the way through the steady rain across the empty lot. There was no sign of movement except in the big ring behind the red stables. There a small figure in a yellow slicker slowly cantered a big palomino around in a circle. In an adjacent ring were two more horses, a roan thoroughbred and a Shetland pony, both standing patiently in the rain.

A tall, thin woman wearing a blue Gore-Tex jacket, blue jeans, and white rubber boots leaned up against the fence of the main ring and watched the exercise girl take the horse through its paces. She turned as she heard our footsteps crunching the gravel behind her.

"Top!" She smiled and walked over to give me a hug. Becky Lane was well over six feet tall. She stooped slightly to give me a peck on the cheek.

"Hi, Beck," I said and made introductions.

"Are you all right? What are you doing in town? Are you staying for lunch? Mom's not here right now, she's down in Atlanta doing the Arlene booth at a convention of travel agents. I know she'd love to see you. It's been years. Step under that overhang—you're getting soaked," she said. In the presence of a stranger, her nerves took over and she spoke too quickly, not pausing to hear our answers. She was more comfortable with horses than humans.

"A year, only a year," I said. "I was down Oktoberfest before last, remember?"

"No," she laughed.

"We can't stay, Becky. I've got a business now."

"So this is it? You just stopped by to say hello?" She turned back to the ring. "Lindsey, canter, keep the rhythm. I need to see him hold the gait for a while. Thatta girl."

"That, and I also wanted to pick up a trunk I left here when my parents moved. It's full of books and pictures. Your mom let me stick it out in the barn."

"You came up here to get a box of books?"

"Long story. My aunt's doing a family project and wants my high-school yearbooks. I'm going down to Florida next weekend and thought I'd take them down," I lied.

She nodded abstractedly, obviously more interested in why the palomino was picking up one of its hind hooves as it ran. "You need me to help or can you get it?"

"We got it," I said. As we turned, I heard Becky call my name. I turned back.

"Hey, you haven't seen that worthless brother of mine have you? He called last weekend, but we were out and he didn't leave a message. Bob John's looking for him."

"Nope. Bob John asked me, too."

She bit her lip. "How is Bob John?"

"OK, I don't see him all that much anymore. Busy with my business these days. You know. You miss us?" Trying to make a joke to ease the tension.

She laughed fragilely. "Nope, I've got these guys to remind me.

That sneaky palomino is always faking a limp to get out of work. He's like Dee Lane. That high-strung thoroughbred is like you, and that cute Shetland's like Bob John."

"Nice animals," I said.

"Gentle too, except for the pony." She stared at me, looking vulnerable, and I could see the gawky, socially awkward girl she'd been back in high school. She misread my lack of response and rolled up her sleeve. The rain fell on a hideous yellow and purple bruise that covered her whole forearm.

"Good God, Beck! Did you have a doctor look at that?'

"No, but it's OK. Not the first time he's bitten me," she said and turned, "Lindsey! Pacing, keep your pacing." She turned back to us. "You see Bob John, tell him to come up sometime."

I nodded and we walked away. "There's some history there," I said.

"No joke," Benny answered.

"That's why people leave small towns —history everywhere."

"Big towns, too," he agreed.

We walked toward the barn, picking up our pace to get out of the rain. "Here's why we came up here. Whenever Dee Lane goes away for an extended stay, he brings his Ferrari up here and puts it in the barn so it won't get banged up or scratched. Place looks like hell and probably has timber rattlers under every old board, but the floor's concrete and the roof is sound," I said. We walked carefully around the puddles. "If the car is here, then he plans to be gone for a while. If it's not, maybe he's not gone."

"Would anyone else know that?" Benny asked.

"I doubt it."

I pulled the hasp loose and tugged. The top of the door wobbled, but the bottom didn't budge.

"It's old and sagging. We're going to have to lift it," Benny said.

It took both of us to lift it and pull it open. The only light came from the door we'd just opened and cracks between the vertical planks that made up the walls. The space was stuffed with old farm equipment, stacks of lumber, boxes. Broken chairs and the like hung from rafters.

"What's the whirring sound?" Benny asked.

"Who knows? Bat, owl, something. Watch where you step. I wasn't kidding about snakes."

"I don't see a Ferrari."

"This is where it would be," I answered as we stepped inside. But the space in the center of the floor where we stood was empty and covered in dust. Underneath the dust, I could make out the faintest of tire tracks—wide Pirelli racing-tire tread. But the tracks were old and the dust thick.

CHAPTER 13

THE RAIN TAPERED OFF AND BY THE TIME WE PASSED THE exit for Between, Georgia, named because it is midway between Atlanta and Athens, the sun was starting to peek through the clouds. It was too early to comb the bars, even the ones out near the mall on the Atlanta highway that open early, so we decided to start at the university, then visit Groovolgy.

I wasn't looking forward to it. With Vinyl Man, you had only a two-hour window when he was pretty coherent. Afterward, we could start running through bars, restaurants, and anywhere else we could think of.

Dee Lane is intensely private. Secretiveness is a very good trait for someone in his line of work. But he also can't stand to be alone for more than a few hours. He has to find a crowd every night. There's this war going on inside Dee Lane: hermit vs. Rotarian.

He's worked out a compromise. Over the years he has perfected the art of coming across as a friendly, but quiet guy. He's the ideal listener, always smiling and nodding, occasionally offering reassuring, but noncommittal encouragement. He volunteers little, and is careful not to dodge direct questions, although he doesn't always give very full or accurate answers. His view is simple: "Top, people love to try to figure out mysteries. Don't answer their questions and they'll do anything to pry out the answer, ask friends about you, plow through your trash, any damn thing. So give them something boring. Say you sell insurance or inseminate cows or something and look like you can't wait to talk about it. Then they'll leave you be."

The first year after we dropped out of school, we worked on a framing crew, me as a saw man and him as a nail driver, building cheap three-story apartments on land freshly bulldozed out of the pine forests down by a creek near Watsonville. One day at break time, the crew sat drinking our morning Cokes. Five of us shared an old railroad tie the landscapers had dropped in place but not yet dug in. It was a classically humid north Georgia day. Our sweat and the condensation on the soda cans beaded up and dropped into the red dust, making little moon craters where the droplets fell. Dee Lane concentrated on aiming his so that they made a line from the pointy toe of one of his oversized black cowboy boots to the other. He wasn't having much luck, and our advice on moving his head and his can one way or the other didn't seem to help. The straw boss walked over and coughed, and we all looked up.

The man tilted back his hat and said, "Dee Lane, I hear you're getting your Ph.D. in forestry. What do you reckon this here tree is?" He held out a withered leaf.

Without blinking, Dee Lane said, "I'd have to see the bark."

"Yeah, right, I should've brought the whole branch I reckon," the foreman said. "I got one in my yard and I think it's a hickory, but my wife thinks it's just a weed tree and wants me to cut it down."

"Could be a hickory," Dee Lane said. It could be a stalk of corn for all Dee Lane knows about trees and forestry. As far as I knew, his forestry training was the same as mine: a scrapbook of leaves assembled for eighth-grade science class. But it was classic Dee Lane. Helpful, but careful not to say he was studying at the forestry school, and equally careful not to say he wasn't.

So we might learn something from Dee Lane's friends. Then again, we might not. We had two stops to make at the university. The first was on South Campus, then we would walk to the law school on North Campus, then wander on up into town. Parking on campus when school is in session is impossible. We left the truck in the huge east lots and took a shuttle back in to the vet school. From here, we would walk the mile or so uphill into town, making stops along the way.

At the vet school front desk, we were directed to the office of Tom O'Reilly, a professor of genetics who had for years kept a running series of chess games going with Dee Lane. O'Reilly was a medium-sized pleasant-looking man, neatly dressed in khakis, a stylish long-sleeved champagne-colored knit shirt, and dark brown, nubby wool sports jacket. He wore hiking boots polished to a high sheen. We caught him in midflight on his way to class, and only able to give us three hurried minutes. We trotted along beside him as he wove his way through the crowded hall to the auditorium where his class waited. He was obviously popular and nodded continuously in response to greetings from other faculty and students.

He had last spoken to Dee Lane by phone a week ago. There was nothing odd about the conversation. Dee Lane called because he wanted to take a break from their marathon chess tournament. Which, the professor happily added, suited him just fine since he was ahead. I asked the reason for the break. He shrugged, and said

Dee Lane was going to be out of touch. This wasn't the first time one or the other called a break, and he thought little of it. On Saturday afternoon, Tom received an E-mail resigning the last game they had open. That was that.

"Did he say when he'd be back?" I asked. Tom shook his head. I wondered again why he'd wanted to see me on Saturday and made a mental note to check the phone log when I returned. Tom said a few more things and told me he'd also told Bob John the same thing. Another question lurked in the back of my mind, but it wouldn't surface, so I left it that I might call him if I thought of anything else.

Tom was halfway into the room when he turned back to face us. An electronic bell pinged from the small, round speaker inset in the ceiling. He held up one finger to the class to tell them he would be a minute. "It's serious this time isn't it?" he asked softly.

My answer was a bland, unintelligible mumble, but it didn't matter because he didn't wait to hear it. The door swung shut, but not before we saw him take two quick steps and make a little hop across the floor. As he stopped and held up his hands for applause, we could hear a cheer build from the students, "D-N-A! D-N-A!" He pumped his fist and led the chant for a few seconds before holding his hands up palms outward, signaling quiet. It was very different than the classes I remembered. I saw Benny peer curiously through the glass.

Our next stop was the law library, at the other end of campus, up and over a steep hill, across a small footbridge, and up another rise. The bridge ran beside Sanford Stadium, which is cunningly nestled both symbolically and literally in the small valley that separates the two campuses. South Campus is where sciences are taught. It is stark, full of new brick and sparse trees. North Campus, where the liberal arts live, is leafy and serene, and looks like a school that is almost two hundred years old. And nothing could show the rabid love of football that unites the two campuses more than this giant stadium, stuck right slap in the middle.

At the law library, we made our way to our next assignation, but the first-floor office in the annex was empty. A girl passed by and saw us; then, without speaking, jerked her head toward the end of the building. We found Dr. Amanda Houle in the courtyard of the main library, sitting on a barely dry concrete bench with an oversized paperback. A sun with low levels of self-esteem made a tentative appearance. Beside her on the bench were a pack of Merits and a green disposable lighter. She was very pretty, thin, almost waif like, with huge green-blue eyes and caramel-colored hair that hung just below her jaw line. Today she wore a starched white shirt and black skirt, but around her shoulders she wore an old rust-colored afghan as a shawl against the cool wind. Her long legs were clad in black hose. They stretched out in front of her, crossed at the ankle, and she leaned her back against the white sandstone façade.

"Hey, Amanda," I said.

"Hey, Top. Hey, Benny." She closed the book and shaded her eyes to look up at us.

"What are you reading?" Benny asked shyly.

"*History of Knowledge*, by Charles van Doren," she answered. "You know, the quiz-show guy."

"Yeah, he cheated on the show, but he actually is a genius, right?" I said.

"That's what they say," she said. "Real interesting book." I saw Benny slip a tiny spiral-bound notebook out of a pocket and jot the name down.

I paused and she continued. "It's been weeks."

"*What's* been weeks?"

"Since I saw Dee Lane. And no, as far as I know, he wasn't seeing anybody else, and no, he didn't leave anything with me." She smiled. Her nose crinkled when she did that, and she looked about six years old.

"I see you've spoken to Bob John."

"Yup."

"OK, thanks," I said. This was the highest point on campus, and a brisk wind whistled around the corner of the building. My over-shirt was still damp from our visit to Arlene. I jammed my hands into my pockets. Benny was wearing a red-and-black warm-up jacket and black driving gloves, and his hands hung loosely beside him. He liked to keep his hands free.

"Hey, Top, isn't there anything else you want to ask me?" she asked.

I stopped. After a moment of silence, she said, "Well, had you asked, the answer would have been, 'No, I'm not seeing anyone right now either. I'd love to.'" I felt myself turning pink.

Benny looked away politely. Amanda's mouth dropped open. "You're blushing. Jesus H. Christ, you're blushing. I didn't know they made those anymore. How sweet!" She made a small moue.

Benny's mouth twitched furiously and he squinted into the dis-tance. I forced a sheepish grin. "Things are pretty intense right now. I'm a little slow." I said.

"Like that's new. OK, I've waited this long," she answered cheer-fully. She didn't seem too worried about our missing friend. Benny shifted slightly but perceptibly, as a reminder.

We cut across the grass to the quadrangle and walked through the arches onto Broad Street. Dee Lane's store was on the far side of the CBD, a little hole in the wall with a sign over it that read "Groovology, Inc." The glass was filled with posters and home-made advertisements for local music events.

Inside, the store was a dark and narrow lane which ran straight to a plywood counter in the back. On one side of the room were floor-to-ceiling bookshelves filled with thousands of CDs. On the other were equally high industrial shelves with wooden orange crates filled with old albums. A long table with half a dozen pairs of head-phones and no chairs filled the center. Behind the counter was Vinyl Man, equally comfortable on either side of the technology divide but, as his name suggested, with a sentimental bias toward the old 33s, 45s, and 78s. Something in the background sounded like a semi full of cats crashing through the wall of a fork factory.

"Dudes," he said. He waved at me and went through a convoluted handshake with Benny, who as a musician rated higher in Vinyl Man's social register than I did. He reached behind the counter and handed over two flimsy folding chairs. "Sit down, dudes. Business sucks completely right now. Tell me a story. What's happening out there?"

Business at Groovology was never good, but Dee Lane had no need of profits. He just needed a W-2 for the IRS. Even had the business been better located, it's likely that Vinyl Man's eclectic merchandising and just plain weirdness would have kept business marginal. Today he wore a skintight purple shirt and almost-matching pants that he'd probably purchased used over at the Potter's House. His spiky hair and thin Vandyke beard were dyed a horrible bright crimson. Despite the cool weather, he wore Birkenstock sandals. His real name was Leonard, and I didn't blame him for using "Vinyl Man."

"Great music, man," Benny said. As best I could tell, he was completely serious. Vinyl Man bobbed his head happily.

"I guess Bob John's been by to see you, too?" I asked.

"Effing A, and I told him jack shit, man. Jack shit. Narcs blow, dudes," A fine spray of spittle ushered the words out. He tapped his foot furiously.

"So what are you going to tell us, then?"

"I don't know, dudes, what's the question?" His voice was strained and his lower lip quivered. It didn't take much to set the Vinyl Man off. I'd seen him chase an elderly woman down the street with a baseball bat because she didn't handle a used Sinatra album by the edges. The record was worth a whole buck ninety-nine. Benny saw Vinyl's fragility and smiled gently. He surprised me by walking over and throwing his arm around the clerk's emaciated shoulders. Vinyl Man looked up at him gratefully, and Benny patted his shoulder as he would a child's.

Before Vinyl Man started hearing the choir inside his head and taking the heavy doses of schizophrenia medications, he'd been a reasonably well-regarded music critic, with a radio show and a regular column in an Atlanta newspaper.

"OK, then, when did you last see Dee Lane?" I asked.

Vinyl Man grinned. "You know."

"Know what?" I asked.

"You know," he wagged his finger at me conspiratorially. "You know."

I bit my lip, frustrated, but with no idea how to break through. Benny interceded, "Tell me, brother. I missed it."

"I saw him Saturday, man, when he left to see Top." Vinyl Man grinned. "I helped him load his bags and his briefcase and that huge, effing heavy duffel bag in the Toyota, dude, and he took off to see the Toporino. He knows." He pointed at me and gave an exaggerated laugh. Ha Ha Ha.

"What time of day, Vinyl Man?" I tried to keep my voice smooth and stay still so I didn't spook him.

He made a face and opened his hands. "I don't remember, man."

"Vinyl Man, try, man. Help me here," I said.

He grabbed the edge of the counter so hard that his knuckles whitened. "I *am* trying, man. You have no idea," he said through gritted teeth. There didn't seem to be anything to say to that, so we waited.

Finally, a few dozen twitches and sighs later, he mumbled, "Afternoon."

"Thanks, Vinyl Man. I'll come get you next week, and you can sit in next time we play, OK?" Benny said. Vinyl may have nodded. We folded the chairs and handed them back across the counter. He took them and placed them carefully against the rear wall. Without looking back at us, he sagged onto the four-legged stool, his hands dropping into his lap. They lay there open and exhausted. His eyes stared at a little spot down on the baseboard.

"You going to be all right, dude?" I asked. He nodded sadly. We left him there, completely spent from the effort of concentrating through the drugs for ten minutes. He would never be all right. But we couldn't help, so we moved on.

CHAPTER 14

THE REST OF THE AFTERNOON AND NIGHT WAS A BUST. WE stopped in twenty bars, I drank half of twenty beers, and Benny drank enough soda to take out the stains in every garment in America. We started at a low-slung cinder-block building out on 78, a hard-core alkie joint with no name—just an ancient neon sign that said "COCK AILS."

Across the highway was a similar-sized building, but this one was surrounded by a ten-foot-high fence festooned with signs and topped with razor wire. In the twenties, poor young women had worked there painting radium numbers onto watch dials. Most got jaw cancer from licking their brushes to sharpen the points. The company was long since bankrupt, and although it was on the list of Superfund sites for cleanup, so far the fence was the only visible sign of progress. Along the side of the building, a set of old painted drums rusted ominously.

Even though we got to the bar just as it opened, there were already four or five cars in the back lot, a lot surrounded by a six-foot stockade fence that kept away the prying eyes of spouses and employers. It was pitch-black inside, the whole place lit only by a few dim bulbs near the bar. It was still early to be here, and everyone sat away from the light, in pools of dark, each space marked by the glowing red tip of a cigarette. Here they only served straight drinks—triples—and the only mixer available was a beer back.

All the regulars here loved Dee Lane because he would sit and listen to their sad stories and, more often than not, buy a few rounds. But Stanley hadn't seen him for a week. We spent the evening going from bar to bar—Paolo's Pizza, the Blue Frog, and the row of student hangouts downtown. We stopped several times throughout the evening at Dee Lane's favorite, Sluts and Mullets in the Normaltown neighborhood.

Sluts and Mullets pitches itself as a bar for locals—hence the name. Truth was, most of the patrons had at one time been students themselves, and were just people who'd come to the university and for one reason or another, settled in. Still, the house band was excellent and the beer was cheap. But no Dee Lane, and no one we spoke to had seen him.

Perhaps it was coincidence, but some other bar hoppers appeared to be working the same route. In particular one African-American guy, thirty-something, clean-cut, was in several of the places we went. And on our last stop at Sluts and Mullets, I was convinced that I'd seen the thin blonde with the small mole earlier at the Blue Frog. No brown Oldsmobile, though. We got home around two and tumbled wearily into bed, my legs aching.

CHAPTER 15

I WOKE IN A DAZE TWO HOURS LATER. IT TOOK A SPLIT SECOND for me to process the kaleidoscope of red, white, and blue lights on the rafters of the gym. Car doors slammed and there was a huge pounding at the metal door in the far wall. For a moment, I considered the possibility that it was a trick. It wouldn't be the first time the bad guys pretended to be cops to make sure the mark didn't come out firing. After a moment's consideration, I left the SIG behind, under the pillow. And that's why the hitters use that particular ruse—it almost always works.

The pounding continued, rhythmic now. *Boom, boom, boom.* Someone yelled my name. The voice had no discernible accent. The sounds echoed across the near empty gym. I reached the door and pounded back. Their banging stopped. "Who is it?" I yelled. "Let me see some ID."

"Top, it's Bob John. Open the door."

I hit the release bar and the door swung open. It had started misting again. Bob John stood there, wearing pin striped pajama tops stuffed into dress slacks. A portion of the tail of the pajama top peeked out from the top of the fly on the trousers. He wore a dark blue standard-issue windbreaker on top, and it shown slickly. His hair was uncombed and matted down, and his glasses sparkled with tiny water droplets. Lights from the three patrol cars threw wild shadows through the doorway. Behind Bob John stood two sheriff's deputies, each holding a pump-action shotgun. Others lurked behind the cars, their faces Halloween masks of dark shadow and flashing light.

"Harlan Winslow," he said.

"Yeah, Harlan," I answered. "He works for me."

"Not anymore," Bob John said sadly. He held out a Polaroid. I couldn't make it out, and turned back in to hit the lights. I threw all four switches and the room lit up completely. I covered my eyes for a second to give them time to adjust. When I could see, I looked at the picture in my hand. It was the naked upper torso of a fat, polka-dotted Harlan.

"Pulled him out of the Oconee River an hour ago. Just starting to bloat. Immediate ID, couple of kids smooching saw him wash up at the dam at old mill. They knew him from the library. You recognize the marks?"

"Burns," I answered.

"Yeah, cigarette burns. And his fingers were chopped off. He was tortured, Top, but the stupid idiots overdid it and killed him. Shock, the doctor thinks. Bunch of amateurs."

"Christ!" I said numbly. It had to be about the missing money. Jealous husbands might cut something off, but it wouldn't be fingers.

"It's all happening now, Top, and goodness knows where it's going to end up." His head dropped wearily.

He stood there, not saying anything, while the deputies watched us impassively. One whose face I could almost see chewed gum in a slow rhythm. Finally I said, "Want me to come with you?"

"What for?" Bob John said. "Unless you got the bag, there's not a gosh-darned thing you can do about this situation. Have you got the money, Top?"

"No."

"Then go back to bed." He turned and walked away.

CHAPTER 16

I SLEPT ANOTHER COUPLE OF HOURS AND WOKE UP JUST before sunrise, smoothly surfacing from a deep dream. It had been about Dee Lane and Gillie. Nothing special, just the three of us laughing as we walked along a path in a park. I didn't recognize the park, nor had the three of us ever really been together there, but it was a pleasant false memory, and I woke happy, but slightly befuddled, and lay there for a moment while my mind sorted out the dream from the morning reality.

In the dream, Gillie was bursting out of a tight white T-shirt and designer jeans, and Dee Lane was the same as always, clad in black from head to toe. He wore round Jennifer Warren–style sunglasses, but with orange lenses. Dee Lane and I walked on either side of Gillie and we had our arms thrown over each other's shoulders. The last thing I saw before I woke was his long lantern-jawed face, split by his usual sardonic barracuda grin.

I rose and pulled on last night's pair of jeans, and sat on the side of the bed in the gray dawn of the gymnasium. The dream wouldn't let go, and I sat foggy, trying to puzzle out the dark pool of emotion lapping against my good mood, then suddenly, guiltily, remembered Bob John's visit. Harlan was dead, at least indirectly because of me. I thought of the other thirty-five people who worked in and around Polymath. A Colombian sociopath named Menes was convinced I had his money. He probably didn't even need the cash, probably had bags full of the stuff laying around his rec room, but would still, on principle alone, feel compelled to recover this particular million and a bit. I thought about Soames, and his argument that I'd become reckless, a danger to those around me.

A wave of angry indignation rose in the back of my mind and swept away the remainder of the dream, and washed over the faint guilt of Harlan. As the wave receded, it left behind the wet, salty grit of determination.

I lay back down on the covers, and covered my eyes with my arm. Later, when I woke, it was broad daylight and I was completely chilled from sleeping bare chested on top of the covers. I rose shivering and jogged to the locker room, showered and made my way to the office. Gillie and Benny followed me a few minutes later. Benny set three mugs on the desk, and Gillie filled each from a thermos. She reached in the pocket of her slacks and pulled out a small flask. She raised her eyebrows. I nodded and she added a symbolic slug of Jameson's to both her own cup and to mine. Instead of moving to the round table, they sat down in the two chairs across the desk from me, which signaled something, although I wasn't sure what. We raised our cups in a silent toast to Harlan.

"You OK?" Gillie asked. Yesterday's storm had blown through, and in its place was a November-like day, with clear blue skies and a loping wind. From the windows, bright flying buttresses of sunlight slanted down between us. She sat back, a foot or so farther away than normal, where the light would not blind her. But the resulting shadow highlighted the black rings under her eyes that the makeup could not cover.

"Not really," I answered.

"Me neither." She said, and took a long sip of coffee. Benny held his cup cradled in both hands and gazed impassively through the steam at a point several feet over my head.

"Now what?" I asked.

"We have to shut down," she answered. "At least until this thing gets settled."

"What?" I asked, stunned.

"We don't have a choice," she said.

"Gillie, we've got a brand, customers. We can explain a day or two, but not any more than that. We'll lose all of the corporate accounts. We shut down and we lose it all. I thought you—of all people—would know that."

"Who killed Harlan, Top?" she asked. Benny stared into his coffee cup, not looking at either of us. She used one hand to rake her curls straight back and away from her face.

"I don't know. Probably someone looking for the money."

"Right, Top. This is not going to end here, every junkie and red-neck backwoods sociopath in north Georgia is going to show up looking for that damned money."

"We can protect Polymath," I said. "Me and Benny."

"Yeah, until they follow the next one of us home, and the one after that. You can't protect all of us, Top."

"So what do you want to do, Gillie?"

"Shut down for a while. Until this is over."

"We could move it," Benny said. I looked at him in surprise.

"How?" Gillie asked. "What would we do with all the gear? How would we get space?"

"Space isn't hard," he said. "The university has that incubator building where the ag extension building used to be. You said one of the dot-coms in there just went out of business. Wouldn't they have desks, phone lines, the works?"

"What about the servers? How long would it take to set everything up?"

"We bypass the coding program, just forward the calls to a switchboard with Gillie and a couple of temps who log the inquiries, drop in a server, set up a dozen PCs tied to their LAN, and we could be in business by tomorrow morning. We're heading into the weekend, anyway. We do a blast E-mail to clients telling them we got flooded out by a frozen pipe or something. That will explain any hiccups," Benny said.

"Are you sure?" I pushed.

"George runs the incubator building, doesn't he Gillie? I mean, he could probably help us out. Maybe we can move in, get started, and the paperwork could catch up. What do you think?"

I shook my head. "That still puts you guys in danger."

"I don't think so," Benny said. "Harlan's tall and blond and he was wearing dark clothes. If he left here late, some imbecile probably thought he was Dee Lane. Fits with the idea of a bunch of goobers out chasing a big score. If that's right, they'll come after you or the school. We can handle that."

I caught the pronoun shift, but left it alone. "Goobers?"

"You know, goobers," he repeated.

"What do you think, Gillie?" I asked.

"Let me call George. Maybe it would work," she said. "Before I do, though, let's make sure we have all the questions worked out." Gillie borrowed a pad of paper and a pen, and filled the page. While she worked, she pushed the pink tip of her tongue out of the side of her mouth. I couldn't take my eyes off it, and when she finished and looked up, she caught me staring and gave me a quick wink.

As she and Benny rose to leave, she clicked the top on the pen. "Progressive?"

I shook my head. "I'm not into it today." She was trying to perk me up, and I had no interest in being perked.

"Chicken!" Her words were playful, but the expression on her face communicated a need I couldn't quite identify, but interpreted as a yearning for normalcy. Maybe we needed some routine to counterbalance the insanity of the last twenty-four hours.

For a moment, I held her stare. Then I gave in, reached into my pocket and pulled out a roll of bills. Progressives could get expensive. I said, "What's the category?"

"Predictions of failure, people," she said.

"That should be easy. Go!" I answered. She dropped a dollar on the table, and I tossed one on top of it. "A dollar," I said. "That's a confident start."

She grinned, waggled her eyebrows, and reached in the pocket of her jacket for a list. In progressives, it is important to get the wording exact; a lot of quotes can be pretty similar when you are in a tight category. "First one. 'You'll never make a living playing that guitar,'" she said.

"Brass plaque on the front of the house John Lennon built for his aunt," I answered. We both threw a five-dollar bill on the pile and each took away a one.

" 'He has never learned anything, and he can do nothing in decent style,'" she read.

"Johann Georg Albrechtsberger, composer and teacher of the young Beethoven," I said. She tossed a ten on the table, and I matched it. She didn't pick up the five, meaning she was letting it ride because she had what she thought was a winner coming. She would save it for last and let the pot build.

" 'He is overage and certain to prove mediocre,'" she read.

"Francesco Basily, principal of the Royal Conservatory of Milan, rejecting Giuseppe Verdi's application," I said. "Is that the last?"

"One more." She tossed a twenty on the pile. "It's a hard one."

I tossed my own bill on the growing pile. "Shoot."

" 'They will never be truly important,'" she said triumphantly.

I folded my fingers into a tent and buried my face in it, concentrating. "They will never be truly important. They. Obviously a group, not an individual. Except for choirs and orchestras, the fame of groups is a twentieth-century phenomenon, 1930 on. Maybe advanced musically. Glenn Miller, The Yardbirds, Steely Dan. Probably rock 'n' roll, because you worked so hard to lead me away from Lennon. Has to be someone who actually was important—rules out heavy metal. Somebody who wasn't obvious. So no supergroups. Rules out Cream. Traffic. The Eagles."

"Fascinating, sharing your thought process with us, but do you know or not?" She put one hand on her hip.

"I'll take a shot. A magazine article about the Stones in the mid to late sixties."

She smiled triumphantly and scooped up the cash. "Close, but not close enough. Warner Brothers, 1967, about the Grateful Dead. I win. Even though I know you took a dive."

"Did not!" I protested.

"You tanked and you know it," she said.

"Why do you say he tanked?" Benny asked curiously.

"Because he never loses. Except on progressives, and then only when the pot goes over twenty bucks and he gets a case of the guilts over taking money from his friends," she said cheerfully. "But no matter, I picked up thirty-five bucks."

I scowled. "I can't even lose without taking a load of crap"— paused, then continued—"Benny, could you hang around a minute?"

"OK," Gillie said, "I guess that means I go. 'Bye, guys."

"Leave the thermos, please," I said. She did, and then ostentatiously pulled out the flask and set it down on the desk as well. I poured coffee into both our cups.

CHAPTER 17

YOU THINK I COULD TALK TO MENES?" I ASKED.

"You could try, but there's no guarantee that in the middle of the meeting he wouldn't blow your head off."

"That crazy?"

"I've seen a lot of guys act crazy to build a reputation, and I've even seen a few that probably were a little off, but this guy is genuinely disturbed."

"What if I met him in neutral ground? Say, at Danny's."

"Top, there are no guarantees with this guy. He could open up in Danny's. He works to his own set of rules. But Danny's is probably the best option you've got. Except for the fact that I can't back you up there."

"That's bullshit," I said.

"Yeah, and it's been bullshit for as long as he's been open, and for a hundred years before that. But if I walk in there, you know what will happen."

"I need you there."

"Your call, but you know the risk."

"I know the risk without you." Benny said nothing, but I could see he was pleased with my insistence. He picked up an apple from the bowl on the desk and tossed it up in the air. As it started to come down, he flicked his hand in a motion like the number 9, and just like that, four quarters fell to the polished oak surface. Without expression, he wiped the blade of the razor on his jeans and shoved two of the quarters over to me.

I called the number of the bar in Atlanta, even though I wasn't sure they'd be open yet. Someone, probably the bartender, answered and had me wait while he went to get Danny. When the old man picked up the phone, his first words were "Take me off the fookin' speaker."

"No," I answered.

"Who the fook am I talking to besides yourself then, Top?" Danny said in a lovely soft Irish tenor.

"I don't know, Danny, but my guess would be half the federal government," I warned.

"I know about them. Those barstards listen in on everybody. I mean in the room with you. Do you have the nigger with you?"

I winced. Benny shook his head softly, telling me not to respond. "I need a meeting with Menes," I said.

"You surely do, laddie, before you get your fookin' wee pecker cut off and stuffed in your smart mouth." Danny cackled. "Better bring a duffel bag with you."

"I don't have the money, Danny, and I don't have any idea where it is."

"Bloody good luck with that fookin' answer, boy."

"Can you set up a meet?"

"Five for me trouble."

"Three," I countered.

"Call me in an hour from a secure phone, and I'll give you a number to call."

"An hour. Good."

"Think nothing of it, laddie. It's me pleasure. 'Bye, Top. 'Bye, nigger," he hooted and hung up.

We sat there quietly in the midday sun. Later, I walked down to the kitchen and made a new pot of coffee, which I poured black and hot into the thermos. I finished the little flask, and then I started in on the bigger bottle of Laphroiag from my credenza. It was a waste of good whiskey, since the adrenaline buzz burns off the alcohol before it can do its job. I wanted to apologize to Benny, tell him that not all of us were like that. But you can't repent other people's sins, only your own. In the South, we truly believe the days of Jim Crow are dead, and that we're beyond the fire hoses and attack dogs. But people like Danny make me wonder.

Benny left to start packing up and I sat there most of the afternoon, thinking. After an hour, I opened my bottom drawer and pulled out a cell phone registered to a Korean grocer from Birmingham, but never used. The time for the meeting was set for the next afternoon at 3:00 P.M. I felt better knowing that we were now in motion, but still, all in all, the day sucked. Dude.

CHAPTER 18

ROUND SEVEN, I PUT A STOUFFER'S DINNER IN THE microwave and nuked it, but the adrenaline was still running and I couldn't eat much of it. I nibbled a few tortellini, then threw it away and ladled myself a dish of vanilla ice cream with butterscotch sauce. I got down most of that, and wondered how long you could live off coffee, alcohol, and ice cream. Add cigarettes and Twinkies, and I had the five basic trailer-park food groups.

After dinner I pulled on a sweatshirt—we heat only the occupied parts of the school—and made the rounds, just like any other night, except this time I stuck a nine-millimeter automatic in my right rear pocket. I started with the band wing, the farthest part of the building, and worked my way back, checking every window and door to make sure it was latched. I had finished, and settled back down in my office with my feet on the desk and a TV clicker in each hand, flipping through the channels on two of the TVs in the wall, when a ping came from the computer behind me. I muted the sound on the sets, turned, and saw a small flashing red icon, and a black-and-white image of someone walking away from the front of the school. Whoever it was walked quickly to the passenger side of a dull-looking sedan, got in, and the car pulled away quickly. I heard the faint sound of tires on gravel.

I swung my feet down and stood up, grabbing the gun off the desk. But before I could move, the telephone rang. I looked at the screen of the front of the school. Nothing. The phone rang again. I hit the icon quickly, and the computer screen split into twelve different images, the entire outside of the school, all of which would cycle every fifteen seconds. The little round dot above each was green. There was another ring, and I picked it up.

"I left you a gift on the front step," a voice said.

"Who is this?"

"Go check out your gift, and you'll see."

"Are you crazy or do you think *I* am?"

A different voice answered, with a very different voice, warm, smooth, lethal. Once Benny had let me hold the Huddie Ledbetter razor and I'd run my finger down the flat side of the blade, still warm from Benny's pocket. This voice was like that blade: warm, hard, with a very faint but still ornate etching that suggested this was no everyday shaving tool. "We saw each other in a bar today. We have a number of mutual friends. Your lines are tapped. The package on your front step holds a telephone."

"I was in a lot of bars today," I said.

"Yes, but only one where you drank Guinness with a South African and left a case in the bathroom. I was wearing a gray suit," the voice said.

"How do I know it's not a bomb?" I asked.

"Oh, please! Because you're not a fool. There are easier ways," Morton said. The blinds were open, and as he said that a red dot appeared on the frosted glass wall. "Oh, and stand near a window when you use it." I hung up, walked to the front door, and slowly opened it. Sitting on the mat was an odd-shaped telephone. It looked like one of those old cell phones from the seventies, a three-pound brick. I held it up to my ear.

"That's better," Morton said. "Sorry for all the melodrama, but our cousins at DEA will be listening to anything you say until that duffel bag turns up." There was a click after he finished speaking.

"What is this thing?" I said.

"The phone?" Morton replied after a pause.

"No, Morton, I've got hold of my wee willie, and I can't figure out what it's for. Of course I'm talking about the phone!" I took a step back and the phone began to hiss. I stepped close to the glass again. There was another pause, and he answered. "It's an Iridium phone, works off a satellite," he said. *Click.*

"I thought that company went bankrupt and dropped all their satellites into the sea," I said.

Pause. "Not exactly. We bought the system." *Click.*

"This is a lot of trouble for a clean line," I said.

Pause. "Procedure. Anyway, it's not completely clean. If your hallway is bugged, someone can still hear your half of the conversation. If you really want to be sure, take the phone outside and walk around. Don't walk in a straight line, or a parabolic could pick you up, although I doubt they have that sort of manpower on you." *Click.*

"No, thanks, I think this is good enough."

Pause. "I'd like to meet in person, if we could."

"Why?"

"To offer you a job."

"Why?"

Pause. "Why do you think? We have jobs that require skills like you have, and we've been following your career for quite a while. We have a thick file on you." *Click.*

I, too, have a thick file on me. "Where'd you find out about me?"

Pause. "Edgar Haggenfuss talent spotted you for us." *Click.*

"I find that hard to believe," I answered. That hadn't been in the file.

Pause. "Foosball did a number of assignments for us over the years, long after he officially left the Agency," he said. "He was my agent." *Click.*

"Bull," I said.

Pause. "Call his wife Laurie if you don't believe me. She gets a government pension." He laughed heartily. *Click.*

"Laurie gets a pension from the CIA?"

Pause. "Of course not. She gets one from the USDA, but you and I both know Foosball wasn't filing crop reports from all those places you two went." *Click.*

"None of my business, Morton. What do you want with me?"

Pause. "A retrieval assignment, in fjord country. Person, Chilean passport, but really German. Eighty-year-old man in poor health. Will take a bit of finessing to get him out." *Click.*

"You're still chasing renegade SS?"

Pause. "We're still chasing missing Jewish money stashed in Swiss and Caribbean accounts, and we want old men who know lists of account numbers and use them to fund Hamas. What do you say? We'll pay well, better than Shaw's. You'll be completely independent, no micro-oversight, complete deniability, of course. And it gets you out of town until this missing-millions stuff blows over." *Click.*

My pulse raced and my mouth was dry with excitement. I saw my reflection in the dark glass of the front window. I was smiling from ear to ear. And then I remembered Lima.

"No, thanks," I said and hung up. I walked back to the office and tossed the big phone onto a chair, sat down, and poured myself four fingers of fine single-malt.

This felt wrong. Suddenly I have to get out of town, my regular way to do that goes away, and then a stranger I've seen only once in my life shows up offering me the perfect job. Foosball had called it a tiger trap. You hunt a tiger by systematically sealing off every avenue of escape with beaters. Then light a fire behind the animal, driving it into a funnel where the rajah with the big-bore rifle waits atop an elephant. Sometimes a beater or two gets killed. I thought of Harlan.

I now had two good reasons to get out of town, and without Shaw's, nowhere to go, except with Morton. Was I in a tiger trap? And if so, why me? Did the husband of the woman I'd lost in Lima hold me responsible for his wife's death? He might have enough weight to move the CIA. I tried to think of who else I might have crossed badly enough to engineer something like this. That assumed that they wanted me. It was still very possible that this was all part of something bigger designed to catch Dee Lane or Menes. Maybe I'm a beater, too, and just don't know it.

And if I was in a trap, who was in on it? Dee Lane? Soames? Bob John? Was Morton's offer just coincidence or the mouth of the funnel, the illusion of escape, but nothing on the other side but an elephant and a shooter? And if so, why go to all this trouble for a part-time librarian? I smiled at my reflection in the dark glass. Dee Lane's paranoia was catching. I poured more whiskey, and drank it down like water.

CHAPTER 19

Buzzz, buzzz, buzzz,
Changes all the rules.
Gives me nerves of steel.
Makes me cool.
Makes me stronger.
Makes me mean.
Gives me rocky hard-ons,
And happy, happy dreams.

It does, too. Intense, euphoric dreams are part of the run-up of an adrenaline high. I woke smiling again, the darkness of the previous day forgotten, dreaming in rhyme. This time, though, the dream was not some concoction of crossed neurons, but a real memory. It was 1988. Bob John, Dee Lane, and I had just arrived at the university, and were playing volleyball on the quadrangle between Reed and Brumby, the two high-rise freshmen dorms. September in Athens can be the hottest month of the year, and this day was a broiler.

On the berm facing the western sun were twenty or so beach towels, each inhabited by a glistening tan female body. A few read.

Most lay on their backs, their eyes hidden by sunglasses, or on their stomachs, bikini straps undone and young breasts flattened against the towel. In the dream, these were almost—but not quite—visible, no matter what angle we peeked from, just like they'd been on that day twelve years ago. None of them paid us any attention, except for three girls cheering us from a huge bedspread-sized towel at the base of the hill. Each sipped from a large plastic Coke cup. As the game went on, they became drunker and louder. We stood, waiting for a serve, when a pretty brunette with big hair and smeared pink lipstick peered over the rim of her glasses and said audibly, "I like that one, the Top."

One of her friends looked at me, surprised, then grinned. She turned and almost fell into her friend's lap. To steady herself, she laid her hand on the brunette's arm. "Shhhugar, you're right," she slurred. "He looks just like a top. A little old top."

"What do you think he'd say," said the first one, "if I told him I'd take him home and *spin* him?" She emphasized the word "spin."

Dee Lane turned to me and mouthed the word "Spin?" He lifted his aviator-style mirrored sunglasses to give me an exaggerated wink. Bob John doubled over in a fit of the freshman giggles and turned away.

The rest of the game passed in a fog. Every time I caught Dee Lane or Bob John's eye, they burst out laughing, and I turned beet red and missed the next ball. Instead of concentrating on the game, I pondered what "spin" might mean. As it turned out, it meant nothing. A half hour later, the girls gathered their gear and staggered back to Brumby. They disappeared through the big glass doors, and I never saw any of the three again. They melted into the huge mass that is the university, either dropping out or settling into orbits that never again intersected with mine.

But the new nickname stuck. I loved it. It fit—I do look like a top. The guys in the game spread it like a virus through the enormous dorm, giving me both identity and status. Soon everyone referred to me as "Top." "Honus" ceased to exist, save in some deep recess of the registrar's computer. Even my parents and old friends quickly adopted the new moniker. It was a nice dream to wake up to. I whistled my way into the locker room to brush my teeth.

I am suited by temperament to hunting, not to being hunted. I can't just hole up and wait for a carload of rented gangbangers to come after me. My brain was running like a bird dog, racing across the fields in big looping esses, sniffing for smells and chasing faint scents riding on the wind. The buzz was flowing, and I was as happy as I ever am.

I didn't shower, but pulled on a pair of loose green shorts, running shoes, gray sweatshirt, watch cap, and gloves. From there I walked down to the office and opened the big steel safe. Over the sweatshirt I slipped a small shoulder holster with a twenty-five–caliber pistol. I closed the safe door on two rifles, two shotguns, and four more pistols—all legal. The illegal stuff is hidden in a footlocker under the stage in the auditorium.

The additional weight and loss of balance created by the gun were nuisances, but ones I considered unavoidable given the circumstances. Over the pistol I snapped a lightweight nylon shell. I practiced ripping open the front a time or two. The snaps didn't pull quite as easy as I wanted, so I finally settled on closing every other one.

Outside, it promised to be a beautiful mid-February day. It was already a cool fifty degrees, but sunny, with a wind beginning to rise off the fields, causing the tops of the pines to sway and whipping the budding branches of the Bradford pears in the field. Last year, we'd planted one hundred and sixty of those on what used to be the sports field. They formed neat rows, evenly spaced, with the trunks wrapped in burlap, held upright with cushioned wire struts attached to stakes pounded into the clay.

Today I planned to make a spiral, making three ever-widening rings around the school. First I would run a couple of laps along the property line that surrounded the eleven acres on which the school sits. It sounds like a lot of land, but schools are large buildings. Eleven acres is only about seven hundred feet by seven hundred feet, and the complete circuit is slightly more than a half mile. Then I planned to use the mountain bike to make a two-mile circuit on the dirt roads and farm paths that run along the ridges and fields overlooking Winterville Elementary. Finally, I would ride the bike six or so miles along paved roads in a long jagged star around my property, finishing off with a mile cool-down ride back in. With the residual adrenaline load I was carrying, ten miles should be just enough to take the edge off so I could settle down enough to hit the phones this morning. I hoped the legs held out.

If Menes or Bob John had any cars watching the school, there was a good chance I could get a peek at them by using the bike. Runners and cyclists are so ubiquitous, and so obviously unthreatening, that most people just ignore them. Last week at Polymath, we had an inquiry from someone asking about a whodunit where the villain was the postman, who almost got away with murder because every witness swore no one had come from or gone into the shop where the body was found. The client wanted to point out in his speech that what is seen every day soon becomes invisible. For the record, the answer to the inquiry was *The Invisible Man* by G. K. Chesterton.

I ran the inside perimeter briskly, enjoying the cold on my legs and cheeks. Yesterday's rain made the track muddy and loose, so I ran along the brown grassy side of the lane. Small dried-up weeds and brambles reached out and snagged my socks, occasionally whipping my shins. Gradually I opened it up, and by the time I'd finished my second circuit, I judged I was on an eight-minute-mile pace. There was a slight throb in my left knee.

In the locked maintenance shed were my bikes: a Pagliani for the street, a high-tech Trek mountain bike, a Schwinn classic for cruising, and hanging on the wall, the mangled frame of my old Waterford racing bike. That remnant was all that was left of that ambition. I took the Trek down, pinched the tires, then rinsed and refilled the bottle with the cool, sweet mineral-rich water of north Georgia. Satisfied, I took off.

The ride was uneventful. There was a cruiser parked in full sight about three hundred yards down from the turnoff to the school. I thought I recognized the young trooper inside from two nights before and nodded, but he didn't respond, just watched me with an impassive stare, his eyes hidden by mirrored wire-rimmed shades. Most of the cars on the road I knew, and most of the exceptions were either elderly or obviously local. I saw a few delivery trucks, any of which could be Bob John's outfit.

Around a curve, four pulpwooders stood behind their truck, pissing steaming streams into the ditch. The oldest one, a middle-aged redneck with long, greasy brown hair under a cap that read Stihl, grinned a smile that showed more than one missing tooth, and raised his free hand to wave. The three younger ones looked ahead stolidly. I waved back and rode on.

There was one spot of interest. Up on top of the ridge, two deep ruts and a fan of mud suggested that a vehicle may have parked too long and become stuck. I laid my bike down and walked the area.

The car had been pointed away from the road, parked in a spot that would have given them a clear view of the top and rear of the school. In the grass, someone had emptied an ashtray. The butts were dry. Given the rain over the last few days, they had been dumped late yesterday or early this morning.

Maybe the two different types of cigarette butts meant a carload of Blade's men spent the night up here casing the school. And then again, maybe it meant a double date came up here to neck, or a load of teenagers parked to drink a couple of six-packs. I looked in the grass for the more obvious signs to prove the alternate theories. There were no condoms or newly dumped beer cans in sight. Still, it was a long shot.

Back on the dirt road, I could make out two long, thin tractor-tire marks. Only one tractor makes that kind of track: an ancient John Deere Model A. It has a very narrow wheelbase that allows farmers to get in and out of spots modern, safer, wider tractors can't get to. The only Model A likely to be running this ridge belonged to Russell Driggers, who hauled feed back to his turkey farm by cutting up and over the ridge instead of driving around on the paved roads. By cutting through, he didn't need to clean off his tires before he went on the highway. I made a mental note to call Russell to find out if he'd pulled the car out or at least seen them parked there, climbed back on my bike, and finished my ride.

CHAPTER 20

A HALF HOUR LATER, SHOWERED, I SETTLED IN MY OFFICE, and flipped on the terminals, coffee in hand. Almost as soon as I sat down, the telephone rang. It was Gillie, reporting progress and giving me the back-door number so I could call in without having to call the old number and wait to be forwarded.

"How is it?" I asked.

"Top, I have to say it's nice. Chaotic, but it's light and clean and very professional. We'll have to work hard, but we'll be ready for Monday. The place feels good. I'm relieved to be away from the school after what happened to Harlan." She sounded a bit guilty. I pictured her as I listened, her mouth close to the receiver.

"Is Benny there?"

"Just left on his way to join you. He says you're headed to Atlanta this afternoon?"

"Yeah, be back around sundown, I hope."

"Benny's two guys, EJ and Dice, are still here. I never spent much time with them before, but they seem like nice kids. They're plugging things in and moving stuff around. I think I'm going to try them on the switchboard later, unless you need them out there."

"No, go ahead. Temps didn't show up?"

"Do they ever?"

"In my experience, no."

"You got it," she said. "Topper, you sound good. I was worried about you yesterday."

"I'm good, I feel good, now. How are you?"

Instead of an answer I heard the rustle as she covered the mouthpiece with her hand and a muffled exchange. She came back on. "Top, sorry, but I gotta go, babe. There's cable all over the place. George is here trying to get the desks together. Maggie's sitting on the floor with her keyboard in her lap right now. We've got a backlog of over five hundred inquiries. I'll talk to you later when things quiet down, OK?" The telephone clicked before I could answer.

I called Russell Driggers on his cell and asked him about the ridge. I also tried to talk to his father, but it turned out he'd left that morning for a funeral down in Albany, pronounced All-Bain-ee, and wouldn't be back until the next day. Then I dialed Bob John's office. The man who answered his phone wouldn't tell me when he'd be in, or if he was in, or whether or not he'd call me. Instead, he told me to give him a number and stay close to it.

An hour later, the phone rang.

"Top, it's Bob John."

"Hey, Bob John. I thought I'd check in."

"Check in?"

"Tell you what I'd found out, see how the Harlan thing's going."

"Well, Harlan's not our jurisdiction. As a courtesy, the Athens PD is keeping us in the loop on this one, but murder investigation's more their field than ours."

"Have they told you anything?" I asked.

"Not really. Fingers chopped off with what looks like a butcher knife or large hunting knife. No fibers or any of that stuff—the river washed it away. His clothes and his wallet still haven't been found. They think maybe robbery, but we think it's part of all this. The word's all over the streets that whoever brings the bag back gets to keep half, and your name keeps popping up."

"Did they find his car?"

"Not yet."

"Anything else?"

"Lots else, Top, but none of it worth much. We're still looking for the money, but there are no changes to your bank account, or anyone else's except Amanda Houle's. She just bought a new car and paid cash. That sort of stuff. Chasing stuff that probably won't amount to anything, because you can't know what might be important."

"And that's it?"

"Why am I doing all the talking here, Top? I thought you said you had something for me." His voice sounded tight and tired.

"Somebody's watching the school." I said.

"Really? Clarke County's got a cruiser on the highway. I have a team in camouflage in the woods. Athens PD may have someone around as well. Everybody's watching the school."

"Do you have anyone up on the ridgeline at night?" He was silent so I continued. "Somebody parked up there so long last night that they got stuck. Russell pulled them out this morning for twenty bucks. He said it was a puffed-up bodybuilder and a small woman. Dark brown Oldsmobile Achieva, maybe ten years old, with Dekalb plates. Said they were looking for a quiet place to talk and got stuck. Wink, wink, nudge, nudge. "

"Maybe it was," Bob John said.

"Russell didn't think so. He's pretty sharp. Said it felt like the woman was in charge, not just there for entertainment. You know he's also in the army reserves. He said he thought he saw what looked like a nightscope in the backseat, and the guy was carrying."

"What's Russell's number? I'll send someone out to have a look," he said thoughtfully. "Atlanta plates, huh?"

"Dekalb plates. Danny's got a bartender and a waitress who could fit that description," I answered. I rattled off Russell's cell-phone number. He'd probably be out in the barn getting his equipment ready for spring tillage now. I also gave Bob John the number at the house. Russell's father was the local Neighborhood Watch captain, a job he took very seriously. Since his stroke ended his farming career, he sits on the porch every day with binoculars, a notebook, and a cordless phone, rocking and taking notes in a slow, shaky hand. He might have seen something as well."

"OK, Top. Thanks. Is that it?" His voice said he was ready to move on.

"Somebody's been in Dee Lane's house. It needs to be secured before the teenagers find it's empty."

"OK, I'm going to use your name on the warrant application. That OK?"

"You won't need it. You can see the break-in from outside."

"Fine. That it?"

"Your friend Morton called me, offered me a job."

There was a lengthy silence. "Watch out. The folks he works for only hire outsiders to do stuff they think is too dangerous to risk their own people on. You give any thought to my suggestion that you take a vacation?"

"Decided against it, but I'm going down to Jacksonville for the day and take a look around."

I could hear him getting cautious. "Stay out of this, Top. You have no business in this."

"How do you figure?"

"Stay out of it." He hung up the phone.

In the spring when the diamondbacks come out of hibernation, anyone walking in the woods is careful to make a racket—clomping around, whistling, rapping trees with a stick. That way the camouflaged snakes can feel you coming and get away. I could only assume that Bob John had someone in place down in Jacksonville, and I wanted to make enough noise that I didn't surprise anybody. Like those rattlers in the spring, undercover agents can be a bit edgy. I thought of the conversation with Soames.

Benny and I locked not only the exterior doors, but secured all the interior doors with keys, and chained and padlocked the big double doors to the gym, auditorium, and band room. We took the key to the front door off Benny's key ring and put it on another big ring with thirty or so keys we'd bought at a yard sale a few years ago. After some debate over timing, we set the alarm to go off in exactly three hours. I brought along Morton's Iridium phone, thinking we might well see him and I could return it.

Then Benny hid on the floor of the truck as I drove out. I turned left, away from the highway, eased up the road, and pulled the pickup in beside the Clarke County cruiser. I rolled down my window. The young trooper stared at me impassively. I made a circular motion as if I was rolling down a window. With obvious reluctance, he hit the power switch and his window dropped.

"I appreciate you being out here keeping an eye on things," I said equitably. He gave a curt nod in response.

"I'm headed to Atlanta now. I'll be gone for the afternoon.

Benny should be back from town in an hour or so. Here are the keys to the school. Why don't you go sit up there and have a cup of coffee? Fresh pot's made. Refrigerator's full of Cokes. Go to the bathroom, whatever. Make yourself at home in the lounge." Behind his shades I could picture his pupils getting larger with excitement. The courts could only interpret this as an invitation to enter, allowing a plain-sight search without a warrant.

"Sure, thanks. Gets boring out here. Maybe I will." He tried to hide his eagerness and did so poorly that he dropped the keys I tossed him. He scrambled out of the car to pick them up. We left him standing beside the car and waving, a goofy grin on his face. The poor kid had no idea that by accepting those keys, he'd just put himself in line for a serious ass chewing.

As we drove away, without moving my lips, I said, "This is pretty devious. I sort of wish Dee Lane was here to admire it. He loves this complicated stuff."

From the floorboard, Benny answered, "He sure does."

CHAPTER 21

MENES SWEPT IN WITH AN ENTOURAGE, TWO BULKY dark-haired men in matching double-breasted shark-skin suits and wraparound sunglasses. Neither was a bodybuilder, like Danny's guy. They were just fat. Both wore crew cuts. One was in his early thirties and the other was much younger, and could have even been in his late teens. Raoul Menes, the man who owned the cocaine trade in the entire southeast United States except for Florida, paused at the door while his eyes adjusted to the dim light. Then with both of his hands, he slicked back his gelled hair. It was a gesture of habit, since his hair was tightly pulled back into a ponytail, and didn't need the attention.

Menes was only about five eight, but he carried at least two hundred pounds. He wore a dark gray custom-tailored suit with a black shirt, buttoned to the top, without a tie. His fat hands sparkled with gold and diamonds, and a massive gold chain hung around his neck. A ruby the size of the tip of my little finger perched on one shortish earlobe. He spotted us in an empty corner and weaved his way across the room, jewelry glinting and sparkling as he walked. His minders followed him closely, doing their best to look like they thought bodyguards were supposed to look, peering around, hands in their jackets.

When he reached the table, he stuck out his hand. "Top?" I looked at his pudgy hand with its five little sausage fingers. He held the hand outstretched for a minute, then shrugged and dropped it when I didn't take it. I noticed he nodded at Benny briefly before he sat down. He smiled at me, and with his corn-pone accent, said, "I didn't expect him to be here. Danny hates blacks, hates them. No offense, Benny—everybody knows that. He's not completely comfortable with us Latinos, neither. I'm surprised he didn't sic that go-rilla Sid on you." It was my turn to shrug. He looked at the bar curiously. "I don't see him anyway. Today's your lucky day, partner." His accent was pure southern redneck, no hint of Latino.

The heavy waitress was working the room alone today. In contrast to her desultory manner of a few days ago, today she moved briskly, taking orders and fetching drinks. Occasionally, she would glance worriedly toward the bar, where Danny himself was mixing drinks, his face a dark red frowning mask. Menes waved to the waitress. She acknowledged him with a nod, but it was still a few minutes before she could make her way over. Menes ordered a Rob Roy, a martini made with Scotch. His sidekicks both asked for light beer. Both Benny and I declined refills. My leg jiggled beneath the table.

"Danny looks pissed. What's going on?" Menes asked.

"Ask him." She jerked her head toward me.

"He don't talk much. That's why I asked you, honey," Menes said. He said "asked" as "ast." His tone became less affable. The waitress jutted out her jaw and stared defiance for a half second to show her independence, but then answered.

"We're already working shorthanded today, and that mother-fucker pulls Sid's arm out of its socket just because Sid tells his little colored buddy that we don't want to serve him. Tough guy here sends Sid to Dekalb General," she said angrily. With a melodramatic toss of her head, she left to get the drink orders. When she moved her head, I could see tattoos on the back of her neck, starting at the hairline and running down into her shirt. They had crisp edges and bright colors, in contrast to those on the webbings next to her thumbs. The tattoo on the left hand was a shakily drawn little swastika in black-green ink, and had the look of a jail-house special. On the other hand was one of similar quality, but this time the drawing was of a cross.

"Is that what happened?" Menes asked me. "Did you pull poor Sid's arm right off?"

"It's one version. It leaves out the part where poor Sid grabbed Benny by the back of his neck and waved a leather sap at me, and the fact that I probably saved the stupid jerk's life," I answered. Menes looked at Benny, who appeared philosophical about the whole thing.

"Top here sounds like a righteous badass. That right?" Menes asked Benny.

"Yes," he answered. I was not sure how we'd gotten on this topic.

"Reckon you could you take Chuck and Desi here?" he asked me.

"If I had to," I said.

"Screw you, you pencil-neck geek," the one on the right said. This was the younger one.

"Stop stealing material from Freddie Blassie," I answered.

"What?" he said dumbly.

"Who's Freddie Blassie?" Menes asked.

"A wrestler from the sixties, Classy Freddie Blassie. He invented the phrase, 'pencil-neck geek,'" I answered. "Also, my neck's twenty inches. It's bigger than yours."

The goon I'd corrected started to say something, but Menes held up his hand to silence him. "Why do you think you could take him?"

"Those sunglasses may look cool, but they mean he's almost blind in here. *I* can barely see, and my eyes have been adjusting for thirty minutes. He's right-handed, carrying his weapon quick-draw style on the left side. But he uses a belt holster, and he's gained some weight since that suit was made. It'll take him five minutes to undo those buttons and get his jacket open, and then his shirt's so tight he might not be able to lift his arms," I answered.

"Screw you, punk, I'll take you and your little girlfriend, here." he pointed to Benny.

"Desi," Menes said placatingly. But he was enjoying the big bodyguard's anger. His eyes danced with pleasure, and you could see him weighing whether to continue his instigation or move on to business. The tips of his sharp canines gleamed over his thick, rubbery lips.

"Fuck you!" Desi said to me, rising out of his chair. "Fuck. You." He jabbed his finger in my face.

"Desi," Menes repeated.

"What, Mr. Menes? I can't let this *maricon* diss me like that," the man lisped, putting both hands on the little table and leaning toward me, inserting himself between Menes and myself.

"Desi," Menes said more sharply. The man stopped and looked around at his boss. "Let me introduce you to Mr. Keirnan's associate, Benny Culpepper." The bodyguard stopped still, and his eyes dropped to the table. I could see the color draining from the skin behind his ears and then the paleness start to spread across his cheeks and up his temples. He licked his suddenly dry lips. Menes's amusement increased. "Well, I see you've heard of him."

Desi looked ill. "Go ahead and sit down, Desi. Go on. Don't worry about it, most everybody's afraid of little Benny. I might even be myself a little bit." He held up his thumb and index finger to show just how little. Menes leaned back, satisfied, and lit a fat cigarette, a Davidoff. He washed the smoke down with a pull on his drink and said, "Well, enough fun and games, fellas. Your meeting, Top."

"I don't have your money," I said.

"Then you sure as hell better find it."

"How am I supposed to do that?"

"That ain't my problem, fella." He parked the cigarette in his lips and squinted around the smoke to examine the nails on the hand that held the cigarette. Satisfied, he held up his other hand for inspection. He frowned and poked at a hangnail with the tip of a fat finger. I had no idea how he could see it in the gloom.

"I need you to call off your men," I said.

"My men ain't been near you. You think they wouldn't stand out down in Nowheresville? Stand out like a hickey on Miss America," Menes said.

"So you didn't kill one of my people?" I asked angrily.

"Could be I'm the cause of it—I'll give you that. But you said my men, and my men haven't left the city limits of Hotlanta." The cigarette between his lips bobbed up and down as he spoke.

"Why don't I believe you?" I felt Benny pull his feet under him and get ready to move.

Menes removed the cigarette and stared at me, his smile gone. "I posted a reward and let things go from there. Did that get your man killed? Maybe. I could give a shit one way or the other. But none of my men are 'on you.' And no one calls me a liar, cock-sucker." A hint of a Colombian accent crept into the final word, "cocksooker."

"Call off your dogs," I said.

"Then give me my money." His voice rose both in volume and pitch. "Give me my goddamned money."

'I don't have it," I said tightly.

"You listen to me, you smart-mouthed shit," he reached smoothly inside his coat. I tensed, and my hand dropped below the table. But he came out with a sheet of paper folded into quarters, which he tossed at me. "Read this." It was a very slick move. I reached for the paper, and as I did he stuck his hand in his coat again, but this time came out with a chrome-plated Colt Python, which he leveled between my eyes, pressing the round steel mouth hard against the bridge of my nose. Below the table, I held the SIG pointed at his crotch.

CHAPTER 22

I F YOU MOVE, BENNY, I'LL KILL HIM." MENES SPOKE TO HIS minions, "If that little black bastard twitches, put a bullet in him. You won't get a second shot with Benny. I mean, if you think you see something that might look like a twitch, shoot the little asshole." They both scrambled to get their guns out of those suits. Desi stood up.

"Read it!" Menes said.

"I've got a nine-millimeter SIG pointed at your balls," I said. The two bodyguards froze.

"I figured. Now read the paper!"

Suddenly there was small pop, and one of the buttons from Desi's shirt skittered across the table. For a fragment of a microsecond, Menes and I glanced at the button, and while we did, Benny reached over and lifted the pistol from Menes's fingers. The Colombian's empty hand still hung in my face until I swung the SIG up and swatted it away. I pressed the black barrel between his eyes. Chuck and Desi looked confused. They moved their useless guns back and forth between Benny and me. Benny put the shiny Python on the table and sucked his finger.

"You OK?" I asked. I could feel my heart pounding, and my breath rasped in my throat.

"Yeah. I stuck my finger behind the trigger, and Mr. Menes pinched it when he tried to shoot you," Benny replied calmly.

"Put the guns down, Des and Chuckie," I said.

"It's Chuck and Desi," the young one said.

"Put them down," said someone in a rolling Irish brogue. "You too, Top." Danny stood behind Benny, siting down the barrel of an AR-15, the civilian version of the M-16. I put my gun down. Chuck and Desi did the same. Behind Danny, the rest of the room watched with interest, but no one dived under tables or screamed or did anything silly. Danny's attracted a knowledgeable clientele.

The heavy waitress stepped around him, bending to keep her head below the muzzle of the gun so she didn't shield us from Danny, and tiredly collected all four guns on a tray. She walked back to the bar, where she clunked them down beside the cash register. "Pick them up when you leave," Danny said, and lowered the assault rifle. He backed up to the bar, turned, and lifted the gate. But instead of putting the rifle away, he left it out, where he could reach it easily.

Menes sat seething, his jaw locked and eyes slits. He pointed at the note. The dimness of the bar made reading impossible. I pulled out my key chain with the little flashlight and managed to make out the writing. It was a printout of an E-mail from Dee Lane.

"E-mails? And you're running a criminal empire?"

"It's double-encrypted, asshole," he said through gritted teeth.

"So it says somebody was supposed to come see you last Monday with a package and it's signed Dee Lane. I don't know anything about it," I said.

"Tough!"

"Listen, Menes. I'm going to try to find the money, and I'll even bring it back if I do. But if anybody else gets hurt, all bets are off."

"You are out of your damn mind to threaten me," Menes said. He rose quickly and his chair toppled behind him. Without another word, he spun and walked over to the bar, picked up his Colt and slid it back in his holster. Chuckie and Desi scrambled after him. Menes threw a bill on the bar. Danny picked it up with the hand not resting on the rifle. They stalked out of the bar. Once they disappeared through the door, Danny laughed and came over to our table.

"Ye're a regular fookin' diplomat, Top," Danny said as he tossed me the SIG. I caught it and slipped it back between my legs. My muscles were so tense my thighs felt like logs. "Piss off a stone-mad idjit like Menes for no reason."

He picked up Menes' overturned chair and sat down into it. "I'm getting too old for this," he complained. His face looked old. The skin around his eyes sagged into deep pouches, and a spiderweb of wrinkled skin was visible under his ears. Without his asking, the waitress came over and set three Guinnesses on the table. Danny and I gulped greedily, to wash away our dry mouths. Benny sipped his soda.

"I can help you here, man," he said. He studiously avoided looking at Benny.

"How?" I asked.

"I know Menes. He's got some cash-flow problems, it's making him crazy. I can calm him down, work the exchange, get things stabilized so to speak. Keep you alive," he answered.

"What's in it for you?"

"What do you bleeding think, Top?" he said with real exasperation. "The money. A cut. I'm sixty-fookin'-six years old. I should be retired to Florida, playing golf and fishing. Instead I get up every bloody morning and stand on my feet for ten, twelve, fourteen bloody hours. I can't even sleep at night because my daughter Moira has moved back in with her little one. I mean, jaysus, I love them, but I'm an old man. I need to get out of all this."

"So, sell up and retire," I said.

"Yeah, on what? Do you know what the IRA's pension plan is? When I had to bolt, they robbed a fookin' bank and gave me the money in a paper sack. That was it. Thirteen thousand Irish pounds in a paper sack. So I bought a passport and used the rest to put a down payment on this place. Now the neighborhood's gone straight to shite. Crack whores on the corner. I'd be lucky to get what I bought it for twenty-five bloody years ago." I noticed he didn't use the N word today.

Before I could answer, a man approached. It was Morton, the CIA slash DEA agent. He still looked far too elegant to patronize Danny's. Today he wore a tan cashmere sports coat over sharply creased brown slacks, along with a windowpane-check shirt and red knit tie. He held out a cell phone to Danny. "It's for you," he said.

The Irishman looked surprised, then took the phone. He listened for a moment, then said, "Jaysus fookin' Christ, I'm on the way." He stood up and stabbed a finger at me, "Get out of me fookin' bar, you damned Judas. Sit here and drink my stout while you set a trap for me own flesh and blood. You bastard. Get out and take your fookin' Oreo with you." He stomped away, mumbling under his breath.

Morton winked. He said, "That was Bob John Wynn. They just arrested Danny's daughter and another guy trespassing at your school. Apparently they had some very illegal weaponry on them, and now they're being held on federal charges."

"Thanks for the update," I said.

"Mind if I sit down, finish our conversation from the other day?" he smiled.

"We're just leaving," I answered.

"Next time, then," he smiled and politely waved us toward the door. And we left.

CHAPTER 23

I T WAS A LONG TRIP HOME. THE ADRENALINE HAD BEEN running high, and when it released I was exhausted, that deep weariness where it takes an effort to lift the foot to the brake and concentration to steer. Benny did not appear to have aftereffects from the confrontation, and he drove us smoothly and expertly through the dense traffic. The trip back was mostly silent, each of us lost in our own thoughts. We finally got back about 8:00 P.M. The lane was full of tracks, but by then, except for a dark blue Dodge, the parking lot was empty. As we swung around the circular drive, the headlights caught Bob John sitting on the front steps of the school, wrapped up in a light parka, hands resting on his knees.

We parked right in front. Benny went up the steps and by Bob John with just a nod. I paused and said, "What's happening, Bob John?"

"Nothing much."

"Do you think the two that broke into the school are the ones that killed Harlan?" I asked.

"Don't know yet. Be heck to pin the murder on them even if

they did it. Not even any fiber evidence on Harlan's body. But we've got them good on the trespass and weapons charges," he said. "How was Danny?"

"Didn't Morton tell you?" I answered.

"Yes, to be honest, he did," Bob John admitted. "I heard he was pretty pissed off about us putting his daughter and her pal in jail."

"That skinny waitress is his daughter?" I asked.

"Yep. It sounds as if the meet with Menes got a little intense, too," Bob John said.

"Yeah, real intense. Come on in," I said. We went inside, but instead of going to my office, I led the way back to the gym. I unlocked the door and flipped on the lights. Bob John slipped off his loafers.

"Do you want to move the bed?" he said.

"Screw it, let's shoot around it." I rolled him a ball and said, "Go." He shot and I rebounded, and I shot and he rebounded. It was a comforting, familiar rhythm, and I felt my neck muscles begin to unlock. After a while, I asked him, "How bad was today?"

He was about to put it up, but stopped and rested the ball on his hip. "Pretty bad. You had us figured out—we couldn't resist the chance to take a look around. As soon as you were out of sight, we came barreling in. Then we spent an hour arguing jurisdiction with that nincompoop from Clarke County. Just when we got that straightened out, Danny's crew showed up. Major takedown. They had a backseat full of guns, including an Uzi. Then we were just getting started again when that darned alarm went off. Jeepers, it's loud."

"In the fifties they put in this huge klaxon to warn the community about fires, tornadoes, nuclear attack—you name it. It's still hooked up," I said.

"Well, it rattled us. Of course, we thought we'd tripped it. Never would have dreamed you just put it on a timer. We were all crouched on the floor holding our hands over our ears. All your neighbors came by to see what was happening."

"How'd you turn it off?" I asked.

"We tried everything. Pulled breakers, you name it. Finally Gillie and George showed up and switched it off."

"I hope you didn't kill the power to my computers," I said.

"I wish we had." He laughed. "I wish you'd been here so I could have killed you. But I don't think we did. Look at your alarm clock, it's not even blinking."

"Good," I said.

"Key ring was a nice touch. Guys couldn't believe that except for the one that opened the front door, not a single key fit any lock in the school. Kept pushing each other out of the way to take a turn," he said, and lofted a long jumper from the top of the key. "Off," he said as soon as he released it.

It clanged on the left side of the rim, and ricocheted toward the bleachers. I chased it down. "I didn't have much choice, Bob John. The school's a target. With the parking lot empty and me and Benny out of pocket, I figured somebody might break in while we were gone. I didn't want them tearing the place up. I figured I'd get you guys to watch it for me."

"You could have just asked."

"Really?"

"No, probably not," he admitted. "But you took a risk. If we'd found anything, it would be legal."

"Not sure about that. First of all, there's nothing here. Second, searching takes time. It would take you more than one day to thoroughly search a building as large as the school.

Third, if you had to pick locks or use an acetylene torch on those chains to get into the classrooms, I'm not sure a judge would view that as reasonable."

It wasn't much of a risk at all. The only thing we really worried about them finding—the gun locker—was well hidden behind a false wall inside a basement accessible only through a trapdoor on the stage floor. That trapdoor currently had three hundred pounds of heavy velvet curtains rolled up and stacked on top of it. Other than that, there was nothing to find.

"That's pretty devious for you," Bob John said. "The spirit of Dee Lane must be rubbing off."

"Yeah, I said the same thing to Benny," I said, chasing down a rebound.

He dropped a long three-pointer from the corner. "Now I'm warmed up. You ready?"

"So you make the shot and then you call it!" I griped.

He grinned. I tried the shot and hit nothing. "H," he said.

CHAPTER 24

I HAD PLANNED TO GO TO JACKSONVILLE THE NEXT DAY, BUT instead had to go downtown to sign the papers to prosecute Moira and her friend Ralphie for criminal trespassing. They were long since gone, bailed out by Danny. In the mug shot, the skinny-as-a-stick waitress from Danny's bar wore a tight leather jacket zipped up all the way. After I finished with that chore, John Slocum, the Clarke County sheriff, wanted to yell at me for a while, and did. Then I went home.

When I got there, the sweepers had just finished and were repacking their van with strange-looking devices. Their leader, Bud, held out a plastic Tupperware container full of electronics. "This is a serious infestation, Mr. Keirnan. Very high quality equipment. Really, really cool. Timed, voice activated, dormants, independent power sources, the works," he said with professional admiration. I didn't volunteer any guesses on why they were there or who they belonged to. When I first called him from the pay phone at the Starvin' Marvin, he was very explicit about not wanting to know any details. "You did want them pulled, none left in place, right?"

"Do people usually leave them in?" I asked, curious.

"Oh, yeah," he said, as if the explanation was obvious. "By the way, there's also a tap on your land line, but nothing I can do about it. It's at the phone company switch. And somebody's scanning for cell-phone calls around here. I don't know if that's important."

"I don't know. Thanks for telling me."

I started to write a check. He looked confused. "I don't take checks, but your office manager and some guy were here already. She gave me the money."

I wondered why Gillie had come out on a Sunday morning, but shrugged it off. Instead of a tip, I told him he could keep the hardware. He grinned from ear to ear, and I suspected that he would make more reselling that than he did on the debugging. If I'd wanted to be a nice guy, I could have just given the stuff back to Bob John. But if he'd wanted to be a nice guy, he wouldn't have put it there in the first place.

I took a nap and worked out, then bored, logged into the server and began helping out with the inquiry backlog. I'd just sourced the quote, "Do your own thing," originally "Dooth with youre owene thyng" from "The Clerk's Tale" by Geoffrey Chaucer, when I heard a small ping.

The sound came from my computer. There are fifteen security cameras on the school, twelve external and three internal. The cameras are digital, which means the resolution is a bit rough, but also means they can be programmed to analyze the data stream and if the scene changes too much too fast, raise an alarm. The images can also be sent directly to my computer screen. About 6:00 P.M. the warning came. I keyed through the cameras. On the second one, I saw the fuzzy shape of Dee Lane's recent ex-girlfriend centered in the tiny frame. She stood for a few seconds, looking for direction, then spotted the small sign and walked out of the camera's field. When I opened my office door, she stood there, looking a bit tentative.

"Hi, Amanda," I said.

"Hey, Top." She looked around curiously. She was dressed as if she'd just come from work at the library, wearing a blue plaid skirt and pink blouse, with short black heels. Her hair was held back with a faux tortoiseshell band. "Where is everyone?"

"This week we've had some plumbing problems, had to move everyone into town for a while. Just me and Benny holding down the fort. And it's Sunday."

She nodded and smiled, but didn't say anything. After a minute of us smiling and bobbing at each other, she said, "Look, I don't know any more about the questions you asked me. I haven't talked to Dee Lane for a long time. We're done and finished. I got tired of waiting for you to call. So I decided to be bold and here I am. Bad idea." She grimaced and put up her hands as if to push away.

I opened the door all the way and laughed. "Good idea. No, great idea. This place is like a morgue with everybody gone. Come on in."

She opened the small knapsack and pulled out a bottle of chardonnay. "Do you have a corkscrew?"

"Sure," I said. She wandered around the office looking at the plants while I opened the wine with the Swiss Army knife from my pocket. I poured it into two ceramic Polymath mugs.

"Très elegant," she laughed when I handed her one. I made an apologetic face.

"Cheers," I said, and we clanked cups.

She took her wine and walked to the floor-to-ceiling bookshelves that cover the east end of the office, stopping in front of the center section. "I've never been here before. This is quite a collection of tops. Do you haunt yard sales on weekends? That's sort of at odds with my image of you as a brooding Mike Hammer type."

"Most of them were given to me. You know how it is, how you never know what to get someone. With me, everybody just gives me tops. I've only ever bought one."

She picked up an art deco metal top from the twenties. It would have been thrown with a wooden launcher, instead of a string. "What's this?"

"It's called a window breaker," I said.

"Oh!" She smiled, then pushed down the plunger on a large metal Ohio Arts top from the fifties. It whirred and wobbled on its base. "And this?" She held up a carved wooden top. It was obviously old, dark from a seeped-in layer of grime and the oil from countless sweaty hands.

"If you look at the base you can see C.S.A, a date, a regiment, and some initials. A Confederate soldier whittled it. It's pretty hard to get a wooden top round enough without a lathe," I said.

"This is the one you bought," she said. I nodded. She went through the rest of the shelf and I explained the difference between string tops, launchers, and finger spinners. She was fascinated with the giant Malaysian fighting tops. But at the end she returned to the old wooden one. "Do you mind me handling it?" she asked. I said no, and she held it under the light to try to make out the worn-down letters.

Finally she gave up, so we refilled our wine and I gave her a tour. I didn't want to end with my bedroom, so the gym's where we started. She kicked off her shoes without my asking, and made a slow circuit of the court in her stockings. Then we walked the linoleumed halls, and I showed her the classrooms we'd already fixed up, where Polymath is housed. We wandered to the old band room where Benny and his informal brass ensemble practice, then looped our way back and poked around some of the older classrooms. She doodled on one of the chalkboards and got half stuck in one of the smaller desks, and I helped her wrestle out. The library got a few words of professional admiration. Along the way, we finished the bottle, and grabbed another of similar background from the fridge in the lunchroom.

The last stop on the tour was the auditorium. I swung open the big doors. Benny had taken off the closing arms to be refinished, so they stayed agape where I left them. Through the opening only a few seats were visible in the dark. "Be careful," I warned, "There's scaffolding everywhere and some of the flooring's torn up. Let me get the lights before you get too far inside."

I felt carefully for the switch. We'd taken the plate off and I didn't want to poke my finger into a box of bare wires. When I found it, I flipped it on and the fluorescent bulbs in the ceiling flickered to life, throwing a harsh white light over the huge room.

She entered slowly, taking it all in. When built, it was intended to be not just the auditorium for the school, but the community center, and was sized accordingly. From where we stood, we could see the balcony rising over us on the left, with a crumbling back wall. The floor canted slightly and ran down to the stage at our right. In addition to the wide aisle that ran across the expanse, three aisles on the sides and center funneled down to the stage. Stacks of braces and planks were stacked just inside the door against the wall. The curtains were down and rolled back into the fly space behind the stage floor. In the center aisle, one scaffold rose up to about five feet below the ceiling. I waited for her reaction.

Her eyes followed the scaffold up to the ceiling. "You replacing the ceiling?" she asked.

"Tinplate. They used to lay out a small square of tin, usually from a can or a small drum, on an anvil and pound it perfectly flat, then they'd tap it over a carved mold. Nail enough of them together and you've got a ceiling."

She looked at the complex curlicues and flower patterns in the metal. "It's fantastic. There are hundreds of panels up there. How many different designs?"

"Fourteen."

"But each one also fits into the bigger pattern as well. It must have taken forever to make them."

"It's going to take forever to refurbish them. Every single one has to be scraped and repainted. Some have rotten wood underneath that has to be replaced. We figure we'll end up tearing some when we pull the nails. Then we'll have to make some new pieces by hand. Want to help?"

"Maybe," She smiled. Then, looking away from the ceiling, said, "Pews."

"Not original, donated in the fifties, when Queen Street Baptist built its new church."

"They've picked up some self-expression since they got here." She pointed to the carved names and dates on the back of each seat.

"You haven't seen self-expression yet," I promised. "Come on down this aisle so you can see around the scaffold."

In the center aisle, we had torn up part of the floor and laid a pathway of planks. I reached out my hand to help her maneuver, but she ignored it and held onto the top of the pews instead. When we passed the scaffolding, I stopped and pointed to the far wall proudly.

"Oh my God!" she said. "It's beautiful. What is it?"

"A fresco." The huge mural covered almost the entirety of the wall, from just above the tongue-and-groove wainscoting to the small row of windows along the ceiling.

"Who did it?" she asked, transfixed.

"In the thirties there was an artists' colony in Madison County. They were potters, mostly, but somehow they got a WPA contract to decorate the wall."

"It looks pretty political. 'Workers of the world, unite' stuff," she observed.

"You got it. They fled the Pacific Northwest and built a little community on a small lake about twenty miles from here. Called themselves the Goode People Farm."

"Down here? I never thought of the South as a safe haven for commies," she laughed.

"I don't think they were communists, more than likely a peaceful offshoot of the Wobblies, which was even worse. And there was no good place to hide. There were antiunion massacres by vigilantes out west and public executions in Boston. One out of every three adult men in Indiana was a member of the Klan in the thirties. It was just a lousy time to be an anarchist. At least here they had good-quality kaolin to make their pots," I answered.

"Wow, this is some room," she marveled. "I had no idea."

"I don't think anyone knows it's here, or there would be a committee from the university out here telling me what I can and can't do." I shifted the subject. "Some of them went on to become pretty well known." I named a famous painter from New Mexico.

"So is it valuable?"

"I doubt it. What would you do with it? It's a fresco, hard to move, and you'd need a twenty-by-seventy open space to hang it."

"It's really beautiful, Top."

"Promise you won't tell anyone? Although maybe it's a bit late to ask."

She looked at me strangely. "No, it's not too late." She paused. "Can we finish our wine here?" Without waiting on my answer, she used her hand to scrape most of the dust off a portion of the first-row pew. After refilling our cups, I settled on the steps cut into the center of the stage, right in the middle of the plank where countless kids had worn a groove walking up on honor days. She sat across from me, shoes off and legs crossed under her, and we talked about her arrival at the university, and the path that took her to the law library.

"I flunked half the 'I' test." she laughed.

"Eye test?"

"No, 'I,' the letter." She drew a capital I in the air with a fingertip. "You know, the SAT. It's designed to tell if you're illiterate or innumerate. If you're neither, they send you to premed. If you're innumerate, then you go to prelaw."

I saw it coming. "And if you're illiterate," we said in unison, "you go to Tech." We laughed more than the feeble joke deserved.

She'd done well, and was accepted to the law school—no mean feat. But after two years, she decided that she'd rather be Mrs. Chip Bazemore than a practicing attorney. "In hindsight, I think I was really looking for an excuse to quit law school before I actually had to set foot in a courtroom. Poor Chip was the one I picked," she said ruefully.

"What happened then?" I asked.

"Oh, you can guess. I made it six months as a Junior League wife in Augusta and hightailed it right out of there." She laughed. "Left behind a very relieved and grateful Bazemore family. Came back and now I'm getting my library-science doctorate."

"I thought you had it," I said. "Dee Lane always called you 'Dr. Amanda.'"

"Nope. Got another year of courses and then have to write a dissertation. But I take courses and work at the same time, so it's not too bad."

"You like the library?" I asked to keep her talking.

"I love it. I really like the stories in the law. And the people who work there. Librarians are good human beings." I nodded agreeably.

She wagged her finger. "So far we've talked about the school, and about me, and nothing about you. That's the problem. You're a lot like Dee Lane. I talk to you all night, and at the end of it, don't know any more than when we started."

So I told her the story of how I got my name at a volleyball game, but instead of laughing, she looked puzzled. "I don't get it," she said.

"Well, I look like a top," I said. "Physically. Built-up torso, skinny legs?"

She looked skeptical. "Show me," she challenged.

"I don't think so."

"Come on," she cajoled. "Are you wearing underwear?"

When I nodded, she wheedled, "Please. Come on. Just show me. Close your eyes and pretend to be a supermodel." She donned her innocent six-year-old face and folded her hands into a mock prayer. I gave in, and shucked off the flannel shirt, dropped my jeans and stood foolishly on the edge of the stage in my stocking feet, shivering in a T-shirt and briefs. She gasped when she saw my legs.

"What are those from?" She stood and ran a light finger down the thick scar tissue. There are four of them, one on the inside and one on the outside of each knee, big, sweeping curves like those on the scroll of a viola.

"Those are why I got into weight lifting. I hurt my legs and had to stop riding my bike." I pulled up my pants.

"How?" she persisted.

"In my hometown, every year they held a criterium," I buttoned the shirt.

"What's that?" she asked.

"A closed-course bicycle race. One year I decided to enter the novice race. About halfway through, I got all pumped up with the yelling and the cheering, and went right to the front. Took off. Just me on a breakaway with a couple of guys from the local cable TV station following behind on a motorcycle."

"Let me guess. You went too fast and crashed?"

"Boy, did I crash! There was a blind turn at the bottom of the hill. I came flying around it, carrying way too much speed and really laying the bike over, and right there in the middle of the road was a Slushee cup with this huge puddle of slick red goop. Down I went."

"You broke your legs when you fell?"

"No, I broke my legs when those dopes on the motorcycles ran over me," I admitted.

She tried to hold her face still, but then it exploded. She held up her hand to her mouth and tried to contain it, half-choking as she tried to stop laughing. "I'm sorry, really I'm sorry. But the way you told it!"

I smiled. "But that's why I look like a top. I couldn't really get around for almost a year. My dad put a weight bench in my room to keep me from going nuts."

"But you've still got the cute legs," she complimented me. She's right—some of the muscles are still there, the defined thighs and the knobby calves, each of which looks like someone

144

has stuffed an orange in a sock. But they still look small compared to my overdeveloped chest and arms. I didn't want to blush again, so I changed the subject and we talked about Polymath for a while. Then the wine was gone, and it started getting chilly in the big room.

She rose to go. "Thanks, Top, this was really cool. I had a lot of fun, and I'm sorry I laughed." She started chuckling again and tried to stifle it. "Sorry, I know it's not funny." I escorted her outside.

"Nice car," I said, looking at the new Accord.

"The old Tercel was falling to pieces. This one is great," she said.

"If you hear from Dee Lane, you'll let me know, right?" I said.

"Sure. You're really worried about him, aren't you?"

"I am," I admitted.

"Top, we're done, I don't expect to hear from him. But if I do, I will let you know ASAP."

"Changing subjects. It's probably too late to ask, but could you not say anything about me walking around an empty stage in my underwear?" I asked.

She looked thoughtfully at me through the open window. "Way too late." She grinned and drove off.

Her lights crept up the lane, disappeared for a brief second, and then reappeared on the highway. I didn't go in until I saw her crest the far hill. When her taillights vanished, I went back to my office and poured a dollop of Macallan into my wine cup. Drinking whiskey on top of a bottle and a half of wine. The buzz was thirsty tonight.

Above the conference table, one TV screen showed a soundless Larry King interviewing an equally mute Sissy Spacek, and on another a silent Foghorn Leghorn lit a stick of dynamite, tossed it down a hole in a tree, and covered his ears. None of it registered.

Instead, I sat and stewed, thinking about the fact that before people thought I had a million and a half dollars, I'd never gotten a visit from Dee Lane's girlfriend. Correction, *ex*-girlfriend. Then I thought about that for a while.

CHAPTER 25

I ROSE EARLY AND WORKED OUT, SHOWERED AND DRESSED. I
made a pot of Illy coffee, drank one cup, and poured the rest
into a thermos. By 8:00 A.M., the coffee, a cell phone, and I were
on the road south. I popped the Books-on-CD edition of *Perfect
Storm* into the slot on the dash, and settled in for a long drive.

There is no good way to get from Athens to Jacksonville. Jacksonville's on the coast, right across the Florida line, and is connected to the rest of the world via a large airport, a huge natural
harbor, and two major expressway systems. From downtown Jacksonville, you can drive straight to Miami, Los Angeles, New York,
or Boston, without ever needing to turn the wheel or detour off the
interstate system. Jacksonville is a very easy place to get to. The
problem is that Athens is not a very easy place to get *from*.

The remoteness is deliberate. The legislators who created the
university were looking for a place so isolated that students would
be driven to study without distraction. Their original choice,
Watkinsville, was crossed off the list because it had a tavern.
Instead, they moved another seventeen miles into the hills, and
founded Athens. The only expressway connecting the small city to

the world runs due west, the opposite direction from where I wanted to go. Nothing runs south or east toward Jacksonville but a series of two- and four-lane roads, roads that weave their way slowly through an endless string of small, sleepy forgotten southern towns.

This morning was foggy, but cold, and I could feel a change on its way. I started on 78 east, then cut down 22 through towns with names like Maxey's, Sparta, Sandersville, Tenille, and Wrightsville. At Wrightsville, which the sign at the city limits proudly proclaimed was home of Herschel Walker, the Heisman Trophy–winning running back, I stopped at the Hardee's for three sausage biscuits, an orange juice, and a fresh coffee. From there, I planned to continue down toward Soperton until I hit I-16, which would take me south and east to Savannah, where I would pick up I-95 for the final 140 miles. In all, it was 380 miles, one-third back roads and two-thirds interstate.

As soon as I took my first bite of biscuit, the cellular phone rang. "Hewwo," I mumbled around the food.

"Top, it's Gillie."

"Hey, Giwwie." I tried to balance the small phone on my shoulder while I picked up the orange juice. I took a quick gulp and washed down half the food.

"Terrible connection," she said. "Are you all right?"

"I'm OK. Got to check something out today. Benny's staying back and working on the auditorium ceiling."

She hesitated, then said, "I've got to call him. We need some rewiring done."

"Sure," I said. There was a moment of awkward empty space. "Are you calling me or returning my call?"

"Returning your call, but always happy to talk to you, boss." She put a playful huskiness in her voice.

"Same here, but I need you to do something. Gillie, did you check the phone logs for Saturday afternoon to Sunday night? I needed a list of all calls, even hang-ups."

"Sorry, I forgot. We've been busy with the move and all. Do you know what you're looking for?" she asked.

"Any sort of a message from Dee Lane." It was unlike Gillie to misplace a request, even one made while she was naked.

"I'll pull them. That it?" she asked.

"No, I forgot, Vinyl said he helped Dee Lane load up a bag to bring out to the school Saturday. Was anyone else besides you working that day?"

"I'm not sure, I can check. Maybe EJ or Dice, although they usually head for Atlanta at five-oh-one on Friday. I'll check the computer and let you know. Here's something for you to work on while you drive. We got a good one today. "Who first said, 'Ask not what your country can do for you, but what you can do for your country?' Five bucks. Call me when you figure it out."

"That exact phrasing, John Kennedy. But back in 1920, Kahlil Gibran said, 'Are you a politician asking what your country can do for you or a zealous one asking what you can do for your country?' It's a translation from the Arabic, so it's hard to match precisely."

There was a moment of silence, followed by a sigh. "How do you do that? You know, you'd probably be some sort of genius if your mind wasn't stuffed with things like that. I owe you five."

There was a pop, and I lost the connection.

CHAPTER 26

I T WAS A LONELY MONOTONOUS RIDE DOWN LONG SLOPING roads lined with pine trees and occasional road-killed carcasses. Every quarter hour or so, the sameness was broken by a town, usually signaled first by the appearance through the fog of a sprawling rose-brick high school, flanked by a flotilla of yellow buses. Then came a glittering mile or so of Wal-Marts, MacDonalds, and Ford dealerships, a few blocks of old, genteel columned houses with yards full of azaleas, and finally the town center, a sad, dilapidated square with a few scattered statues. No matter how small the town, there was always one monument to the Civil War, and another to World War I, usually a bronze statue of a doughboy, flat helmeted and bayonet in hand. In some of the larger towns, there was also something commemorating World War II, and in a few, even a marker to Vietnam.

Around every square was a ring of shops, most of which were closed and shuttered. A few beauty parlors, insurance agents, bars, and junk shops held on gamely. In almost every town, gang graffiti marked the brick walls and overpasses, mocking the virtues of small-town life. These little islands were less like Smallvilles than they were miniature Detroits, with decayed economic bases, hollowed-out city centers, and dangerous, drug-eyed kids.

I drove through these slowly. This part of Georgia has a long and well-deserved reputation for speed traps. Every year huge wildebeest herds migrate across the Serengeti plain. Packs of patient crocodiles lie in wait where the rivers are shallow. The big shaggy animals gather, then make a panicked dash across. The crocodiles, which need to eat only twice a year, pick off the incautious and the stragglers.

In the sixties, back when thousands of northeasterners drove their V-8s down Highway 301 to winter in Florida, the police department in Ludowici was so avaricious that one governor, Lester Maddox, actually used state money to erect billboards at the city limits warning drivers to slow down. I was safer in my truck than in a Mercedes-Benz with Pennsylvania plates, but I still stayed pretty close to the posted limits.

It was a familiar trip. Up these same roads Dee Lane and I had driven vans full of marijuana and later, cars with suitcases of cocaine in the trunk. For four years, five or six times a year, Dee Lane would drop by and ask me if I wanted to make some extra money, I'd say yes, and we would take a long bus ride to Jacksonville or Daytona. There we would be met by Matthew, a thin vegetarian with long brown hair, a perfect Jesus beard, and a battered Volvo whose bumpers were plastered with stickers urging us to "Commit Random Acts of Kindness" and "Save the Whales."

Matthew's job was to drop us at the junkyard, or parking lot, or wherever we were supposed to pick up our vehicles. There we'd see three or four identical vans or cars. Each vehicle was a couple of years old, clean, and painted an inconspicuous green or beige. There was usually some sort of signage on the side. We'd be given our start time, route, and contact point. Then, at ten-minute intervals, we'd leave the yard to drive to Atlanta or Charlotte.

It was never clear which vehicles really held the dope, and which were decoys. My career as a courier was pretty uneventful. I was never stopped by the police and never had to call "Mom," using the number I'd been told to memorize. But Dee Lane was plugged in to the next layer of management. He said sometimes vehicles did get stopped, and once we even lost a load. But most of the time it was just boring driving, seven or eight hours of staying carefully within the speed limit. We got $5,000 each per trip.

Dee Lane loved these trips. Like all good smugglers, his pulse is as slow as that of a marathoner, and it never seems to vary, no matter the situation. Dee Lane can stand in a customs line with a suitcase full of coke and never have a droplet of sweat break out on his upper lip, even if customs is strip-searching the entire plane ahead of him. He seldom carries a weapon. For protection he depends on his rep and the complex web of misinformation he has spun around himself. That—and a keen street sense.

I drove on autopilot, half-listening to my CD, reminiscing and observing. I reached the interstate after two and a half hours, and by 10:30 I neared Savannah. The fog had burned off, or been left behind, and with it the small towns and tired landscape. I now entered the sprawling trappings of the new South, rows of pretty, new four-bedroom houses perched on the edges of golf courses, malls, and bustling traffic. Twenty years ago, it was impossible for those not from Savannah to ride through the town without gagging, due to the rotten-egg odor emitted by the paper mills. Now, though, it was just a faint whiff, a testament to technology. Steady streams of traffic poured down both sides of the big highway.

I hated those trips. Operatives and smugglers are totally different breeds. My gig is to jack my pulse up to 120 and run like that for two or three days or even longer, riding the buzz, senses rubbed raw, shooting at every shadow. Driving the van was a way to make money. I always wondered how Dee Lane could ever enjoy a profession where a good night was one where nothing went wrong. Where's the fun in that?

CHAPTER 27

ACROSS THE STATE LINE, AT YULEE, I TURNED OFF, HEADING toward Amelia Island, which held the small airstrip where Dee Lane was last seen. A long drive like this makes my legs stiffen, and both knees throbbed. I was looking for a place to grab a hamburger and go to the bathroom, when out of the corner of my eye I saw a highly polished black Ferrari Testarossa parked on the corner of a small used-car lot across the divided road. Food forgotten, I changed lanes abruptly and did a quick U-turn, ignoring the blaring horns.

As I pulled into the lot, a tall, pimply young man in a white polyester-blend shirt, Members Only windbreaker, and poorly knotted tie skipped out of the trailer-office to meet me. His name tag said, "J. W. O'Bright."

"Good morning, sir. What can I do for you?" J. W. extended his hand and smiled. He had a wispy mustache, parted his thin hair in the middle, and wore glasses with chewed earpieces.

"I saw that Testarossa. Thought I'd come take a look. You don't see many black ones," I said.

"No, sir. It's a custom job," he answered. I strolled over to the car and walked around it. Someone had washed it recently and buffed it to a perfect shine. Our faces were reflected in the deep black paint. "Pretty car."

"Oh, yes, sir, it is that," J. W. said, and used the tip of his tie to dab at a blemish on the windshield. That said better than words who was responsible for the hours of buffing that would have been required to bring out this glow.

"How much you want for it?" I asked.

"It's not for sale, sir. We have some fine vehicles if you're in the market, but that particular car belongs to a big Ferrari dealer down in the city. They were supposed to pick it up day before yesterday, but something else come up, so they'll be here this afternoon or tomorrow."

"You drive it?"

"Oh, no, sir. Too rich for my blood," he lied badly.

"Well, if it belongs to someone in Jacksonville, how'd it get up here, then?"

Car salesmen are trained to be obliging, and instead of just telling me it was none of my business, he struggled to make up a story. "Well, sir, it's like this. An old Italian fellow from New York was driving it down to Miami and got this far and just got tired. These cars don't ride good at all. He called the dealer, left the car, and I drove him to Jacksonville Airport. So it doesn't even belong to the dealership in Jacksonville, really. They're just kind of handling it for him." He watched earnestly to see if I believed him.

"Isn't that something?" I agreed. "Can you tell me how to get to Amelia Island?"

"You're probably headed to the resort, down on the south end.

It ain't hard at all, a straight shot over to Fernandina Beach and then right."

"You got a map we could look at?"

"Sure, come on in the trailer," he said heartily. "Normally my assistant would be here, but she took her lunch break late today. Something to do with her kids."

Inside, the heating was turned on and the air was warm and stale. There were two small desks, and it looked as if there really was someone else who worked here. I closed the door and pulled out my wallet. Carefully I took out four fifty-dollar bills and laid them side by side on the desk. J. W. stared at them and at me, suddenly scared. I sat down in the visitor's chair.

"J. W., what do you say you lie to your friends and I'll lie to mine, but let's not lie to each other, OK? No old Italian man from New York suddenly got tired of driving a Ferrari with Georgia plates and gave it to you. I figure the guy who really left it asked you not to talk about it. That's fine—he's a friend of mine. I understand you're a man of your word, and I can respect that," I said. He looked at the door again, hoping his co-worker would finish her business and get back soon.

I kept going. "So here's what we're going to do. I'm going to tell you what happened, and you're just going to fill in the details. And if you do a good job, I'll give you two hundred bucks and not tell the guy who left it here that you drove it around, which I'm sure wasn't part of the deal."

"Look, mister—" he stammered.

I interrupted him. "J. W. I'm not kidding around here."

He swallowed dryly and looked hopefully at the door.

"OK, here's what I think happened. A tall guy, six-three or so, with straight blond hair, probably needed a shave, left that car here. He paid you to drive him to Amelia Island and not to say anything. He told you to park the Testarossa in back, but it's so sharp looking, you couldn't resist cleaning it up and putting it out front, especially when it was supposed to be gone a few days ago. How am I doing?"

He nodded and I pushed a fifty across the table to him. "Good. Tell me more about the guy who left it."

"But you already know."

"Yes, but I want to be positive you're not just taking my money."

"Oh, sure. Well, like you said, he's tall, although I'm six-two and he was way bigger than me, so I figure six-five at least, maybe six-six." I nodded encouragement. He continued, "And he was dressed all in black, with a black leather coat that came down to here." He motioned somewhere below the desk.

"Anything else?"

"Sunglasses. He had these wire sunglasses with little tiny green lenses. Must have been the size of a nickel. Looked real strange at seven on a Sunday morning."

"You just happened to be here on a Sunday morning?" I pushed another fifty across the desk.

"No, sir. He called a couple of days before and told me he wanted to look at a car on the lot, an old 4-4-2 stuck in the back row. We don't keep cash or nothing around, so it's not a big deal to meet somebody after hours. Do it all the time," he said, voluble now, proving Pavlov right.

I shoved the third fifty across the table. "What was the exact time you dropped him off, and what was he carrying?"

"He didn't seem to be in much of a hurry. He told me about the car, and how he was a lawyer from Tennessee, right across the state line, but taxes are cheaper in Georgia so that's why he had those plates. Just got a divorce and wanted to get rid of the car before his wife found it and gave it to her new boyfriend. You probably know about that, the tennis pro? That's why I figured it wasn't you and it was all right to talk to you. You don't look like a tennis type." A lot of times, when people talk for money they ask you to do that: to confirm that these are special circumstances and that they're not really snitching. So I nodded at all the right points, but didn't say anything to break his flow. "We stopped and had a doughnut, too. Finally got to the airfield about eight-thirty or so. He was carrying a backpack and old brown briefcase." That would have held the book Dee Lane had been working on for years. I pushed the final fifty across.

"You see him get on the plane?"

"Yeah. No. I saw him walk toward it, though."

"Very, very good, J. W. Now I want you to do something for me." I reached into my back pocket and pulled out my wallet again. This time I took out a hundred, which I placed on top of the stack of fifties in front of him. "I want you to put that Ferrari in the back and cover it up. There's a cover for it in the trunk. And I want you to forget I asked you any questions. You got it?"

He nodded, but I could see he didn't get it. "Come with me, will you?" We went out to the truck. I reached under the seat and pulled out the pistol. I didn't point it, but held it loosely in my hand. His eyes grew big. Behind the freckles, his pale skin lost the rest of its color.

"J. W., this is not divorce stuff. It's really serious. I need to be sure you understand I mean it when I say I want you to keep your mouth shut tight." This time he nodded furiously. "It's OK, J. W., nothing's going to happen to that guy. Or to me. Or to you. I just can't take a chance that you start blabbing to impress the girls down at the bar, and one of them tells their daddy, who tells somebody else, who tells somebody else, and first thing you know, the police are knocking on my door. I want you to promise me you understand our deal."

He didn't say anything, too afraid to speak. His chin trembled uncontrollably. "I think we're OK here," I said and got in the truck. He nodded, and kept nodding as I turned the truck around, and started to pull out. I swiveled my head to check for traffic before pulling back onto the highway. As I released the brake, I heard a shout behind me. J. W. ran up to the window.

"You're about to go the wrong way. Fernandina's to your left," he said.

"Thanks, J. W., I saw a Wendy's up the road. I think I'll grab a bite," I answered, and headed back to the entrance to I-95. Dee Lane planned his disappearance down to the smallest detail, and he'd sold his Ferrari. That meant he wasn't coming back soon and that no one was going to find him. He'd left a trail a mile wide leading straight to that jet, so there was little or no chance he'd been on it. Did that mean he was alive? Hard to say, but it improved the odds.

It helped me narrow the time window. Vinyl Man helped him load the bag in the Camry around sunset, and he'd left Athens no later than midnight. That meant that somewhere in that six hours, the bag disappeared.

Dee Lane loves Brazil, in part because that's the only place he's ever been caught smuggling. A customs officer once opened his carry-on bag to find two bottles of Johnnie Walker Black. "But sir," he protested, "you cannot have two bottles of liquor."

Dee Lane smiled and said, "But I don't have two bottles."

"How not, sir?" asked the puzzled officer.

"That one belongs to you." Whereupon the customs agent smiled, put the bottle beneath the counter, and told Dee Lane to zip up his bag. And Dee Lane is especially fond of Florinapolis, reputedly home to the most beautiful beaches and the most beautiful women in the entire world.

I smiled at the mental image, then switched off my cell phone and popped in a Schoenberg CD. I needed to think.

CHAPTER 28

I WAS EXHAUSTED BY THE TIME I REACHED WINTERVILLE. I'D driven almost solidly for 700 miles, thirteen hours down and back. Even though it was only around 11:00 P.M., I could feel the tiredness in a tight strip across my shoulders and neck. My mouth felt like a used sweat sock, and the inside of my eyelids like sandpaper. There was a small amount of bitter, almost-cold coffee left in the bottom of the styrofoam 7-Eleven cup between my legs. I drained it as I turned off the highway and eased over the washout onto the lane that led to the school.

I could see the glow long before I made the last turn. The old brick building hunkered in the center of the glare like a dark frog on a lily pad of light. Every outside light blazed, including the floods at the corners, the big lights over the main entrance, and the yellowish security lights in the parking lot and over the rusted-out jungle gym. I stared at the entrance. The doors were propped open with the little brass doorstops we'd refurbished so carefully, but seldom used. Most of the interior lights were extinguished and rows of dark windows sat in quiet tension, the sole exception a bank of six windows on the front left of the building, where my office is. There, the shades were lit with a faint glow, and narrow ribbons of light leaked out around their edges.

Carefully, I killed the headlights, cut the engine, and coasted to a stop. I pulled the SIG from under the seat and took the .22 from the glove box. Slowly I eased out of the truck. The only sound was the pinging sound the hot engine made as it cooled in the night air. I stood and waited. Behind me, the pitch-dark treeline loomed, and creepy crawlers ran up and down my exposed spine. As quietly as I could, I pulled the slide back on the nine-millimeter and slid a cartridge into the chamber. I waited for someone to make a move.

Nothing happened. I stood perfectly still for five minutes, five minutes that felt like five hours. Eventually, as my ears adjusted, I began to hear other sounds. First, a distant hum of traffic, then a few moments later, I picked up the faint lilt of music playing in the background. Gradually I heard more of the tune. Brass. Four-four time? Da da da dada, da dada dada da. John Philip Sousa? I knew only one person who listened to that stuff. I slammed the truck door as loudly as I could and walked up the steps. As I got closer, the music became louder and the beat more insistent.

The door to my office was open, held that way with a chair from the conference table. Through the opening, I could see Benny. He sat in my Herman Miller ergonomic superchair, his feet propped up on the desk, smoking a huge cigar. The butt of another cigar lay in a glass ashtray, which was perched precariously on the corner of the desk closest to him. Also on the desk was an almost empty bottle of clear Rumplemintz schnapps, a glass, and a fine dusting of ash. When he saw me, he smiled and held up the remote control. The music died. With his other hand, he motioned me in.

"Hey Benny, what's up?"

"I'm waiting," he said solemnly. The office reeked of cheap

tobacco mixed with pot. As I watched, Benny dropped his jaw and blew a series of perfect smoke rings. His words were slurred, and his head bobbed a time or two, but each time he snatched it back before it hit his chest, and smiled again. The cigar he was smoking and the stub in the ashtray both still wore their red-and-gold paper bands.

"Who you waiting on?" I asked.

"Whoever." I laid the pistol on the desk, but didn't sit down. He sat there, swaying drunkenly. But cobras sway drunkenly, too, and that doesn't make them look any less lethal. I didn't move.

"I've never seen you get high before. Are you OK?"

He ignored my question. "You know, I used to love this stuff, back in the bad old days. Haven't had a drink or a smoke in four years and seventy-three days. You want a drink, Top?"

"Sure." I picked up the bottle and walked behind him to the credenza for a mug, holding my breath. He didn't flinch or even appear to notice as I walked behind him, but I was sure he'd be following my movements through the reflection in the dark window glass.

"You ever seen somebody die from a razor cut, Top?"

"No, I haven't."

"First fight I saw was two hookers. I was just a kid, hanging out in this bar in the neighborhood, running errands for the dealers." He took another gigantic puff.

"These two women get into it. First thing you know, they pull out blades and started swinging at each other." He looked into the distance. "It was so quiet, man. All the music stopped and nobody said nothing. Everybody just watched these two old whores make big passes at each other in this little cleared-out space between a couple of tables. Them razors made a whistling sound. Sveeep. Sveeep. Then all of a sudden one just moved her hand a little bit, and the other one stopped still—dropped her hands and just stood there. The first stepped close and put her arm around the girl's neck like she was kissing her, but she was whispering something in her ear. She said what she had to say, and stepped back, and the one that was cut stood there swaying. Dead as dead can be and didn't even know it. Then she just crumpled in a little pile on the floor. And all of sudden the place was jumping, people screaming and running over tables and shit, getting out of there before the po-lice came. The winner stood there, grinning her ass off, blood all down the front of her blue dress. I picked up the dead girl's blade and got the hell out of Dodge. That was the very first razor that I ever owned."

"You trying to scare me, Benny?" I asked carefully. The electricity sang up and down my arms, and I could feel the blood pumping through the thin membranes of my mouth.

"Why you ask me that?"

"I come in here, you're wasted, and you're telling me weird shit about what it sounds like to get your throat cut. What am I supposed to get out of that?"

"You shouldn't have brought this down on us, Top. This"—he hesitated, searching for the word and gave up—"this is what I came out here to get away from. I had all of this I wanted back in the city. Not right that it's here."

"I don't know what I could have done to stop it."

"Yeah, well. It's here," he said stubbornly.

"You don't have to stay," I said, too quickly.

He looked at me, hurt. "Yes, I do."

I felt like a jerk. After a few minutes, Benny said, "You find out anything about Dee Lane?"

"Maybe."

"Find out where he is?"

"No, but it looks like he planned to go away—for a long time, it looks like. I don't know, but I've got a gut feeling he might have headed to Brazil. No reason to think it, just occurred to me."

"You can't call him and find out what's going on here?"

"I'm not sure exactly where he would be. I'll E-mail Shaw's and get them to send someone, but I wouldn't count on hearing back. Dee Lane's not easy to find when he doesn't want to be."

"Hell of a mess," Benny said.

"Maybe he doesn't know what he left behind. Probably sitting on a beach, drinking rum and pecking away on his laptop, and maybe he's got no idea that all hell is breaking loose back here."

"How could he not know?"

"I haven't figured that out yet," I admitted.

He shrugged his indifference and lifted his hand. My shoulders trembled with the effort of holding my hands still, both the one that rested on the edge of the table and the left one, which I held down beside my leg, a quick reach from the small automatic that rested in the small of my back. He reached not for his pocket, but for the armrest and using the black rubber slab for balance, swung his feet down, reached over, and picked up the bottle. The little man poured the last of the liquor into the glass and took a sip. He smacked his lips.

"Aaahh. You know why I'm so fast, Top?"

I shook my head.

"But you know my name?"

"Benjamin Bell Culpepper."

"You know who James Thomas Bell was?" Before I could answer, he said, "Of course you know—what am I talking about? You know everything. Tell me about him, Top."

"Benny."

"Just tell me, man, come on. I know you know." His eyes, which were unfocused a minute before, narrowed and locked on mine. A humorless smile creased his face. There was a single clear drop of schnapps balanced on the end of his thin mustache.

"Cool Papa Bell. Played for the Pittsburgh Crawfords in the old Negro Leagues in the thirties. Fastest man to ever play the game. Any color, any time, any place. Once stole home from first on a sacrifice bunt. Another time he walked, then stole three bases in a row. They say he told the pitcher every time before he did it, 'Get ready now, I'm going on the next one.' And outran the pitch."

"Yeah, that's him. Cool Papa Bell was my granddaddy. You didn't know that did you? My grandmama was pretty, and those baseball players come barnstorming through town, they could have any girl they wanted. They say my daddy was Cool Papa's illegitimate son. So my mother's family named him James Culpepper. Slick, eh? Cool Papa. Culpepper? Get it?"

I spoke again, "Tell me what this is all about, OK?"

He stared at me for a moment, and then suddenly covered his face with his hands. I still didn't move. "They got Vinyl Man," he mumbled. "Did Bob John call you?"

"*Who's* got Vinyl Man?"

Benny was mumbling something. I picked up the big pistol wrong-ended and rapped it down hard on the desk. "Hey, tell me about Vinyl Man," I said too loudly.

He lifted his head and stared at me. His quiet tears ran down to disappear into his small, neat goatee. "Bob John called. Police drove by Groovology about six. Doors wide open, but the place is empty. Couple of hours later, got a call from the Home. No sign of Vinyl Man. Left his meds. Bob John thinks somebody snatched him, maybe the ones who got Harlan."

"Vinyl Man?" I slumped in my chair.

He hesitated a moment, covering his eyes. "Leonard Marks. Twenty-eight years old. A pitiful loser and a pitiful little job. Loved the horns. Couldn't get enough. Jazz, Miles, big band, whatever." He looked at me again.

I knew my mouth was open, and swallowed hard. After a minute, I said quietly, "Vinyl Man had a big bull's-eye on him from the word go. Everybody should have seen it. We should have seen it. Bob John should have seen it. Especially after Harlan."

"Well, we didn't see it, and they got him," Benny replied with surprising bitterness.

"I can do this."

"Do what?" Benny asked.

"Find him. Get him back." I reached over and picked up my glass and finished what was left in it. It tasted like peppermint schnapps always does: like somebody mixed kerosene with Karo Syrup.

"How?"

"We'll find him." I sounded like a child. Because I said so. That's why. That's how.

He stared at me, eyes glistening, before he finally stood up. He tottered a moment, then gained his balance. As he passed by me, he lurched and brushed against my shoulder, then weaved his way out through the door. "I believe you," he mumbled over his shoulder.

I left the office door open and propped open all the windows, even though it was probably down to the high forties by now. The ashtray and schnapps bottle I dumped into a plastic bag, and twisted the neck tight. I tossed it into the covered garbage can out front, making sure the lid was on tight enough that the raccoons would have to work to get it off. I turned off most of the exterior lights, locked the doors carefully, then went down to the storeroom and fished out a down sleeping bag.

Unfurling it on the office floor, I lay down on top of it and covered my eyes. Before I fell asleep, I remembered the .22 tucked in my waistband and reached back to remove it, but found it already gone. I thought back to Benny's bump as he passed by and smiled. A little message. Maybe getting soft in his old age of thirty-something, but he was still Benny the Blade Culpepper, the fastest man between Philadelphia and Mobile. I quickly fell into a light dreamless sleep.

CHAPTER 29

I WOKE ABOUT 4:00 A.M., WIDE AWAKE, NO CHANCE OF GOING back to sleep. Nor did I want to. I'd had another of those cheerful, Technicolor adrenaline-rush dreams, but this one starred the dead mother and daughter from Lima. The mother looked much as she did in the photos her husband Armando gave me: tall with a thin Spanish nose and a sallow smoker's complexion. In the picture, she was probably twenty-five at most and very beautiful in a classic way. The little girl, Consuela, was pudgy and wore a pageboy haircut. All of her pictures showed her with a gap-toothed grin.

In the dream she was pale and the sleeve of her school tunic was stained with red brown blood, just as it had been. But she laughed and danced anyway, while her mother smiled and applauded her pirouettes. Her mother wasn't bleeding at all in my version, but of course it had poured out of her in a pink froth that night. Her leg had a hole in it, and half her chest had been gone when she'd died in my arms as we ran across that stone courtyard. Consuela ran ahead. I dodged right behind her, trying to shield her with my back, but a bullet went right around me and nicked her and another hit her mother's foot. I came away without a scratch that time. Not even a scraped knee.

In the dream, I yelled at them to come with me, but they just kept on playing together, dancing and laughing. I grabbed the mother's hand and tried to pull, but it slipped right through mine, so I grabbed it again, and again it slipped away. They sang something in Spanish, but I could understand only the word for "doll." Adrenaline dreams are usually intense, but happy. This time I woke in a pure panic, heart pounding and shoulders jerking as I fought to rise. I sat upright and gulped big breaths until my heart slowed, the stale taste of schnapps like gasoline in my mouth.

I pulled on my socks and Converse All Stars, checked E-mail, and saw a new one from Bob John. He wanted to know if we were available for breakfast. I answered, then folded up the sleeping bag, stuffed the small cell phone in my pocket, and made a circuit of the school, pistol in hand. Everything was quiet.

In the gym, I lifted for a half hour, mostly arm work, curls and extensions. I took it easy, working mostly with fifties, careful not to pull anything. It felt good and when I was done, I climbed on the stationary bike. But I couldn't get into it. The rhythm wouldn't come. After fifteen minutes, I gave up and toweled off. I picked up a basketball and took a quick uninterested shot, but let the rebound bounce away.

I had two hours to kill before we left for town. So I pulled on an old flannel shirt and went to the auditorium. The back wall was bowed and cracking, and we'd planned to tear down the lath and rebuild it when we finished the ceiling. It was mindless, dirty work, requiring no finesse—just the energy to swing a ten-pound sledge and pull on a pry bar.

I couldn't smash the dream, which lingered on the fringes of my consciousness like a bad radio jingle, so I smashed the old wall instead. I worked down it systematically, moving backward, leaving a path of broken sticks and plaster on the floor ahead of me. I'd been working about thirty minutes when I felt the phone buzz in my back pocket. I dropped the sledge, wiped my sweaty hands on the back of my jeans, and fished the phone out with two fingers.

"Top," she said.

"What are you doing calling at this hour, Gillie? Is everything OK?" I asked quickly.

"Yeah."

"You shouldn't be at home. Why don't you go to a hotel? On Polymath."

"No, I think we're OK. George called his cousin, and Athens put a cruiser out front."

"That's good."

"I didn't wake you, did I? I figured you might be up. If you were asleep, I figured you wouldn't leave the cell turned on. And if you were awake, then you would answer." I could hear her sip something, probably a cup of coffee.

"You were right. I couldn't sleep. I'm in the auditorium."

"You're not working on the ceiling without help, are you? That scaffold's not too steady."

"No, tearing out the back wall."

"Good. Leave the ceiling until someone can help you with it. I'll come out on Saturday."

"You don't have to do that."

"Oh, I'm beginning to miss the old dump. How about the wall? Can you tell yet why it's bowed? Is the brick collapsing?" she asked.

"I can't tell. The whole place is just one big cloud of plaster dust. We'll have to let it settle."

"Oh," she replied. I sat listening to the phone, but all I could hear was her breathing.

"Why are you up?"

"Oh, Top," she laughed. "It's five A.M. I'm always up at four, four-thirty, five. That's when I do the laundry and make the kids' lunch and do some of the cleaning. When I get home at night, I have to make supper and work with Robbie on his homework. He's a bright kid, but it takes him a while to get stuff. When he gets it, it's in there forever, but if I didn't work with him, he'd get so far behind he'd never catch up. So the morning is my time to get ahead a little bit. I'm sitting here on the couch wearing an old robe that belongs to George, folding clothes."

"Do you need some time off from Polymath, Gillie?"

"I need some time off from kids, but I'm not going to get that for the next seventeen years," she laughed.

The phone went quiet again.

"You didn't answer the question, Gillie."

"I know. Maybe I do, Top. I've been thinking maybe I should cut back some. We've needed the money, but George is supposed to be getting a big raise. Running the incubator's more responsibility. Maybe I *will* cut back some. Let me think about it."

I closed my eyes and grimaced. Be careful what you ask for. Or offer.

"We miss you, Top. *I* miss you."

I didn't answer.

"You're not going to say, 'I miss you, too, Gillie'?" she laughed.

"I *do* miss you," I said.

"Too late, Top," she sighed. "You've had all the chances you deserve. It's too late now." Neither of us said anything for a while.

"So are you around tomorrow at the school?"

"Not clear yet. If we get any leads on Vinyl Man, I'll chase those up."

"I don't care about Vinyl Man, Top. I mean, I *do* care, but finding him is a job for the police. You should leave this to the experts."

"You know better than that. They've got Vinyl, and the same thing could happen to him that happened to Harlan. And we don't know where Dee Lane is, and they could come after any one of us next," I said.

"That's bs. You love this stuff. I can hear it in your voice when we talk. You're happy as a clam that all this stuff is happening."

"Gillie, give me a couple of days, and we can sit down and sort things out."

Instead of answering, she said, "How many insurance policies do you own, Top?"

"None."

"That's wrong. You have three: a health policy, a small life policy, and key-man insurance. You signed the applications a year or so ago, and Polymath pays the premiums. But the point is, you didn't know you had any." I could hear the exasperation in her voice.

"I don't know where you're going with this, Gillie."

"Where I'm going is you had a chance and you didn't take it. You always talk about loyalty. You're loyal to your friends, you're even loyal to that damn school, but how about loyalty to us? You blew it," she said. I was too tired to track. I could hear her crying softly into the phone.

"Tomorrow," I said. "I will come by to get the phone logs and we can talk."

"I don't want you to come by tomorrow and talk, Top. It's too late. Oh, shit, I don't know what I mean. I'm sorry I called." The phone went quiet in my ear. I sat there for a few minutes. Then I laid the phone down on one of the pews, where I would hear it if it vibrated, and resumed my demolition.

CHAPTER 30

T HE BUSY BEE RESTAURANT IS LOCATED IN A NARROW storefront on Broad Street in downtown Athens. The main room is square, with rows of old red vinyl booths across the front and down the side. There are probably a dozen square tables in the center. The cash register is on a small plywood-stained-walnut counter across the back. Behind the counter is the door to a private room that the Kiwanis and other clubs use on a rotating basis, and a swinging door to the kitchen. To get to the bathroom, you have to go outside, down a small alley, and around a corner into the back of the kitchen. Health regulations won't let you cut through.

The ceiling and floor are both brown. It's hard to tell what color the walls are, because every inch of the surface is covered by hundreds of fraternity paddles held in by screws. Somehow—every year—they find room for more. In the spring the place is full of pledges with magnifying glasses and flashlights assigned to ferret out the faint signatures of long-dead brothers. Some paddles are supposedly a hundred years old, which would make them roughly the same age as Mina, who had gone to get our two coffees and an English-breakfast tea.

We avoided the topic of Vinyl Man. Bob John and I argued a bit too passionately about whether the Hawks should have traded Mutumbo. It was a stupid argument, but Bob John's E-mail suggesting breakfast was time-stamped at 3:34 A.M., telling me he wasn't sitting idly until Vinyl Man's body showed up in the river. If he didn't want to talk about Vinyl, it must mean that there was little new to be said. Benny ignored the conversation and sat staring straight ahead, looking pretty much normal except for the black wraparound sunglasses and the sheen of sweat that covered his slightly greenish face.

Mina flatfooted it back, slapped down the drinks, and demanded our order. Her eyebrows were drawn on at slightly different angles, two thin brown lines, one pointing at three o'clock and one at ten. Her face was heavily powdered, and her hot pink rouge, matching lipstick, and black pageboy wig gave her a vague resemblance to silent-film star Theda Bara. Very vague. We ordered meekly, not that it mattered. Mina was senile and had been as long as anyone remembered. We knew that in the worst case eventually her baby sister Veronica, who wore similar makeup but looked more like Buster Keaton, would peer through the small opening where the orders came out, see us sitting here, and we'd get something. But what or when was uncertain.

"Tried to call you yesterday," said Bob John.

"I turned off my phone and forgot to turn it back on," I said.

"Reception stinks on I-95 anyway," he said.

"Yup." I sipped my coffee, not knowing if I was supposed to be impressed at his knowledge of my whereabouts.

"Last night we went into Danny's bar and his house on a trumped-up warrant. Found a couple of unregistered weapons, but we'll have to give them back. It was an Alabama warrant," he said.

An Alabama warrant proper is where one deputy goes to the front door and another to the back. The one at the front knocks and the one at the back yells, "Come in." In this case, I assumed he meant the DEA called in their own anonymous tip.

"No Vinyl Man," he finished.

"Do you think he'd keep him there?" I asked.

"Who knows? As a rule, criminals just aren't that smart. But his whole crew was accounted for. I also think if he had him you would have gotten a call." When Mina placed his coffee on the table, Bob John filled it with two sugars and so much cream that it rounded at the top and almost overflowed. He leaned over and carefully slurped a quarter inch of it down. He poured in another creamer.

"What about Raoul?" I asked.

"I don't think so. Same reason, he would have called," he answered.

"So there's somebody in the mix we don't know about," I said.

"Oh, heck, yeah. With that reward out, there's probably thousands of people in the mix we don't know about." He smiled grimly and nodded at my hands. "What's the white stuff?"

I glanced down at my fingernails. Plaster dust was caked around the cuticles. "I was cutting cocaine."

"Don't joke like that!" He looked around.

"I couldn't sleep, got up at four, and tore down some of that lath on the back wall of the auditorium. It's impossible to get all that plaster dust cleaned out of the cracks and crevices."

He nodded. Gingerly, he lifted the still-too-full cup to his lips. Just as he did, we heard his pager hum and he sloshed a bit over onto his hand. He quickly put the coffee down, wiped his hand on his napkin, and looked at the LCD readout. "I'll be right back," he said and slid out of the booth. Outside, through the glass, I could see him dialing his cell phone.

"Veronica just saw us," Benny said.

"Good," I said, "I'm hungry." Over Benny's shoulder, I saw Bob John pacing in a tight circle as he talked. Then Mina moved into my line of sight. She dropped four plates on a table near the front window. The fraternity brothers at the table tried to protest that they had ordered something else, but Mina cut them off, waving her finger in their faces and telling them that she knew the national president of the Kappa Sigmas and would call him personally. The four kids, all of whom wore the white and red T-shirts of the Pikes stared openmouthed. She tore the check off and hurled it at them, and stomped off to the coffeepot. They looked at each other dumbfounded. She came back and started to refill our cups, but Bob John's was still almost full. She turned to me, but didn't pour.

"You don't look like you need any more," she said, turned, and moved away. Bob John moved in right behind her and slid into the seat. I raised an eyebrow.

"Something else, got to go," he said. Before he could rise, Mina stepped up and slid three plates onto the table.

"Eat some of this before you go," I said. It wasn't close to what we ordered, but it was a good choice. Veronica sent fruit for Benny, a heaping order of pecan pancakes, and one of scrambled eggs, grits, and bacon. Bob John and I quickly split the pancakes, eggs, and bacon. He ate without talking. I managed to get down one pancake and a slice of bacon. It tasted good and I wanted more, but my throat was too tight to swallow it. Benny gingerly popped a strawberry into his mouth, and let it sit there, without chewing. Bob John stood up, wiped his mouth and reached for his wallet at the same time. I waved him off. He took a last gulp of coffee, then left quickly.

Benny held his napkin up to his lips and carefully spit the strawberry into the white paper. "Now what?" he said. He took off his glasses and stared at me intently.

"Now we go talk to all those people who won't talk to Bob John." I stood and dropped a ten and a five on the table.

CHAPTER 31

W E FIRST STOPPED AT THE HOME, WHICH WAS A HUGE old mansion on Prince Street. Even though it was only seven-thirty or so, we found the manager at his desk, a tired-looking forty-year-old heavyset man with a graying beard. He came outside and we sat on the front steps while he smoked a cigarette. He clearly was concerned for Vinyl Man, but didn't know anything beyond what he'd told Bob John and had been relayed to us. No calls. Nothing unusual. No one new snooping about.

Around eight, we left the Home and walked over to West Hancock, where Groovology was located. Benny jiggled the handle and pushed lightly on the frame, but nothing budged. A row of unconvincing silver tape ran around the edge of the front window, supporting the security-firm sticker plastered on the door. There was no yellow tape across the door, just a black-and-white sign that said CLOSED. We cupped our hands and peered through the dark glass and at rows and rows of dark shelves.

It was still early—Athens beats to university time, not local—and the street was quiet. Groovology sat on the line between the good end of Hancock and the not-so-good end. Uphill were T-shirt shops, latte bars, and even a few law offices, both up-and-coming and down-and-going. Downhill were a few night-clubs and small businesses, a large auto-parts store, and the local mission. As we stood there, a car pulled up in front of the Potter's House, then pulled away. Across the street, a sixty-year-old man wearing khakis and a short-sleeved plaid shirt walked up to the door of a barbershop. In front of the shop stood a striped pole. Stricklin's was painted in gold leaf on the plate-glass window. I looked down Hancock to Prince.

"Look at this, Benny."

"Look at what?"

"You can see the roof of the Home from here. It's a five-minute walk, right down this street, turn right, and one block down."

"And? We just walked it in three minutes. You're not the fastest walker in the world, even when you're all wound up like today."

"So this is downtown Athens, at five-thirty in the afternoon, and Vinyl Man disappears in a five-block area. Probably right from the store," I said. "Is there a back way out?"

"Didn't they have it nailed shut because Vinyl was paranoid about kids stealing the records? I remember Dee Lane saying something about Vinyl Man coming down here at all hours of the night to check up. So he nailed it shut," Benny said.

"I never heard that."

"Well, Dee Lane talked about it once at the game, saying if the fire marshal ever showed up he was going to be sent to County," Benny said.

"Then someone saw something."

"Bob John said they talked to everybody, even put out an announcement on the radio to find drivers who might have been in the area."

"Someone saw something," I said stubbornly. The man across the street rolled out a green awning that shaded the window of the barbershop. "I think I need a haircut."

Benny looked at my short hair, trimmed every week by Gillie with a number-four attachment on the shaver. "You are looking a bit shaggy. I think I'll walk down to the Potter's House and see if any homeless guys are in the alley, and if they might want to earn a bottle."

Stricklin's was an old-style three-chair barbershop. Behind each chair was a mirror, and in front of each a shelf covered with a white towel, on which lay neat lines of shears, scissors, and razors. A tall cylindrical jar filled with blue disinfectant and a cluster of combs stood beside each set of laid-out tools. There was no sign offering unisex styling or any other attempt at softening the old-style barbershop feel, just a row of wood and leather chairs, a few round wire tables with *Field & Stream* and *Time* stacked neatly on them, and a plastic booster seat. When I stepped inside, the man who had unlocked the door was carefully mopping an invisible spot on the immaculate red-and-black linoleum tile floor. We traded good mornings.

"What can I do for you?" he asked. He wore his name on a small, engraved metal tag pinned over his pocket. His lower right arm sported a blurry blue USMC tattoo, complete with globe and anchor. I noticed that between each mirror was a small planter holding two neat American flags. In the background, I could hear the undulating voice of Paul Harvey.

"Thought I'd get a trim, Mr. Stricklin."

"Don't look like you need one to me."

"Must be hard for an honest man like you to stay in business." I smiled.

"No, not too hard, we do just fine," he said politely. "I've seen you before, going in that place across the street. You must be a friend of that crazy boy."

"Yes, sir, I am."

"You ever serve?" I shook my head. "Then where'd you get that 'sir' stuff? Nobody talks like that anymore."

"Way I was raised."

"I almost believe that," he answered with a tight-lipped smile. "I didn't see anything yesterday, that's what I told the police that came to my house last night." I sat down in the end chair, and rubbed my legs.

"Do you mind?" I asked. "I've been up for a while and walking on this concrete hurts like the devil." I started massaging my calves, hard. The pain began to melt away. I rubbed harder.

"You must not have heard me," he said, smile gone. "I didn't see a thing, honest to God."

"I believe you, Mr. Stricklin, but I also think you were a little too careful in the way you said that. Who else works here?"

"Nobody. You can't afford employees anymore with all the government regulations and taxes and stuff. I used to have a boy that did shoes," he motioned to a shoeshine stand that stood beside the back door. "But he got old and went to live with his daughter in Blackshear, and I never replaced him. People don't get dressed up anymore, anyway, don't worry about shoeshines."

"Why three chairs?" I asked.

"It's none of your damned business why I have three chairs. Who do you think you are to come in here and ask me all these questions? Now I was polite and answered your questions, but I want you to get out of here, right now. Or I'm going to call the police."

He picked up his mop and held it across his chest. "Go on, get up and get out of here. Get." His veins bulged under his pink skin. A half step forward to reinforce the threat.

I wandered down to the Potter's House. Benny sat on a concrete parking wall. Beside him on either side sat a filthy man with brown clothes and stringy long hair. He waved me closer. "Top, Dave and Lewis. Lewis and Dave, this is my friend Top. These guys talked to the police, Top, say the cops talked to every single person on the street. No one saw anything—like Vinyl Man just vanished."

"OK." I looked at one of the two. "Tell me, how many people work in that barbershop down the street?"

The homeless men looked at each other. Benny sighed. "Come on, guys, I already gave you five bucks each, five more if you answer my friend's questions." They didn't answer. "Let's go. You both reek. I want to get out of here, and you two want to get to the liquor store."

"Not open yet," one said through a mouth without teeth. He wore a filthy jacket that, on closer inspection, appeared to have belonged to a Georgia Tech football letterman. If it was his, he'd lost some weight since graduation.

"How many?" I said.

"Three," the other one answered. "Old Man Stricklin and that Russian couple, Irina and Sergei."

"Where can we find Irina and Sergei?" I said. "What time do they usually show up?"

"Usually they open up, 'cause they live right over the shop in the back room. Not supposed to since they rezoned downtown," he said lucidly. "Nice people. Sometimes they'll give us a cup of coffee if the old man's not there yet. I think they're off the books.

Stricklin probably doesn't even pay taxes on them." I gave the one with the Tech jacket a ten, and slipped the helpful one a twenty.

"Are they there every day?" I asked.

"Except Sundays. Shop is closed on Sundays," he said. Yesterday was Monday.

"Thanks, fellas," Benny said.

"Thank you," the lucid one—Dave or Lewis—said politely.

CHAPTER 23

S
O, YOU WANT TO GO SEE THESE TWO RUSSIANS?" BENNY SAID.
"Yeah, let's hope we can catch them in the apartment, so
I don't have to deal with Stricklin again."

We crossed the street and walked back toward the barbershop,
but cut across a vacant parking lot and angled toward the rear of
the building. At the back of the shop, a gray wooden staircase led
up to a small open landing, and an aluminum storm door. On the
landing we could see three clay pots, a small hibachi-style grill and
a half-used bag of charcoal briquettes.

"This the only entrance?" Benny said.

"I didn't see a staircase inside. I would have seen it, I think," I said.

"You want to both go up, or me to wait in case the old man
comes around?" Benny asked.

"Why don't you wait? Let me see what's up there," I said. I left
him there and walked softly up the stairs. Just as I reached the
landing, the door opened and a pretty girl with short, bleached hair
with black roots and a round Slavic face stepped out. She wore a
man's T-shirt that came down to her knees, and an open housecoat
over it. She looked surprised to see me, then opened her mouth to

yell. Before she could get the sound out, I spun her around, clamped a hand over her mouth, and shoved her back into the apartment. On the sofa was a thirty-year-old man, same hair, shirt-less, wearing blue jeans. On his shoulder was a huge NBA-style tattoo, but this one was of a pack of Marlboros flanked by a can of Bud on one side and a can of Coca-Cola on another. A red-white-and-blue banner ran under the decoration. I could see how he and Stricklin would get along. Several *People* magazines, an overflowing ashtray and a half-drunk cup of coffee sat on the low table.

"What the hell?" the man said with a thick accent. He jumped to his feet and banged a toe on one leg of the table. I saw his eyes water. He looked around for a weapon, found none, and balled up his fists rather unconvincingly. His arms were flaccid, and there was a roll of flab around over the top of his jeans.

"Easy," I said. "I just want to ask you some questions."

"Let her go," Sergei said, taking a step around the table.

"Irina, I'm going to let you go. If you scream or something, I'll report you to the cops and you'll get in big trouble. Now just be cool." I turned her head around and looked into her scared round eyes. "Be cool. Just be cool, OK?" She nodded.

"Get the hell out of here!" Sergei ordered.

"Two questions, then I'm gone," I said.

"Who the hell are you?" he said.

"A friend of Vinyl Man's. You know Vinyl?"

Irina nodded. "Poor boy." Sympathy softened her features.

Sergei peered around for a weapon without being conspicuous about it. "Sergei, I do this for a living. If you go for that knife on that counter, I'm going to take it away from you and beat the crap out of you. You know what 'beat the crap' means? Now be cool, comrade."

"Go to hell, comrade!" he spat, but stopped fidgeting.

"Did you see who grabbed Vinyl? Yes or no."

The couple looked at each other. "No," Sergei said.

"No," the woman agreed, then said something to Sergei in Russian. He raised an eyebrow, then shook his head. "No."

"Come on, guys, let's not do it this way. You have to know I can make you talk, and then turn you over to the police. Don't tell me that where you come from, you don't know how this works. Just tell me the truth and I'm out of here."

"But Mr. Stricklin said—" Sergei said.

"Look, this is between me and you. No one has to know. I'm not going to tell Stricklin, and I'm not going to tell the police you told me. Did you see anyone grab Vinyl?"

"Not exactly," the woman said.

"What does that mean?" I asked.

She pulled the worn chenille housecoat tighter around her and looked at the man. He put his arm around her shoulders and spoke, "I saw four guys hanging around that afternoon. One came out of the alley behind the store, said something, then all four went inside. But we were busy then. Irina was doing a manicure and I had to do a shampoo and cut, so I was away from the window for five or ten minutes. When I came back, they were gone."

"Describe them to me," I said.

CHAPTER 33

WELL, I SAW IT, BUT I DON'T BELIEVE IT," BENNY SAID. "Half the Athens PD goes over that street all night long and can't find a witness, and you find two in thirty minutes. How lucky can you get?"

"It's not luck, and it wasn't thirty minutes," I said.

"No, I know it's not," Benny ambiguously said. He continued, "Any special sort of car you want me to borrow?"

"Just one that won't stand out too much. If you can, find another one of about the same size, make, and color, and swap the front plate with the back one on the car you get. No vanity plates," I said.

"Got it," Benny said. "EJ's driving me in. I'll be back about six or so. Where do you want to meet?"

"I don't know yet. I'll have to call you. You need anything from the school?" I asked. I turned off College and into the incubator parking lot. Through a gap between the buildings you could see a slice of one of the football team's Astroturf practice fields.

Benny pulled out his wallet, fished out a key card, and handed it to me. I zipped it through and waited until the arm raised before edging over the metal spikes.

"Yeah, there's a little maroon gym bag in the bottom of my closet. It's got some clothes and shoes in it," he said. "I could use that. How are you going to find out where these four live?"

"Educated guess. When I was out riding day before yesterday, I saw four men who fit the general description of these guys standing next to an empty pulpwood truck. I should have stopped and talked to them. It's February, wrong time of the year to be cutting wood. Too slick and muddy right now. But I was expecting some of Menes's crew—city punks, not pulpwooders. I'm guessing those four were watching the school, and they're the ones who grabbed Harlan."

"But how you going to find them?" he said.

"I'm hoping Russell's dad spotted them. He's sharp as a tack, but he's convinced he's getting Alzheimer's so he writes down everything in that Neighborhood Watch notebook of his. Probably has a record of every time we go to buy a bag of chips. If we're lucky, he'll have a plate. If not, I'm not sure how we'll find them. May have to hack into some databases and see if I recognize their mug shots," I said.

"And if it's not them?"

"Then we'd better hope Bob John finds Vinyl Man, because this is our best shot," I said truthfully. EJ pulled up behind us in a black Honda Civic with spoiler and blacked-out windows. There was a tiny white decal on the rear windshield that showed the character Huey, from the *Boondocks* comic strip, pissing on the Stars and Bars.

"How much do I pay you?" I said, eyeing the car ostentatiously. Benny climbed in the passenger door.

"Not enough," EJ grinned over his Oakleys and peeled away. He jammed on the brakes a few seconds later and crept over the spikes at the exit, then turned left on College and was gone. It was another beautiful day. The pear trees were budded out, and on a few tightly wrapped buds were tiny white lines where some of the more adventurous flowers were peeking out. The breeze this morning was one of those North Georgia early-spring specials, with strands of cool humid air and warmer dry air braided together in long, soft cables that wound between the trees and buildings.

CHAPTER 34

I CARDED MYSELF INTO THE INCUBATOR BUILDING AND BUZZED up to the fifth floor. The elevator opened onto one of those plain Marriott-like vestibules with tan wallpaper and mottled carpet. Perpendicular to the elevator was a floor directory with a half dozen names on it. All of the names seemed to involve colors and poor punctuation and explain nothing about what each company did— Red Rocket.com, OrangeOrange.com. We weren't listed, of course, so I turned and walked to the hallway and looked in both directions. There were several doors, most of which were marked by small glass plaques with the names of companies on them. At the north end, taped across one plaque was a single piece of notebook paper with Polymath hand-lettered on it. I walked down and let myself in.

There was a large unmanned desk just inside the door, covered with paraphernalia that I recognized as Gillie's. To the left, behind the desk, was a wall of windows that overlooked the lot where I'd left the truck. To the right people were working, and behind them a glassed-in room filled with Apple computers and EMC data-storage units. There was a door in the back wall, and beside it one of those frosted glass plates.

I stepped over a bundle of wires held down with black and yellow gaffer's tape, and walked down a row of cubicles. Inside each was one of our researchers, with a headset on, tapping at computer screens. I frowned at the headphones. Bypassing the scrambler program meant that once we returned to normal, we might have some problems reestablishing the blind interface. Other than that, though, everything seemed fine. I walked down the aisle to a chorus of hellos, some out loud and some mouthed silently, and a few thumbs up. Near the back, I reached Maggie's cube. Her headset was on her desk, and she held a pencil clasped between her teeth as she peered at the screen.

"Hey, Maggie," I said.

She looked up, spat out the pencil onto the desk and grinned, "Top." Her grin eased. "Are you all right? You look a little stressed. Legs hurting?"

"Like hell. I drove down to Jax yesterday, and couldn't sleep when I got back. Where's the boss?"

"Went out. I'm supposed to call her if you and Benny show up. I know she wants to see you. Should be back in about a half hour. She just left—you couldn't have missed her by more than a minute."

"That's OK, I'll be here awhile. Do you think I can take any terminal? Same log-on and passwords?" I asked.

"No. Here, let me help you get set up."

I checked voice mail and E-mail. There was a call from Amanda asking me if I'd heard about Vinyl Man. There was an E-mail from Gillie with a quote that began, "All beds are narrow"—uncited, but of course I recognized it as Edna St.Vincent Millay. The e-mail was signed "I love you," which brought me to a full stop. I also pulled the call logs from last Saturday and Sunday. There were three calls from Dee Lane, all between eleven and twelve, and one from a 305 area code: Miami.

There was no ransom call or message—from Danny or Raoul or anyone else. I worried about Vinyl Man. Whoever had grabbed Harlan had little patience. Now Vinyl was off his meds so he would be in full schizo rave mode. It would soon be apparent to whoever grabbed him that he was of little use. I wondered if going after him tonight would be soon enough. Maybe Soames was right; maybe I was creating situations I knew would turn crazy. I rejected the thought.

It took thirty minutes or so to make my calls. I first rang Russell Driggers's dad.

"Mr. Driggers," I spoke loudly and one of the researchers popped his head above his cubicle and looked back at me. I grimaced and pointed to the phone and my ear. "This is your neighbor, Top. How was your trip to Albany?"

He did have a plate for the truck. We talked for a few minutes about that and other things. Next I called the Department of Natural Resources, stayed on hold for twenty minutes listening to Mozart, the elevator music of classical composers, before eventually getting through to the permit section, where I talked to a helpful woman named Blanche. She had no record of a permit for our area for this time of the year. While I waited, I'd hacked into the state Department of Motor Vehicles database. They had a name and a rural address matching a seven-ton white logging truck. Then I called up MapPro and located the rough area where I suspected Vinyl was being held.

When I found it, I dialed EJ, who answered on the second ring. I said, "Truck stop," and hung up. Benny would know I meant the one in Cornelia. Hopefully, Bob John wouldn't. Finally I called

Danny, to see if I could shake anything loose about Vinyl Man, just in case my pulpwooder theory was wrong. He wasn't answering, but 10:00 A.M. is a little early for a bar owner to be up and around, so I left a message.

Gillie returned just as I finished my calls. She swept in in dramatic fashion, holding a tray of Starbucks drinks in one hand and a Dunkin' Donuts shopping bag in the other. Dice followed behind her, balancing four Starbucks trays stacked up in his hands and using his chest to steady them. George followed behind with two more trays. Gillie wore a tailored herringbone suit, in charcoal gray, two-inch black heels, and today her hair was pulled back. Her lipstick was a stark red. It was an outfit I'd never seen before, but seemed appropriate to this office. Gillie put her coffee and pastries down and turned to unload Dice and George. She hadn't seen me yet, and I watched her for a moment before standing up and saying her name.

CHAPTER 35

TOP!" SHE SQUEALED, AND RAN BACK TO GIVE ME A HUG.

I nodded to George and Dice. "Hey, George, how are the kids?"

We went back and forth for a moment while a few of the researchers came out and picked up their coffees. Dice and George distributed the rest and offered doughnuts around. They offered me a raspberry jelly, and I took it, but when I held it up to my mouth, the smell made my tongue feel thick and throat tight. I dropped it back into one of the open boxes and said to Gillie, "Is there anywhere around here we can talk in private?"

"Sure," she said. "The project room in back."

"Could you bring the phone logs?" Hoping my voice sounded normal, not letting her know I'd already pulled the logs.

The project room held a single long table surrounded by black cloth chairs on rollers. Two easels with flip charts sat in the corners near the door. On the wall at this end of the table was a very flat wooden cabinet which probably held a whiteboard and on the other wall a huge built-in TV screen. An exercise bike flanked one side of the screen and a massage chair the other. A few pieces of paper lay strewn across the blond wood surface.

Gillie saw me looking at the massage chair and shrugged. "They also had water coolers with Evian and an espresso machine, but those got repossessed. Supposedly someone is coming to get the TV any day now. I think the bike and the chair are paid for." She closed the door.

"How you doing, Topper?" She smiled.

"Could I see the logs?"

"Top, are you OK? How about, 'Gillie, how are you?' or something?"

"Sorry, I'm focused right now. You know, getting Vinyl Man back."

She looked at me strangely, then smiled. "That's Bob John's job. You should be here, focused on us, focused on me." She stepped close and put her hand flat on the front of my jeans. "Oh, nice. I could see it poking out from halfway across the room this morning." She leaned toward me and I could feel the soft weight of her breasts as she moved her hand lightly up and down on the surface of my pants.

"You want to do it right now, Top? Right here? With all of them right outside? Would that be exciting? I want it, Top. I missed you, baby. Right here on the table," She whispered, and reached back under her jacket to unsnap her skirt.

There was a knock at the door. "Gillie?" It was George's voice. "Gillie, the ACD technician is here."

"Shit," she whispered and buried her face in my shoulder. She lifted her head and called out, "Tell them I'll be there in a minute. Sorry, Top, we've been waiting on this guy for two days. I'll be a few minutes." She straightened her skirt hurriedly and licked her lips quickly. "Top, I hate to ask you, but do you mind working outside?

You can use my desk, but George and I may need the whiteboard with this guy. Here are the logs. Something's wrong with the computer—I had to pull them down manually."

The log was not the usual printout, but a long list written in Gillie's neat, smooth hand. She had highlighted four numbers in yellow, but beside them she'd written, "Called them back. Telemarketers. Nothing from Dee Lane." I nodded, satisfied. There was only one more chore before I left, digging into the UGA geography department's on-line archive. I'd finished printing before Gillie's meeting was done, so I dropped the manila file with the call logs on her desk and left.

CHAPTER 36

THE DAY WAS COMFORTABLY WARM WHEN I CAME OUT. I bent over at the waist and grabbed my thighs, pulling the hamstrings taut. When I stood and turned, beside the truck stood Raoul's thug, Desi. The Mercedes stood on the street, and I couldn't tell through the dark windows if someone was with him. I sauntered over. "What do you want?" I asked.

"El Jefe wants to talk to you, pussy."

"Dizzy, now why are you starting off on the wrong foot like that? Look, fella, I'm cranky, not getting laid regular, so lay off, OK? I might just stomp the living shit out of you. For fun. And since this is my town and I'm the respectable businessman and you're a coked-up punk from Atlanta, just the sort of asshole local cops love to hate, *you're* the one who'll spend the night in the tank. Is that what you want?" I said. I stepped closer and he pushed himself off the truck door.

With the hand inside my pocket, I pressed the button on my key chain that unlocks the driver-side door. Desi heard the click behind him, and half-turned. He realized his mistake instantly, but by then it was too late. I'd kicked him full in the groin. I grinned and raised my hands over my head to indicate the field goal was good. He folded in half and threw up. I skipped around the mess, then slapped him as hard as I could on the face with my open left hand. He went down to one knee in the puke and I reached in his belt and pulled out the Glock.

I grabbed Desi by the back collar of that ridiculous suit and half-pulled, half-dragged him through the lot, across the grassy strip and onto the sidewalk. When I reached the grass, I paused a second to scrub the bottom of my tennis shoes. I dropped him on the sidewalk, stepped back, and kicked the side of his head. He gagged again and rolled over into a fetal ball. I tapped on the rear window of the big Mercedes Benz with the barrel of Desi's gun. Raoul rolled it down. "Are you honest to God fucking crazy, Top?"

"You're the one parking in a traffic lane on College Avenue. Do you know how many sweet young things there are driving down this street, talking on cell phones and doing their nails at the same time? You better pull off the road before you get a Miata up your ass." I left Desi there and walked over to swipe the card. The big Benz pulled up and through the gate.

"Why did you do that to Desi? He say something to you?" Menes asked. He looked out at me from the dark, smoky interior of the car. On the other side, I could see the bare knee of a girl, but nothing else. Today he wore a white silk suit with a dark green shirt and monochromatic tie. A large emerald was pinned to his earlobe. Big black bags hung under his bloodshot eyes.

"Nope, I just believe in punishment as a deterrent. And anytime Desi ever sets foot in Athens again, I want him to associate it with pain. If that other nitwit gets out of the car, I'll give him a lesson in behavioral psychology as well," I said. The dome light went on as the driver's-side door began to open, and I aimed Desi's pistol over the roof.

Menes said in a tired voice, "Chuck, sit down and close the door. I don't feel like playing games this morning. I just want to get home and go to bed." He looked at me and shook his head. "Do you have any idea what a sad day it is when I'm the grown-up one of the group?"

It was a good line, but I held my poker face. "So what do you want?" I said.

"Can you stop yelling?"

No, I couldn't, not with the buzz roaring like a Class IV rapid through me, but I didn't answer. Instead, I said, "What do you want?"

"I'm tired of screwing around, Top, I need that money Friday night. You've got until Friday morning to find it and bring it to me." He didn't bother to go into detail about what would happen if I didn't.

"Yes and no," I said.

"What does that mean?"

"I think I know who's got your money and where, but you've got to go get it," I said.

"So tell me now, and I'll take care of it," he answered.

"I've got to get Vinyl clear before you go blazing in there. Give me until tomorrow afternoon, Friday morning latest."

He considered my offer. "Top, this better not be any of your bullshit. You've got a rep for getting a little cute and a little crazy. I just want my money, partner—no more bullshit."

"I've also got a rep for being straight. Call me tomorrow afternoon. I'll tell you where and when."

Desi staggered to his feet and was pawing his stomach for his gun, the same one I now held down at my side. Menes turned and called to him, "Get into this car, and no more stupid stuff." He turned to me. "And what else? You're not doing this just to make me happy."

"And no more reward. Call it off."

"That's not that easy to do." He pursed his lips and tilted his head, trying to look like a don was supposed to look. The *Godfather* movies ruined these guys.

"Then I'm going to get Benny and we're going to come to Atlanta and settle this thing."

He shook his head, unafraid. "Tell you what, tough guy. When this shit is over, you get your little darky bitch and come on down. Anytime. Bring that stupid flapping grin and twitchy face of yours and come right on down." I raised the gun and sighted at his right eye.

He didn't blink or move his eyes from mine. "Say I call it off. How do I know you're not just blowing smoke up my ass to get some time?"

"Call Danny."

"Why should I call Danny?"

"Call him and ask him. I phoned him an hour ago to set up a meet."

"You know how many times I've heard that line? 'Raoul, I was looking for you to give you the money, man.' What lame shit!" He said the whore's part in a nasal whine.

I didn't answer while he thought it over. "OK, The reward is off. I'll call you tomorrow afternoon. You got a clean number?"

"No. Call and leave a number, but switch the last two digits. I'll call you back in ten minutes. It'll be fast—I'll be calling from a cell. I don't get back to you, it means I'm not there."

"OK. Anything else?"

"Yeah, what am I looking for? Is it really a duffel bag?"

"A big one. Small bills, mostly twenties, few hundreds and tens. Green, new bag. What else you want to know? Don't try a switch, Top."

"Call me tomorrow."

The window on the Mercedes rolled up and Chuck took off, missing my toe by about an inch. They stopped at the curb and Desi climbed woozily into the passenger seat. And then they were gone. Inside my truck, I lay back with my eyes closed, the taste of acid reflux in the back of my mouth. The buzz was roaring, and it sounded like I had an electric shaver stuffed in each ear. One more stop, then to McDonalds to get a shake to quiet my stomach, then home for a two-hour nap. I stuffed my shaking hands into the vise formed by my thighs, and prayed silently for the night to hurry.

CHAPTER 37

I T WAS DEE LANE WHO TAUGHT ME ABOUT BOLT-HOLES.

"Top," he lectured, "there are three rules of bolt-holes. Rule number one. Always have one. Rule number two. Don't tell anyone at all where it is. Not your best friend, not your mama, not even *me*." He tossed back a shot of tequila and motioned for the señorita to bring another. It was early evening, and we sat in the thatched open-air bar of La Ceiba, in Cozumel. We sat at the end of the bar facing the water and the distant lights of Cancún, our feet up on the low stucco wall. Dee Lane's leather jacket was on a chair, but he wore black jeans, a black T-shirt and Ray-Ban Wayfarers. I wore a pair of cut-offs.

"Are you listening, Top?" A good question, since Dee Lane talked only when he was pie-faced drunk, and he got that drunk only with old, old friends who were even drunker than he was. Even then, he spoke barely above a whisper, though the bar was almost empty. "Top, hey, Top, listen to me. Come on, son, lift your head up and *look* at me. This is *damned* important stuff. Top, a *good* bolt-hole can buy you a week. But if anyone, *anyone* else, knows about it, it's good for a day, max."

"What's rule number three?" I slurred.

He leaned back in his chair, almost toppled over and caught himself, lurching straight up. "What? Oh, rule number three. Never use it unless you *really* have no other choice." I nodded with a drunk's exaggerated solemnity. We stopped talking and watched a huge cruise ship slowly back out and begin its careful turn.

Dee Lane was right. You never use a bolt-hole because every time you use it, it becomes less safe. And finding a good bolt-hole is hard work. For my first, I'd rented a small cottage on a quiet lake from two elderly sisters, sweet little old spinsters who one day had their nephew bring over a pry bar, break the lock, and tear the place apart looking for money.

My current bolt-hole was a one-bedroom efficiency in the Button Gwinnett Arms, a sprawling, faux Edwardian complex just off the beltway on 129. Button Gwinnett was one of the two Georgia signers of the Declaration of Independence and famous mostly among autograph collectors. Only three of his signatures are known to exist, the rarest of any literate public figure in American history.

The Arms was ideal for a hidey-hole. I could get to it quickly, only minutes from the school and from downtown Athens. And even better, it was large and anonymous, with a high turnover. Most of my neighbors were young professionals on their way to their first home or a better apartment. They were too busy trying to pay off those college loans to snoop around. Fifteen buildings, each two stories and divided into three sections, were scattered across a few acres of pine trees and azalea beds. Roughly three hundred apartments, and around five hundred people.

I'd never seen any of the other people who lived in my section of Building 5T. But I had run their names through the computers at Polymath. Two of them were flight attendants, one was a young intern at the hospital, and another the recently divorced night manager at a call center owned by Bell South. There were two more apartments in this miniblock, and both belonged to a large multinational engineering company that used them to house relocated employees. Once every few months, I jotted down any new names on the mailboxes and ran them to make sure an FBI agent hadn't moved in.

Today I parked two buildings down, even though the entire lot was half empty, and walked casually up to my building, climbed the stairs, and headed to 204. I unlocked the door, opened it six inches, slipped into the semidarkness and deactivated the alarm quickly. Behind the door, the small folded piece of matchbook I had placed there was exactly where it should be. Still, I looked around carefully before pulling the drapes, removing the length of steel pipe that lay in the runners of the door, and sliding open the glass. Light poured in and fresh air followed, chasing out the staleness.

There was not much to see in the light. Much of the room was filled by the bed and television. The closet door was open, and inside on the floor were two packed bags. One was a nice new Tumi trifold, full of Polo and Tommy Bahama shirts and khakis. The other was a cheap and battered roll-aboard, with a pair of worn work boots, and some well-washed cheap clothes from discount stores. On the top shelf of the closet were two Atlanta telephone books, each with a razored-out section. The white pages held a nine-millimeter SIG, and three extra clips were cut into the yellow pages. The kitchen was unused, but in the freezer were a dozen frozen Stouffer's dinners, and the cupboards were well stocked with canned goods, cereal, and Clif Bars.

On the table beside the bed was a picture of a pretty blond

woman and two kids, the same picture that came with the frame. To be truthful, were anyone to come in here, that probably would not be enough to convince them that this was a typical apartment. At the very least the ISM Super Diamond safe, that sat conspicuously at the end of the bed, would have made them suspicious.

Underneath the safe were three sheets of half-inch plywood. They distributed the weight across the floor and prevented the three-foot steel cube from falling through and killing some unfortunate soul down in 104. Inside the safe was a shoebox full of false ID, including a not-so-good forged New Zealand passport, another genuine one from Paraguay, and a couple of driver's licenses, ten thousand dollars in cash, two dozen Krugerrands, and three more pistols. I used the safe like an end table, and on top were a dozen videotapes, still wrapped in the same packaging they wore when I bought them at Wal-Mart. There were also dozens of books on the safe and stacked neatly on the plywood beside it, mostly mysteries by Connelly and Crais and Block, the O'Brian series, and a stack of thick biographies of famous Europeans I'd been meaning to mine for new quotes. All in all, if I ever needed to hide out for a while, I didn't want to get caught because I got bored watching TV and popped out to the B&N or Blockbuster.

Dee Lane loves the drama of having a bolt-hole and the whole intrigue shtick. I always thought it all a bit silly, but did it anyway. Now I was grateful to have a place where I could take a nap without worrying about getting my door kicked in by the DEA or an SUV full of Colombians.

I went into the kitchen area and poured myself a glass of tap water. The faucet hissed and spat, and the water came out slightly brown. I poured it down the sink and let the water run until it was clear and cool. I drank that glass and two more, but the dry mouth didn't go away. I looked in the freezer for an ice cube to suck on; sometimes that helped. But both trays were empty, of course. I filled them and put them back on the little rack, then poured another glass of water. Sitting down on the side of the bed, I sipped my water and stared at the insistent blinking red light on the answering machine. After a moment, I punched the "new messages" button.

A computer voice read out the date, then a man's voice said, "212-219-0704."

I erased the message and called 212-320-1851. "Hello," said someone in a lilting Scottish baritone.

"It's Top," I said.

"Do you have a number, Top?" asked the voice.

"V34721E," I said. If I needed to call back, I would simply add a digit to every number, and the new recognition code would be W45832F. Not very sophisticated, but good for a very limited communication series.

"We found him in the Seychelles," he said.

"Long way from Florinapolis," I said.

"Nay, same hemisphere. 'Tis all the same once you get the hemisphere nailed down. We relayed your message. He'll be in touch."

"Thanks. Anything else?"

"Yes, he said sorry. Just trying to give you some work and get himself out of a jam. Didn't mean to get you in one. Says to be careful."

"Always. Tell Desk to bill Polymath, and I'll settle up."

"Aye, I'll tell him."

"And tell Desk I may need him to handle some money before too long. Clean it up, spread it around, that sort of thing."

"Not a problem, mate." The phone clicked in my ear. The guy

on the phone was named Ian, and he'd briefed me twice. He was a good guy, gave a good briefing, thorough and careful. Ian would relay the message to "Desk"— probably Soames.

I kicked off my shoes, threw a corner of the bedspread over my feet, set the alarm clock for two hours, and laid back with my forearm over my eyes. My tongue felt thick and cottony, and I wished I had the ice cube. Eventually, I dozed off and slept fitfully for an hour and a half. When I woke up, it was in the middle of a dream, and I had the impression that perhaps I'd woken myself by saying something. But I had no recollection of the sound. The sheets and bedspread were pulled loose from their corners and kicked down to the end of the bed, and I lay on the bare mattress.

CHAPTER 38

THE MEMORY OF THE DREAM WAS FRESH AND HEAVY. IN IT I sat in a room in the hotel in Lima, where I'd waited before going in to retrieve the mother and the girl. It was a run-down Hilton, the only sittable chair a straight-backed wooden one from the desk. Of course, in the real Hilton, the room was twelve stories up and the windows were sealed. But in the dream Hilton, there was a small balcony accessed through two old-fashioned French doors that opened out, and a wrought-iron balcony. In real life, I'd spent the four hours in dead quiet, waiting to go get the mother and the daughter out, sitting in that hard chair and staring out at the brown, dusty Lima sky.

In the dream, I heard someone crying. I looked around to find the source, but didn't get up out of the chair, I just turned and twisted to find the source. Finally I heard someone outside call my name softly and walked out onto the balcony. It was only one story up. Unlike the real Lima, there was no stifling traffic, just a long empty street and on it Gillie and Amanda and Consuela, the little girl from Lima. Gillie and Amanda and the girl were all crying. Little lines of tears ran down through the dust on their cheeks, and no one said a word. The two just stood there, the child behind them, hugging each other, crying, and looking up at me. I looked up and down the street for Benny and Vinyl Man, but they weren't there. It was a lousy way to wake up.

CHAPTER 39

THIS IS THE BEST YOU COULD DO?" I ASKED. WE LEFT THE truck parked in a dark corner of the truck-stop parking lot at Cornelia and drove up Highway 23 through the young night. There was a steady flow of traffic on our side—Atlantans headed to the mountains for the weekend, but the return side of the highway was relatively empty. Benny pulled a black turtleneck over his head. We both wore surgical gloves, and I could feel my hands sweating. But now that we were moving, I didn't care. This felt so, so good. The buzz roared behind me like a tailwind.

"EJ took us to Lennox Mall. The only thing in the parking lot is black BMWs. So we took one. At least it made it easy to swap the plates," he said.

"I don't know what this place is like. If the road is rutted, we may have to walk in part of the way," I said.

"We'd have to do that anyway, more than likely," he said, pulling on black canvas combat boots. "Did you look on that Web site that has the satellite images?"

"Yeah, printouts and the maps are rolled up on the floor behind me. There's a Maglite in my bag."

"Top, we don't need a Maglite. This is a 740i. It's got every type of light you could ever think of, including two different kinds of map lights."

Benny studied the maps for a moment, then looked up. "Hey, Top, I got one. I've been working on it for a while. Progressive. Are you up for it?"

"Sure, why not?"

"You just need to tell me if it's Yogi or bogie."

"Cute! Bogie means somebody else said it? Do I have to say who?"

"Absolutely."

"Go."

"Half this game is ninety percent mental."

"Bogie, Danny Ozark said that. Yogi said, 'Baseball is ninety percent mental. The other half is physical.' You started with a stumper, must have some good ones."

"It gets late early out there," Benny read from his notepad.

"Yes, talking about the outfield in Yankee Stadium."

"If you come to a fork in the road, take it," he read.

"Maybe. Most authorities say yes, but never sourced. What are we playing for, anyway?"

"Twenty. There are only three more. 'It's too crowded, nobody goes there anymore,'" he said.

"Yogi. That was too easy—you're setting me up."

"The doctor X-rayed my head and found nothing," Benny said.

"Bogie. Dizzy Dean."

"I love sports. Whenever I can, I watch the game on radio."

"Bogie. Gerald Ford." I pumped my fist in victory.

"How do you do that? That's disturbingly weird, Top." He shook his head.

"Don't you mean disturbingly costly?"

"I do." He reached back into the bag on the rear seat and pulled out a bill, held it up to the light, and handed it over ceremoniously. I stuffed it in my shirt pocket. He paused a moment. "Top, why do *we* always give you a quote and you tell *us* who said it?"

I thought for a minute. "I don't know, that's just the way the game started."

"What's your favorite quote?"

"I like a lot of them."

"What is it tonight?"

I did not answer quickly. Benny waited patiently until finally I said, "People sleep peacefully at night only because rough men stand ready to do violence on their behalf."

Benny nodded in appreciation. "Rough men ready to do violence. True. Who said that?"

"George Orwell."

"I liked that *Animal Farm* book pretty well, but *1984* was a little too strange," Benny said. I told him most people would agree with him.

CHAPTER 40

A FEW MINUTES LATER, WE REACHED TALLULLAH FALLS, and just beyond that, the divided highway ended. At Clayton, we turned left onto 76, and bored our way deeper into the foothills of the Blue Ridge Mountains. I drove through a canyon of dark pine trees, the only lights the occasional billboard advertising hamburgers and gasoline. We turned north after five miles, and took a dirt road across the state line into North Carolina. A green sign with an arrow to the left showed the way to the Appalachian Trail. Benny used the map and the handheld GPS to navigate us through two more turns, and told me to stop. I looked around and saw nothing except a broken-down mailbox, once painted white, and on the side the remnants of a name painted in uneven black letters.

"According to the map, this is it," Benny said. "It's three miles up a side road."

I flipped the lights to high beam for a minute and saw it, a two-wheel rutted track that crossed a culvert, paralleled the road we were on about fifty yards, and then turned right into the woods. "Look at that drop-off—we may have to walk the whole three miles," I said and beeped the horn a few times.

Benny looked surprised. "What was that for?"

"Change of plans. We're not going to surprise them out here. It's dead quiet and dark as a coal mine. They'll see us and hear us before we make the first turn. Might as well be up front about it so they don't freak out and shoot Vinyl," I answered.

"I hope you know what you're doing."

Me, too, I thought. Then caught myself. Where did that come from? I am the best in the world. No hope needed. Let those guys at the end of the road have the hope. And getting Vinyl back alive would show Soames that I still was the best. Show Soames? I thought. Where in the hell did that come from? It was a strange moment. My mind lurched from one uncomfortable thought to another, undirected and unchecked. While you're thinking, they're shooting. Save the play-by-play for the bar. I shook my head like a dog trying to lose a flea.

"Top, are you OK?"

Instead of answering, I flipped on the high beams, and left them on, then moved up slowly and eased over the edge of the road. We heard the long scraping sound as the undercarriage hung on the berm created by the road grader. We crossed the culvert slowly and edged along the rutted track. We picked our way along the twisting road and negotiated around the deeper ruts. We were quiet, and rode with the windows down. The only sound was the brushing of the weeds that grew between the ruts scrubbing the bottom of the car. At one point we heard running water and crossed a small, sturdy-looking wooden bridge. When the trip odometer said 2.7, someone holding a large electric lantern stepped in front of the car. We stopped. He set the light on the hood and walked around to the driver's-side window.

I shielded my eyes. A double-barreled twelve-gauge shotgun

barrel came through the opening. "Get out of the car," said a thin teenaged voice.

I looked at Benny. "Get out. On this side. Throw out your keys and then get out of this door. I'm going to step back. When you come out, put your hands up in the air. There's a whole bunch of us, so don't get stupid."

"Who is it?" called a voice.

"It's them," the boy said. "I'm going to bring them up to the trailer." The shotgun retreated, and I climbed out of the car. Benny followed.

"Close the door," he said.

"You want me to come down?" the voice said, an older male.

"No, I got it. You stay up there. We'll be there in a minute," he said. Now that we were out of the car and turned away from the light, we could see our captor, a tall boy with pimples and a little darkness on his chin that in a better light might have been a beard. He wore a Michael Jordan sweatshirt and a greasy NASCAR cap that bore a picture of Dale Earnhardt and said "#3." His tennis shoes were caked with red clay mud, and around the edges of each was a thick roll of the sticky soil. The stock on the shotgun he held comfortably had been hacked off, and the barrel was six inches too short. A people gun.

The boy holding it should have looked scared. His eyes should have been as big as dinner plates and his nostrils flared like a thoroughbred's. But they weren't. His eyes were calm and flat. His voice was thin, but steady. I didn't know whether to be reassured because the finger on those triggers didn't belong to a terrified kid, or scared because we were being held hostage by someone who seemed to know what he was doing.

"Throw your pistols on the ground," he said.

"I don't carry one," Benny said.

"No, you coons like knives, don't you? Well, throw that down there. Do it now, both of you." I carefully pulled my SIG out with the two fingers of my right hand and dropped it, trying to hit a grassy spot and keep it out of the mud. Benny dropped a black razor on the ground. It wasn't his good one, and I wondered if he still had it on him.

"I've got forty thousand dollars in a bag on the backseat. All I want is the guy you kidnapped. We'll give you the money," I said.

"You ain't going to 'give me' anything, motherfucker," he said. "Anything you got is ours now. What you can do is tell us where you hid the rest of it. Come on, let's go talk to Richard." He waved the nose of the gun up the road. "Coon, grab the lantern."

"Donnie, what's happening? You OK down there?" called the voice. "You want Carl to come down?"

"No, I said I got it, goddammit," called the kid. He was not leaving us many options. He stood four feet back, right on the edge of the ring of light thrown by the lantern, and moved both his gaze and the gun continuously between us. Both hammers were back on the shotgun, and it wouldn't take much of a pull. With that barrel, it would throw a wide pattern, and one shell would probably kill both of us. I shifted a few inches, and over his shoulder, through the trees, saw a bare bulb of low wattage.

"Get the money," he said.

"OK, but be careful with that gun. This car cost me 80 K; I don't want it shot up like an old stop sign." I stepped aside and opened the door, then moved behind it and pulled the .22 from my waistband. He glanced at the car, then his eyes came back to me and saw the gun. His mouth made an "O." I shot, and kept on shooting, six quick pops, emptying the pistol before he fell. Benny kicked the barrel of the shotgun away, in case the gun went off, but instead it came loose and went skittering off into the brush. It was over in fifteen seconds.

"Donnie?" said the voice.

I nodded at Benny. "We got Donnie," he yelled in a flat black voice.

"Donnie? You OK?" The voice was higher pitched now, afraid or angry.

Benny switched off the lantern and I reached inside and killed the car lights. From the duffel, I took a plastic bread bag and a nightscope. I tucked the bag in my pants and slipped on the nightscope. The world turned green. I looked at Donnie. Most of the slugs had hit him in the throat, but two hit him in the face, probably as he started to fall. One eye was gone and part of a cheek. I could see broken teeth.

"You didn't have any choice, Top. We couldn't have taken him out barehanded, and you can't knock anybody down with a .22," Benny said quietly.

"You sons-a-bitches. Donnie better be OK. If you've hurt him, I'm going to skin this crazy asshole alive, swear to God!" Richard yelled.

I reached over and rolled Donnie over. I pulled out his wallet and stuffed eight hundreds into it, replaced it, and rolled him back. Whenever possible, confuse things a bit. As I straightened up, I felt the nausea and grabbed the bag. When I was finished, I tied the throat of the bag tightly and wiped my mouth on my sleeve.

"Here's your gun. I got the keys," said Benny. He stuck his hand inside the car and popped the trunk. "Let's put that in a garbage bag in the back so it doesn't smell up the car."

I desperately wanted to rinse my mouth and spit, but we wanted to leave little evidence in case this turned very bad. Instead, I stuck out my tongue and wiped that with my sleeve. "You ready?" said Benny. He offered me an AR-15 assault rifle from the trunk.

"Yeah, sure. Five minutes," I said and moved into the pine forest.

Benny turned around and went to sit on the hood. "Hey, Richard, you ready to deal, man?" He continued to use his down-home voice.

"Donnie better not be dead," said the voice.

"Tell you what," Benny said. "You give us Vinyl Man and we'll give you Donnie. You give us a live body and we'll give you one. Give us a dead one, and that's what you'll get back. How's that?"

"So Donnie's OK?" Richard yelled. His voice was different this time, more forced, and behind him I thought I heard a noise that was suddenly cut off, as if a door had closed.

Benny yelled back, "No, he sure as hell ain't OK. Took a .22 caliber bullet in the arm and the chest. He needs help, doctor help, real bad, but he's alive. He'll make it, but not if we play games, Richard. I heard that door. I know what you're up to." His voice was no longer from the front of the car, but thirty or so feet behind it.

CHAPTER 41

The pine forest was sparse, and I walked out a hundred or so yards and turned right, covering another two hundred yards. I slipped the scope off once I'd negotiated the trees. To my right, I could see the dark end of a blue-and-white mobile home. Streaks of green mildew ran down the aluminum. There was a small uncovered deck on the front, lit by the bare bulb I had seen from the car. On the porch stood a middle-aged man wearing a denim shirt and jeans, and barefoot. He held an AR-15 very similar to mine.

The trailer sat in a small clearing, maybe twenty feet of yard carpeted in pine needles on my side and the rear. An electric wire ran from the trailer back to a small waist-high shed at the edge of the trees, and I could hear the hollow hum of a water pump coming from it. There was also an old trash barrel with holes punched in it set on concrete blocks. Out here, people would either burn their trash or just dump it in a ravine. On the far side was what looked like a sizable clearing, where a white Dodge Ram pickup, a red 1970s Camaro, and the pulpwood truck were parked. A clothesline stretched between two pine trees. A lawn mower was headed under

229

the edge of the trailer, but weeds grew around it. There was a general air of seediness around the whole place.

I kept moving past the trailer and hooked back once I was safely beyond it. When I reached the tree line, I looked carefully for dogs, saw and smelled none and bolted for the dark underside of the trailer, landing on the soft pine needles and rolling underneath it.

The spot where I landed smelled of raw sewage. Many of these homes have do-it-yourself plumbing, usually just an el that dropped from the commode and ran down the hill to a flat place or a stream. This one was either stuffed up or had come loose. The stench was overpowering. I quickly scooted to my left, toward the porch.

From my vantage point, I saw the outline of a man carrying a bolt-action rifle, kneeling behind a tree, pointing down the hill toward Benny. I saw him motion to someone on the road. There had been four the morning I saw them near the school. Donnie, Richard, Ronnie, and Carl. I wondered if more were inside the trailer, but heard no footsteps above me. The man they called Richard crept down the steps and stood barefoot in the yard, not more than five yards away. I crawled out of my hiding place, stood up, took two quiet steps forward, and put the barrel of the automatic rifle at the base of his skull. "Put it down," I said softly.

He laid the rifle carefully on the ground. "Step backward until I tell you to stop." I led him backward two paces until my back was against the wall of the trailer.

"Now tell that guy in front of us to put his gun down and get up here. And the one by the road." He hesitated, and I continued, "Donnie is dead, Richard. You want to die, too?"

"You boys put down your guns and come on back here. He's got me." The man behind the tree turned around and looked surprised.

He looked at me for a moment, and laid the bolt-action rifle on the ground.

"Daddy, you OK?" he said.

"Yeah, Carl, but he's got me good. You and Ronnie come on up here and let's see what he wants. Just do as he says," Richard said.

"Clear!" I yelled.

I heard the BMW engine start and saw the dark mass beyond the drive dissolve into pine trees as it was illuminated by the car's headlights. Benny drove very slowly up the small hill and into the clearing. Ahead of him on the road marched a tall, thin youth, a double of the one we'd shot. His hands rested on top of his head. Benny drove with his right hand. His left rested on the door frame, where it held Donnie's double-barreled twelve-gauge balanced on the BMW's outside mirror, and pointed at Ronnie's back.

CHAPTER 42

W E TAPED CARL AND RONNIE TO TREES USING FIBER tape, the kind that UPS uses on commercial packages. Unlike duct tape, it is impossible to break or tear. We then taped Richard's hands behind his back, and wound a few strips around his head and looped it over the barrel of the shotgun. "You know how this works, right? We go through that door, and anybody's waiting on the other side and slaps at this gun or anything, your brains are going to be spread all over the room," I explained.

"Nobody's in there except the nut, and he's asleep," he said. His left cheek was sunken, and I realized all his teeth were missing on that side. It gave him two profiles, young and handsome on the side I'd first seen tonight, old and haggard on the other.

"Is he OK?" I asked.

"Yeah, yeah, I just gave him a Dilaudid to shut him up. He went to sleep, but he should wake up OK."

"What exactly?" I asked.

"A three. An hour or two back," he said, then bitterly: "Why'd you assholes kill Donnie? He was just a goddamned kid."

"Why'd you kill Harlan?" I said.

"Who?" he said unconvincingly. I bumped the back of his head with the gun. He cursed and opened the door. I pushed him through it and waited. After a moment, I pushed him a little farther and stepped inside. My heart hammered in my chest. The inside of the room was filthy. Beer cans and full ashtrays covered the top of the small coffee table. Underneath it were two crumpled Marlboro packs and an empty Pringles container on its side. The plastic garbage can in the kitchen was overflowing, and beside it stood a full paper grocery sack, the bottom stained with something wet. There were empty drugstore containers everywhere, spilling from the garbage, tucked under end tables and stuck in the cushions of the sofa. Benny slipped behind me, his good razor open in his hand. He moved quietly down the hall.

"So, what's your game, Richard? You guys grow dope? Probably not—too much work," I said.

"We cut pulpwood," he said.

"Maybe once in a blue moon," I said. "When you're not kicking in the back door of a drugstore at midnight."

"Well, you're going to have it your way, whatever I say, so it don't matter, does it?" he said.

Benny came back. "It's clear. Vinyl's tied up with clothesline on a bed in the back, but he seems OK. He's snoring like a bear."

"Did you search the place for the money?" I said.

"Not yet. I'll do that now."

"What do you mean, 'search for the money'?" Richard said.

"Harlan had the bag. He's dead. You killed him. Means you've got the money," I said.

"Are you crazy?" Richard's confusion was genuine. "Why would we have grabbed this guy if we already had it?"

"How the hell do I know how junkies think? I think we'll take a look anyway," I said. "Was Donnie your son?"

"Nephew. Ronnie's twin brother."

"He's dead. Body's down the road over on the side."

"You said. He should've let us come down and help him. Little cowboy always was too macho for his own good. Almost beat a faggot to death one time because he was five dollars short," he said.

I grunted. "How'd you find us?" he said.

"People saw you snatch Vinyl. I remembered seeing four guys who fit the same description driving a pulpwood truck and pissing in a ditch near my house. DNR says no permits to cut timber near my school, so no reason for you to be there. You had the real plates on the truck. Not too smart, Richard. Neighborhood Watch wrote them down and we ran them. All in all, pretty sloppy work."

"Screw you, you just got lucky!"

"And you're lucky we found you, not the police. There's enough shit in this room to put you guys away for life and a day," I said.

"Hey, your finger's not on the trigger is it? You're shaking like crazy, man. I'm about to piss my pants. Take it easy, all right?"

Benny came back. His nose wrinkled at the smell and he stepped carefully along the shag carpet, as if afraid he'd step in something. "I found nothing. But the place is filthy, Top, I don't want to touch anything. This is worse than the worst apartment in the 'Shoe.'" The 'Shoe' was a notorious Atlanta project.

"Did you check the freezer?"

"Not yet. I've got to find something to do the tires with." He rummaged quickly through the kitchen. There was an open Buck knife in one drawer. He folded it and slipped it in his back pocket. When he finished the refrigerator, he carefully kicked over the garbage and jumped back.

"Whew. Richard, can't you people clean up?" Benny said. He poked through the mess with his toe, as if looking for something.

"We been busy, just ain't gotten around to it," Richard said defensively.

"All right, let's pack up," I said.

I saw my captive's knees buckle, and then he caught himself. "Please don't kill us, mister. We ain't hurt nobody!" Richard begged. "Please, please. Them's just kids out there. Carl's only fifteen."

"That's bullshit, Richard," I said. "You killed Harlan and we all know it. And what if I let you go and you decide to come after us?"

"Top, I'll do it if you want me to. It doesn't bother me like it does you." Benny flipped open the razor.

"Please," the man blubbered. "Please." I smelled the acrid odor of urine as his bladder let go. Benny grimaced and looked away. Richard's knees gave completely and he dropped down to the floor, kneeling, pulling the shotgun with him. Luckily for him, my finger was outside the trigger guard. He screwed his eyes shut and bit his quivering lips. I fought the overbuzz.

"Here's the deal, Richard. I'm going to tie you up with that clothesline. You can work loose. We're going to slash the tires on your vehicles and take your guns. Don't even think about coming after us, tonight or ever. If I ever see you again, you're dead, man, and I'm not kidding."

"The guns? I mean, we use them for hunting and stuff," he sniffled.

"Automatic weapons and sawed-off shotguns?" I said.

"Well then, protection. It's dangerous living out here all alone."

"We'll leave your guns at the bridge," I said. "God only knows what would happen if we get stopped by police and somebody runs those things through the FBI database. We don't want them. Richard?"

"Yeah?"

"I'm not shitting about killing you." I said. He tried to nod, but rapped his head on the gun as he raised it.

CHAPTER 43

W E LOADED UP VINYL IN THE BACKSEAT, STILL ASLEEP. Benny drove. We stopped at the bridge, unloaded the guns we'd taken from them, and dropped them in the stream. I threw the .22 I'd used to shoot Donnie in as well. "How much of the money do you have left?" I asked Benny.

"We still have a thousand or so, in twenties."

"Let's throw it in the stream, confuse things," I said. So we did. As we climbed back in the car, Vinyl Man began stirring. He opened one eye and said sleepily, "Top? Benny?"

"Yes, dude, it's us," I said. "Just relax, we're taking you home."

We drove in silence until we got back on the highway and passed through Clayton. By then Vinyl was awake and sitting up, blinking at his surroundings. I tried to drink a warm Coke, but could manage only small sips. Benny watched me from the corner of his eye. My hands stopped shaking, but I was still unsteady.

"Are you going to be OK?"

"It's always like this, when I come down."

Before he could reply, Vinyl Man started howling, a high-pitched keen. He grabbed his knees and rocked back and forth furiously. I turned and shushed him, but he ignored me. His eyes were screwed tight, and he banged his chin on his chest.

"Turn on the radio. He'll respond to music," Benny said.

I punched the on button for the music system and Britney Spears's voice blared from the speakers. Vinyl Man blocked his ears with his palms and screamed in agony. "Top, I said music!" Benny said. Then more insistently, "Vinyl Man, this is a busy place, you need to quiet down. Someone could hear you. Vinyl Man, hush, be quiet. Top?"

I punched the next button on the CD changer and Enya came on.

Benny yelled, "*No, No, No!* Music, we need music." I'd never heard him raise his voice before. Vinyl, stunned as well, stopped his keening for a moment and stared at Benny, then started back again. With both of them making noise, it was even louder this time.

"Oh, Christ, you'd think you could have stolen a car from someone who had better taste," I punched the rest of the CDs. Another Britney and two boy bands cycled through.

Vinyl Man began sobbing. He tried to open the doors, but Benny had the childproof locks on. So he pounded the windows with the flats of his hands. "No, no, no!" he cried.

I quickly turned to the radio and hit "scan." Benny shook his head to the first four. Then, when we reached the fifth, after one bar, he said, "Turn it up."

I cranked the volume up as far as I could. "Vinyl Man, Herb Alpert, 'The Lonely Bull.' Listen to the horns, Vinyl!" Benny yelled. Vinyl Man stopped his pounding to listen, then smiled and sagged back in the seat. His eyes closed again and his hands floated down to rest on the leather seat. Benny sang the trumpet part, "Dah, dah, dah, dah, dah, dah-dah-dah, dah-dah, dah, dah, dah,

dah, dah-dah." Vinyl nodded along happily until the song finished, then smiled rapturously as "25" or "6 to 4" by Chicago came on. He lay back with his eyes still closed, and basked in the brass.

"Six to four," he sang in a sweet tenor. Benny adjusted the mix and beat time on the steering wheel. I stuffed my fingers in my ears.

When that ended, an oily-voiced deejay came on. "This is WWWK, World Wide Rock, the only station that plays the real classics. Stand by folks, for five—count 'em—five in a row," he smarmed.

And that's how we drove back to Cornelia, in a stolen black BMW with a trunkful of guns and a garbage bag of vomit, singing like drunk Japanese businessmen to one oldie after another:

"Brandy, you're a fine girl,
What a good wife you would be,
Your eyes could steal a sailor from the sea."

"From the sea," Benny sang in counterpoint, drawing the final note out and taking it higher than in the original. Vinyl nodded approvingly.

We left the BMW in the lot running with the doors unlocked. With luck it would be stolen again and end up a few hundred miles away with a few sets of prints in it. On the drive home, Benny compromised for me, playing a classical piece by Wynton Marsalis, and he and Vinyl Man nodded along contentedly. When we got to Athens, we took Vinyl to the emergency room at Athens General. I expected him to protest, but he went inside meekly. The ER room staff greeted him by name and led him gently to a gurney. He lay back and they started a drip. A male nurse covered him with a blanket and lay a restraining strap lightly across his chest, but did not lock it down. We called the supervisor of the Home and Bob John, and left messages at both places, then left quickly before the Athens PD could show up.

Outside, we stood for a moment in the parking lot. Benny looked at his watch. "One-thirty. Do you want to head home?"

I shook my head. "You go. I'll call you tomorrow. We'll finish this thing." He nodded and without arguing climbed in the truck, backed out, and drove away.

CHAPTER 44

I T WAS COOL AND I SHIVERED THROUGH MY STILL-DAMP T-shirt. I stuffed my hands in my jeans, and walked down Cobb for two blocks, stopping in front of an older white clapboard home. I walked around to the back, softly crunching the gravel in the drive, and up the creaky wooden stairs to the apartment over the garage. I knocked, got no answer and knocked again. A few minutes later the light came on, the curtain parted and a sleepy Amanda looked out. Without makeup she looked a little younger. She stared at me for a moment and opened the door.

"Vinyl's OK," I announced.

"Are you?"

"Yes. Maybe. Vinyl's OK, though."

"You want to come in," she said, not questioning.

"Can I sleep here?"

She hesitated, then nodded and moved aside to let me in. "My God, you smell. Sorry. Take off those clothes. I'll start the shower."

"Adrenaline," I said apologetically.

"Smells like sweat, puke, and urine to me."

I was too tired to undress so she peeled the clothes off me and took them into the kitchen. My knees trembled and I stood in her living room, naked and cold. I heard a washing machine start up. She came back and led me by the hand through her bedroom and to a small bath. She started the shower, and stood awkwardly beside me, testing the water until it was warm enough, then gently pushed me inside, pulled the curtain, and left. I turned it up hotter and stood under it for a long time, until it began to cool. When I got out, a towel and a pair of men's gym shorts lay on the sink. I dried off, put them on, and came back to the living room. She sat in a chair, smoking, one leg tucked under her, an afghan around her shoulders.

She'd made up a pallet on the floor in front of the sofa. Without saying anything, I got on the quilt facedown, pulled the sheet up to my waist, and closed my eyes. I heard her stub out her cigarette, and exhale, and then the sag of sofa as she laid down on it. She hung her hand over the edge of the cushion and gently stroked my back, her cool fingers tracing swirls and eights across my concreted muscles.

"Is it over now?" she asked.

"Not yet. Vinyl's back, but the people who killed Harlan are still out there, and I've got a target on me until that money is found. And it's possible all this was a deliberate setup, and if that's the case, I have to settle up with whoever did it."

"Why?"

"That feels good," I said as her fingernails began stroking my back in long smooth, soft rakes.

"Any ideas on who set you up?"

"Could be anyone. Government agency, the cops, somebody I don't even know."

"Anyone? Dee Lane? Benny? Gillie? Bob John?"

"I hope not."

"But you're not saying no."

"Not yet."

"Am I on the list, too?" she asked softly.

I didn't answer.

"But you came here," she whispered.

I lay there quietly, feeling her fingers swirl across my back, and hoping it wasn't anyone on her list. And that is how we woke up, six hours later, when Bob John knocked on the door.

CHAPTER 45

WHEN THE KNOCK CAME, WE BOTH WOKE. AMANDA swung her feet down, remembered I was there, and straddled me to get to her feet. She hopscotched over me and turned back. I stared at her pajamas, a very faded gray T-shirt from the Georgia baseball team's national championship in 1990, and a pair of FSU maroon sweatpants. The combination hadn't registered the night before.

The knock came again. "Don't go there," she warned, seeing my disgust at her ugly pj's. "People who live in glass houses."

I looked down at the pair of too-small gym trunks I was wearing. She peeked out the curtained door and said, "Bob John," twisted the bolt, and let him in. She stepped back to let him by, and gave him a friendly pat on the shoulder as he passed. I hopped up, grabbed the pale blue sheet from the floor, and used it to form a sarong.

"Morning, Amanda, Top," he said.

I beamed at him. "Good morning, Bob John. Here to see me?"

"Yes," he answered. "I'd like to say I was such a good cop that I know your every move, but I went everywhere else I could think of, struck out, and was driving by here on the way to the hospital when I thought, 'Why not?' And here you are."

"You two want coffee?" Amanda offered.

"Sure," we answered simultaneously and followed her into the kitchen. She filled the kettle, put it on a gas burner, and put a filter into a ceramic funnel. Bob John reached in his sports-coat pocket and pulled out a tin of Altoids. Without commenting, he opened them and set them on the table, closer to me. Opening the fridge, Amanda removed a Melitta coffee can. I ate five mints.

"Shoot, look at the time! I'm going to be late. Here, four scoops. Black for me. I'm in the shower." She clanked the can in front of me, pecked me on the cheek, and scooted for the bedroom.

I finished making the coffee, poured her a cup and took it into the steamy bathroom. I placed it on the edge of the sink. Before I could say anything, a voice from beyond the plastic curtain said, "Are you OK? It sounded like you were having a rough dream there?"

"No, it was good. I'm OK."

"OK then, now thanks. Out." Back in the kitchen, Bob John was fishing a carton of milk from the fridge. He opened it and sniffed suspiciously, then poured. He sat down at the small oak table and pushed a mug across to me. "To Vinyl Man." We clinked cups.

"Where'd you find him?" he asked.

"Wandering around out on 441, a few miles north of Commerce. Just walking down the road in the ditch, singing like crazy," I said.

"Could you show me where?"

"Sure, no problem."

"You seem happy today. Looked like the dickens yesterday at the Bee."

"Well, I was really worried about Vinyl. With Dee Lane gone, I feel responsible. I shouldn't say it like that. It sounds like I'm talking about feeding his pet goldfish, but you know what I mean."

"You just *found* him?"

"We'd been out driving all night, never thought we'd really find him. Turned a corner and there he was, wearing that silver outfit of his, just walking along."

"Strange, Benny told me a story about guns and shoot-outs and all sorts of stuff." He looked intently in my eyes.

"Really? Wow! Are you sure he wasn't kidding around?"

"He didn't tell me any such thing and you know it. He told me the same story you did. Word for word, except he speaks better English than you."

"See? I told you."

"He'd probably take me to exactly the same bend in the road, too."

"Might be hard to find in the daylight. Things look different at night," I answered sincerely.

"Are you ever going to start telling me the truth so I can help you?"

That had to be rhetorical. "Did you ask Vinyl?" I said sweetly.

"Oh give me a break, Top! Vinyl Man doesn't make sense even when he tries, and he won't even try with us. Told the nurses something about a bridge and a bull and losing a necklace made of the finest silver from the north of Spain and fireworks, and how reading from a prayer book will make the devils quiet down. The only part of that I can decipher is a line from some old seventies rock song."

Amanda came through, dressed impeccably, makeup in place. She placed her empty cup in the sink and turned around. "I don't see the truck in the drive. You better get dressed if you're coming in with me, Bali boy. Your clothes are in the dryer in that little pantry behind you."

"Oh, I'll take him," Bob John said pleasantly. He looked at me and tilted his head innocently, "He's probably going to want to go down to jail to see Benny, anyway. Can we just pull the door to, or do we need to lock up and bring you the key?" Amanda stopped long enough to ask about Benny and jail, and then bolted. I dressed as soon as Amanda left. As I brushed my teeth with my finger and spit into the sink, Bob John folded up the sheets I'd used.

"She'll wash them anyway," I said.

"I know. It's that old camp-counselor training."

"Great. She'll think I did it, score some points."

The car was a dark blue Dodge. As I clicked my belt, Bob John carefully slipped it into reverse, threw his arm over the seat and turned his head to back out cautiously. As the back wheels bumped on to Cobb, I asked, "Were you looking for me to ask about Vinyl Man?"

"No, not really. I figured you'd lie to me anyway."

"You're going to end up twisted and bitter from hanging around all these cop buddies of yours," I said playfully.

"From listening to my friends fib to me, more likely." Then, "How well do you know Amanda?"

"About as well as you." I said.

"I don't sleep naked at her apartment." Bob John smiled.

"I wore gym shorts. Why?"

"In addition to the new car, she paid off two overdue credit-card bills with cash. This week. Any idea where she got that much money?" he asked innocently.

"No, do you?" I said cheerfully.

"She told the woman at the car dealership it was a lump-sum divorce payment that had been held up for a couple of years due to some paperwork. Does that sound right to you?"

"I don't know her well enough to talk about money, Bob John,"

I said. We drove down Prince past the huge antebellum estate of the president of the university, strangely located off-campus in a fading neighborhood. A few minutes later we passed the vegetarian restaurant, The Grit, housed in the old Coca-Cola bottling plant. Great food, and they used textured vegetable protein so ingeniously that it was hard to tell the dishes were meatless—until you farted nonstop for the next two days.

Bob John drove carefully and diligently, signaling as he changed lanes and staying exactly within the speed limit. The vehicle was so obviously a cop car that no one dared pass, and in the side mirror I could see two lanes of impatient commuters lining up behind us.

"Just well enough to stay at her house," he laughed.

"It's the twenty-first century, Bob John, you got to get out more."

"I guess I do. Hey, I heard a good quote the other day. You might be able to use it."

"Let's hear it."

"'Familiarity with danger makes a brave man braver, but less daring,'" he said carefully.

"Herman Melville."

"That's right," he said. "Tell Benny hello for me."

"But you're checking her ex-husband's checking account anyway, of course."

"Oh, yeah, we have to do that. It's policy, you know." He pulled over at the curb in front of the station and smiled. "Hey, you going to take Morton up on his job offer?"

"Don't know yet. Should I?"

"Absolutely not. People who work for those people end up messed up. But I don't expect you to take my advice."

"I might—you never know."

CHAPTER 46

USED A CREDIT CARD TO MAKE THE FIVE-HUNDRED-DOLLAR bail, and the deputy told me to go outside and wait. Thirty minutes later, Benny came through the front door of the police station. He wore a gray sweater, dark pants, black silk socks and carried his shoes and sunglasses. He came over to where I sat on the tailgate of the Ford and stood in front of me. "Shoelaces went missing."

I nodded. "I think there are some flipflops in the bottom of the toolbox."

"Don't say anything, please, I know it was stupid." He stood on the bed of the truck while he rummaged through the Fiberglas compartment.

"Why'd you decide to break into Groovology?" I asked. Benny closed the lid and started to vault over the side, but I called to him, "Wait, let's take a walk. I'll buy you an English-breakfast tea at The Brewpot."

"You think they bugged the truck again?" he said.

"Oh, sure," I said. "I don't think they could resist."

"Do you want me to call the sweepers back out?"

"Tomorrow's fine," I said. He raised his eyebrows.

"OK," he said. We walked down the hill, him flapping pleasantly beside me. I turned my face up to the sunshine and grinned. There is no better place to be on this planet than Athens in the spring, premature as this one was. Benny grabbed my elbow and gave me a little tug, so I missed walking into a small tree set in a planter on the sidewalk. We turned on Lumpkin and headed toward the Pot.

"I might as well get it over with," he sighed. "When I got home last night, I unloaded the stuff, and there on the backseat was a set of keys. I figured Vinyl Man must have dropped them when we took him out of the back. I couldn't sleep, so I drove back in to Groovology to have a look around."

"How'd you get caught?"

"It's embarrassing. That old beat-up alarm actually works, so when I got in I had to take a few minutes to bypass it. I just finished, turned around, and there was this young Athens police officer, and behind him our good friends Sergei and Irina. They'd seen me enter and called it in. Can you believe it? This time they decide to call the police."

I smiled. "Did they give you a hard time?"

"Not really. They know Vinyl won't press charges. They can't prove he didn't give me the keys and ask me to check up, which is what I told them. I have a sheet, but it's pretty thin and pretty old. Just kept me cooling my heels long enough to make a point. John Slocum from Clarke County came over and glared at me for a while, asked where you were. I couldn't tell him since I didn't know."

"Went to see Amanda."

"Uh-huh. Too bad I didn't get time to look around," he finished.

"Nah. Nothing in there." A cool shadow blocked the sun. I looked up and saw a row of cottony clouds move across half the sky. The sun fought to shine through, but lost. I buttoned my flannel shirt and stuffed it into my jeans. We turned into The Brewpot.

"How do you know?" he said over his shoulder as he headed down the stairs.

"Two reasons. First, Bob John and the cops had an excuse to look around when investigating Vinyl's disappearance. I'll bet they took the place apart, looked inside every record sleeve."

He stopped at the bottom and turned around. "And the second reason?"

"There's only one place the money can be."

"And?"

"Where else? In the school."

"And how long have you known this?"

"I figured it out yesterday."

"Wish you'd thought to mention it," he said. "Anything else I should know?"

"Sorry. I had to confirm it. Needed to check the call logs and get hold of Russell's daddy."

"What did Mr. Driggers have to say?"

"Said he saw Dee Lane driving out early on Saturday evening. Then it all made sense. After all, he knew I was getting antsy and needed a gig. He may have even mentioned it to me, but I hadn't understood what he was saying at the time."

"Not unusual for a conversation with Dee Lane," Benny said.

"Still," I answered.

"But why'd he go to all the trouble to stage his disappearance?" Benny asked.

"Who knows?" I shrugged. "This is Dee Lane. There's a quote about Alexander Pope, 'He scarce drank tea without a strategem.' Dee Lane's always plotting and subplotting. Dee Lane would put on a disguise to go to the Piggly Wiggly."

I saw Benny silently committing the Pope quote to memory. "So we had it all along."

"I guess so."

"That does leave one open question."

"Yes, it does," I agreed.

CHAPTER 47

WE GOT BACK TO THE SCHOOL AROUND NINE OR SO. Benny went to dispatch EJ and take a shower while I checked the machine. There were four messages. One was from Bob John and predated our earlier get-together. The others were from Danny. He left a different number from the one I had, but I did not call him back immediately. Instead I spent some of the hours until noon dusting a bit, tidying up E-mail, and reading a few pages of the Polymath bible, *The Oxford Dictionary of Quotations*. I spent most of the rest of the time practicing my throw with the Malaysian fighting top. Fighting tops require a steady hand, and now that the buzz was gone, this morning was a good time to practice.

EJ called just before noon, said, "Done," hung up immediately. I called Danny.

"Yeah," a young woman's voice answered, worn sounding. In the background, a baby cried.

"Could you tell Danny it's Top?" I said.

"Hold on." She clanked the phone down on a table. I heard a grunt, probably her picking up the child, and her voice say, "Quiet, little man, shhhhh, shhhhh." The crying stopped. Then footsteps, and a few minutes later, Danny picked up the telephone.

" 'Tis me," he said.

"Hello, Danny."

"Don't you sound bloody cheery this morning? 'Top o' the morning Top' they'll be calling ye. Heard you found the lad. Well done, keep the fookin' cops out of me arse."

"You still interested in this business?"

"Mebbe." He tried to sound guarded, but was not able to disguise his excitement. "Look, my phone's not clean, here, Topper. Be careful what you say."

"Here's the deal. I've got a package for our friend. He needs to get it today. Can you deliver it?"

"The package?" he gulped.

"No, not *the* package, *a* package. He's expecting it."

"So why don't you run it in yourself?"

"I told you, I want to get *out* of this, not farther in. If I deliver it, I might get drafted, if you know what I mean."

"So, how much?"

"As much as you can get—I'm not paying." He thought about this for a few minutes. "All right, where?" he said. I heard a door open and lighter footsteps. Someone whispered something. Danny said, "Jaysus Christ, Top, you've got balls. Having Elbert Day's son deliver a package for Raoul Menes. You've either got the finest sense of humor outside of fookin' Ireland, or you really are stone mad." He hung up.

EJ had shoved it halfway under the door, because the mail slot was sealed. Not having a place for people to leave packages was probably a habit from Danny's old IRA terrorist days. Perhaps he did not want his old friends to keep in touch. Now Danny had the package of maps and satellite photos, the same one that led us to the trailer. In the best case, he'd pass those on to Raoul. But the other possibility—that he might try to short Menes and retrieve the bag himself—was not bad either.

I sat for a few moments, and thought about EJ being Elbert Day's son and, more importantly, about Benny not telling me, then stuffed a cordless phone in my pocket and joined Benny in searching the school. We did not talk, but worked methodically and patiently. We started in the boiler room in the basement, using flashlights to peer into every cranny and behind every piece of equipment. We looked through old unused closets, behind stacks of desks and boxes of obsolete textbooks, and in four hundred lockers. We stuck our heads into large unused stainless-steel refrigerators and ovens in the cafeteria, and climbed steel ladders in electrical supply closets to aim flashlights into attic spaces. After three hours, we'd finished about one-third of the building. We decided to take a break when the phone rang.

I answered and a voice rattled off an Atlanta number. I hung up, grabbed a cell phone from the office, climbed into the truck and drove past the chicken farm to the new playground. The clouds settled in now in earnest, and a raw north wind blew across the damp ground. I had the park to myself as I chose a bench at random and punched the number in, reversing the last two digits.

"Hello," someone answered, not Menes. There was the sound of traffic in the background, and more distant, a playground that sounded as if it were full of kids.

"Call Danny," I said.

There was a moment of silence while someone covered the receiver and a dull mutter. Then the voice came back on. "If we need to reach you, you around today?"

"You don't need to reach me, today, tomorrow, or the next day," I said and hung up. I laid the cheap Nokia on the ground and smashed it under my foot, keeping at it until it was a stringy mass of plastic pieces. These I scooped up and dropped into a trash can. The Feds are just like raccoons and garbage cans: You can't keep them out, but you can make them work a bit.

When I got back to the school, Benny was sitting on the steps, waiting. He winked, and I followed him into the building, down a shiny hall, and into the auditorium. He pointed to the ceiling. I peered hard, but saw nothing, and shrugged. He led me up onto the stage and over to one corner and pointed again. I closed one eye and put my head close to his elbow, sighting along his arm and saw it, a small triangle of white cloth sticking from behind a torn piece of tin.

It would have taken a strong man to reach up into the ceiling and lay a large bag up there. We climbed up the scaffolding carrying a small folding stepladder, which Benny placed on the boards and held while I stood on it and wrestled the bulky sack down. Of course, it was not a new green duffel, as Raoul had said, but a faded gray canvas laundry bag.

We opened it and looked inside, and saw not packets of bills but a huge mass of loose notes, crumpled and stuffed together. It did not look worth two lives. On the top was a folded piece of yellow notebook paper wrapped around a stack of bills. I opened it and read it out loud:

"Topster. Here's a little job that might work your buzz off for a day or so. This needs to be delivered to a guy. Check messages for address. Be careful, this guy's a little nuts. Twenty-five to you. Off to finish something. Will be in touch."

And that was it. Dee Lane had offered a simple courier run, and it had turned into World War III. Benny climbed halfway down and I lay on my stomach and lowered the bag to him, and he swung it down. He dropped it the last four feet, and it tossed up a cloud of white gypsum dust, but not nearly as much as if we'd dropped it the whole way. Each of us took a corner and we carried it onto the stage. I wrestled up one end of the pile of curtains and Benny forced the trapdoor open a foot or so, and stuffed the bag down inside. We heard it drop, and he helped me pull the curtains back. He swept away the tracks with his feet.

We stood there, grinning at each other, then shook hands ceremoniously. That didn't seem to be good enough, so we shook hands again and this time patted each other's back furiously.

CHAPTER 48

NOW WHAT?" SAID BENNY.

"I say we give it away."

"To whom?" When I told him, he smiled and nodded. "But that's going to piss Raoul and those hillbillies off."

"Hillbillies? First goobers, now hillbillies. Just go ahead and say 'white trash' and get it over with," I said.

"No, thank you."

"Sure it's going to piss them off, but I don't want them to end up happy."

"No, I suppose not," he agreed.

I made a big show of calling Soames, and setting up an immediate rendezvous with one of his people, a Mr. Rockwell, who lived in one of those gated communities in Hilton Head. I told Soames to tell Rockwell to warn the guards at his gated community that Benny and EJ were African-American, so they wouldn't get tossed on sight. By then EJ had returned, and I packed Benny and him off with the duffel bag. I stood on the front steps and waved them out of sight. It was hard to wait for them to leave, but Benny had already risked enough.

As soon as they turned the corner, before the splash from their tires had soaked back into the puddles in the tire ruts, I had already raced back inside. I unlocked two of the lockers quickly. From one, I took two high-tech plastic knee braces like NFL linemen wear, ones that allow front-to-back movement, but restrict lateral twisting. From the other I took a full set of camouflage gear. I pulled both on hastily.

In the auditorium, I managed to drag the heavy curtains from over the trapdoor, and from the gun locker selected two weapons: an Accuracy L96A1 precision sniping rifle, chambered for .300 Winchester Magnums and already scoped, and an HK MP5K, a submachine pistol. I packed two web belts with thirty-round magazines, each about two seconds worth if the HK is set to full auto and stuffed the submachine pistol and the belts into a shoulder pack. I started to close the locker, then decided to add two grenades. I hefted the pack, and satisfied with the weight, pulled the drawstring tight. I stuffed four magazines for my SIG Sauer pistol in the side pockets of the camo pants. I dropped the nightscope, a sleeping bag, flashlight, a handful of Clif Bars and two bottles of water into a carry bag, slung the rifle and the backpack over my shoulder and made my way to the truck.

My plan was simple. I figured Raoul would move quickly to take out Richard and get his money back, but I had timed it so that he wouldn't be able to get to the trailer before dark. I guessed a city boy like Raoul would be nervous making a night raid in the country. Instead, he'd probably get in position and move in at first light.

I wanted to be in my position by then, on the hillside 300 or so yards east of the trailer, hopefully with a clear view of the top of the road and the front of the dwelling. With any luck, I'd be able to set up and take out Raoul from a distance. It was even possible I could even get in the shot in the confusion, and get in and out without being noticed. Not likely, given the heavy flat sound the sniping rifle makes, but possible.

CHAPTER 49

THE SKY WAS LOSING ITS LIGHT AS I ROUNDED ATHENS AND turned north. I drove carefully, taking few chances, not wanting to be pulled over. Not today. Not with a submachine, a sniping rifle, and two hand grenades under a sleeping bag on the floorboard behind my seat. The radio droned lightly in the background, classical probably, but I wasn't paying any attention.

Gillie called at some point. I lied and told her I was working in the shed. She asked if she could come out to the school to see me, but I begged off, using fatigue as an excuse. A few minutes after she hung up, there was a muted ring. I flipped open the small LG and hit the green OK button, but nothing happened. The ringing continued. I looked at the phone, but it showed no incoming call. The ringing seemed to be coming from the glove box. I reached over, opened it, and pulled out the Iridium satphone Morton had left on my front steps, and that I'd put in the truck and never returned.

"Hello?"

Pause. "Top, it's Gerald Morton," he answered. *Click.*

"I should have thrown this damn thing away," I said.

Pause. "I'm glad you didn't. They cost three grand each and have encrypted chips in them. We lose them, the paperwork is unbelievable. If you decide you don't want it, do me a favor, drop it in a mailbox." He laughed. *Click.*

"What can I do for you, Morton?" I was not laughing.

Pause. "I wanted to know if you've given any thought to my offer," he said. *Click.*

"Not much, to be honest."

Pause. "I know you're out of work, Top, and I know you don't want to be." *Click.*

"You think you know. I know I'm thinking about retiring, becoming a full-time librarian."

The pause this time was longer than the regular delay. "You don't want to do that," he said. *Click.*

"I don't?"

Pause. "Perhaps you do, but you won't in six months," he said. *Click.*

"Soames says I should retire," I said.

Pause. "He's wrong. You're not buzzed out, just still recovering from Lima." *Click.*

"What do you know about Peru?"

Pause. "More than we should. Hellmund came to us for help. We told him to sit tight, and that's when he panicked and called the police. So maybe it was our fault. But it wasn't yours. You're just as good as you've ever been." *Click.*

"You can't know for sure." I said.

Pause. "We've seen this before, Top, studied it, analyzed it every way there is to analyze it. Trust me here, the biggest mistake you can make is to go lay on a beach. It will eat you up like a cancer, rot you from the inside. If you get back to work, you'll be OK," he said. *Click.*

I thought about the Technicolor dreams. "I wish I could believe that, Morton," I said.

Pause. "I wish you would, too." This time the click was deeper and more final.

I rolled down the window and dropped the phone onto the pavement.

CHAPTER 50

A MILE AWAY FROM THE TURNOFF, IT BECAME CLEAR MY plan wouldn't work. The trees up ahead reflected red-and-blue lights. To my right, where the trailer would be, I could see a faint orange glow reflecting off the low clouds. I wondered if that was Raoul's work, or if Richard's crew had managed to blow themselves up. I pulled over into the mouth of a forestry-access road, and thought briefly about just turning around. Now that the buzz was gone, I had none of that superhuman energy that comes with the ride—just a dull tiredness.

Instead, I drove a hundred yards down the road and pulled off into a pine-needled clearing. As long as Raoul was alive, Polymath wasn't safe. I hid the rifle in the bushes across from the truck, in case a police car came down this far, slung the backpack over my shoulder, slipped the nightscope on top of my head, and walked back down to the main road. Awkwardly, I began jogging toward the red-and-blue lights.

I ran listening for sounds behind me, ready to dive into the ditch, expecting more police cars to round the bend at any moment. But none came. As I approached the curve, I cut off into

271

the woods, going twenty feet deep beyond the tree line and slipping the scope down onto my face. In the green light, I continued to jog through the thin forest. About ten yards from the road to the trailer, I pulled off the scope and, dropping to my knees, edged out to the roadblock. There was just one police car, straddling the main road. It was dark blue and unmarked, and its lights flashed furiously. A lone cop, wearing one of those blue windbreakers with DEA in big yellow letters, stood in front of the car with a walkie-talkie in one hand and a shotgun in the other.

Then I understood. Menes's speed had fooled us all. This car was here because Bob John's men had a tail on Raoul. They had followed him up here. And that was it. This car might be the only police within miles. If the DEA had any idea Raoul was going for the money, they would have had a small army on hand. There would be helicopters, a dozen cars, and two reporters from CNN. But no. Instead there was just this one poor schmuck, alone in the North Carolina woods. I wondered if crossing the state line had also taken them by surprise.

While I watched him, the cop spoke into the walkie-talkie. And I realized he must have a partner nearby. He could never get a signal in these woods and hills unless the other radio were very close, another walkie-talkie. I had no idea if that agent were on foot or if there were more cars up the road. At any rate, I'd have to be more careful. I hadn't come here to get in a firefight with the DEA.

I turned and headed up toward the small wooden bridge, staying in the woods, quickly settling into a rhythm. Not quite a run, not with the braces and this terrain in the dark, but a quick walk-slash-scramble. The road ran parallel to my path to the left, sometimes in sight, and sometimes not. The land rose and fell, a series of small hills, and little sharp ravines with soft bottoms. After ten minutes of movement, I topped a small rise, ready to negotiate the down slope. Instead, suddenly I found my legs pumping nothing but air. I windmilled three feet or so, landed on the angle of a slippery mudbank, and slid butt first down into the ice-cold water of the creek.

I cursed under my breath, and tried to climb back out, grabbing a handful of roots and digging my toes into the soft bank. Both feet slipped out of the poor footing, and I fell face forward onto the bank, catching myself on my elbows. The bank across the way was higher, maybe six feet or so, and appeared to be the same clumpy mud and loose debris. I turned and began making my way upstream toward the bridge, looking for a place to scramble out. In the bottom of the stream I saw a twenty-dollar bill pinned against a small round stone, washed downstream from where Benny and I had dumped them only twenty-four or so hours ago.

I rounded a small bend. Ahead of me stood the wooden bridge, silhouetted against the sky, maybe two feet above my head, eight feet above the creek bed. And there, standing in the middle of the bridge, was Bob John Wynn. He looked up the road toward the trailer with a bulky pair of night-vision binoculars, and spoke into the walkie-talkie, which he held sideways under the glasses.

Crouching down, I crept closer to the bridge, easing myself up under it, and found a small concrete ledge. Laying flat, I gratefully pulled my aching feet from the cold water. I lay on my back, very still, and looked up through the gaps between the creosoted timbers at the bottom of Bob John's feet.

He turned around and spoke to someone behind them. "We've got them pinned in. There's nowhere to go. Wait until I give the word. We'll turn on the disco lights and the spotlights just as they make the turn and slow down for the bridge. Be ready to fire. We'll pin them right here. Nowhere for them to go."

Another voice said, "What if they try to ram their way through?"

"Shoot the tires. If we can strand one of their war wagons on the bridge, that's just as good. Better. We only have to hold them a few more minutes. Local is on the way." I noted that Bob John said "one of their war wagons." "Wagons," plural, as in more than one car of lunatic Colombians.

"I hear them coming, Bob John. Better get back here," the other agent said. There was the approaching roar of large engines geared down, the growl of fat tires, and an occasional thud, either the vehicles bottoming out or the smash of the tires against the sides of the ruts. Headlights played over the bushes beside the stream.

Bob John turned and scrambled backward. "Now!" he yelled.

The top of the bridge lit up like the county fair, flashing lights everywhere. The area beneath the bridge was illuminated by little slats of light leaking down from above and the blackness turned to gray. I heard a roar as a high-powered vehicle came closer and suddenly shuddered to a stop. The engine revved. Behind it I heard at least one more vehicle.

A voice came from my right. "What the hell?"

A bullhorn from the left said, "Get out of the car and put your hands over your head. This is the DEA."

CHAPTER 51

AYSOOS CHRISTUS, BOB JOHN, WHY COULDN'T YOU just follow these guys back to Atlanta and arrest them there, instead of forcing a showdown out here in the middle of nowhere? You can't really believe they're just going to turn themselves in after committing who-knows-what mayhem two miles up the road. I thought again about his use of the plural, "war wagons."

A door slammed, and someone dropped noisily through bushes and into the stream a few yards away. I swiveled my head, but saw nothing. Suddenly an engine revved, and I felt the bridge above me shudder as an SUV roared across. There was a huge wham and a tearing sound as it plowed into the side of the DEA car. The engine died, and the driver tried unsuccessfully to grind it back to life. From downstream I saw the flash of a muzzle, and I heard one of the DEA guys scream. Suddenly others began firing automatic weapons across the bridge at Bob John's position. I heard bullets ripping into the side of the DEA car and whistling through the trees behind them.

"Get out of the truck, get out!" someone yelled. And directly above me, the back hatch of the SUV swung open and three men crawled out. They scrambled quickly across the bridge. As soon as they were clear, another SUV came roaring across the bridge full speed and slammed into the back of the first one, sending it spinning sideways, one wheel dangling over the edge of the wooden bridge. I wondered if removing the air bags came standard on the SUV criminal model. The driver backed up and charged again, and this time the first one hung over the side of the bridge a moment, then flopped upside down onto the streambed. It was a very new-looking Cadillac Escalade. One rear wheel spun freely.

Someone on the DEA side fired an automatic shotgun repeatedly. The pellets bounced off the front of the second SUV and rained down through the cracks in the bridge. Kevlar panels, probably. I heard the truck on the bridge back up again and charge forward again at speed, and another crash and sliding sound. Up top, guns continued to stutter, and I could feel the vibrations of bullets chewing up the heavy timbers of the bridge.

"Almost clear—ram it again. Go for it, hit it again," someone shouted. It sounded like Raoul.

Suddenly I heard someone say, "The fuck?" right next to my ear. And there, about two feet away from me, frozen in shocked surprise stood Desi, looking ridiculous in his city suit, covered with mud and dark up to the waist from where he'd been floundering in the stream. I lifted my right arm and shot him once in the center of his face. He fell backward in slow motion. Above me, a pair of boot soles moved backward suddenly. I rolled off the ledge and back into the stream, pulled the HK from the backpack and jammed its short four-and-a-half-inch barrel up through one of the gaps between the boards.

"One of them is under the bridge. Somebody's shooting under the bridge."

Somebody else yelled, "Desi?"

The truck began to back up, and I pulled the trigger and sent thirty rounds hammering at the metal underside of the SUV. I heard a scream, then the sound of bullets hitting the harder metal of the engine, and the truck stopped moving. Pulling the small submachine gun down, I yanked out the empty magazine and dropped it into the stream. Before I could replace it, I felt a cool liquid run down the back of my neck and smelled the sharp odor of gasoline slicing through the night air. And just as it registered, the world exploded.

A second later I found myself lying facedown in the stream, gagging as I fought for air. I used my elbows to push my face above the surface of the water, and vomited. Through the loud ringing, I heard someone scream again. I slung the machine gun, and stood unsteadily. Drunkenly I staggered to the abutment closest to the DEA position, and grabbing the concrete lip, pulled myself up and over, and fell heavily into a small ditch. Shakily, I rose to my hands and knees. The DEA car lay crumpled across the road, one pulled-off fender still providing a token barrier. On the bridge, the second SUV burned, and flames began to lick the ends of the timbers themselves. I smelled burning flesh and saw a blackened corpse lying on the bridge behind the vehicle. There was no sign of Bob John or the other agent.

The world began to get louder as my ears cleared, and there came another crashing sound. The flaming SUV shuddered and then slid at an angle toward me. One wheel caught, and it twisted in the other direction, skewing over the far edge of the bridge. Behind the burning wreck I could see yet another Cadillac Escalade, wheels spinning and smoking as it pushed the wreck in front of it. I felt the empty slot in the submachine pistol where a fresh magazine should be, and remembered dropping the spent magazine under the bridge. I swung the small backpack around and groped inside desperately.

The SUV backed up. "Get in, get in, goddammit. We're getting out of here." Doors slammed and the engine revved. The driver slammed it into forward gear and it jumped across the bridge, shouldering the burning wreck over the side, swatting the fender of the DEA wreck out of the way, and roaring up the muddy dirt road toward the highway.

Suddenly, impossibly, after only thirty feet, the massive vehicle skidded to a stop. Incredulously, I watched the backup lights come on as it moved slowly down the slope toward me. I dropped the knapsack and put my hands behind my back. *One.* The driver rolled down his window to see the road better. I recognized Chuck's face in the side mirror. *Two.*

When it reached me, the black-tinted window behind Chuck rolled down, and a chrome barrel slid out. *Three.* And I threw the grenade in my hand as hard as I could at the fat smiling face inside the opening. As I dropped, I saw the barrel jerk upward. The dome light blinked, and there was a scramble inside the vehicle. Then came a blinding white flash, the sides of the truck expanded sideways, the entire vehicle leaped a foot into the air, and a massive concussion rolled across me, peeling the clothes off my back and searing the back of my hands as I covered my head. A door sailed over me and tore into the woods beyond.

Then the world went quiet. I lifted my head. I should be able to hear something, but could not. I crawled up the ditch until I could no longer feel the heat, and rolled onto my back, feeling the cold leaves digging into my raw skin, and gulped the cold night air.

CHAPTER 52

I WANTED TO LIE THERE ALL NIGHT, BUT BOB JOHN HAD SAID the locals were on the way. If I couldn't get back to my truck before they sealed off the area, I would be stuck here, trying to explain an illegal submachine gun and hand grenade. I climbed to my feet wearily, dug the nightscope out of the pack, and dropped the HK inside. Pulling the scope on, careful to keep my face turned away from the burning vehicles, I stumbled through the ditch and made my way into the forest.

One of the DEA agents lay just a few feet from where I went in. Half of his head was missing. And across from him lay another, back up against a tree and hands doubled over his stomach. I felt his neck. There was no pulse. Neither body was Bob John's.

It was steeper here—almost vertical—and I worked my way carefully down the bank. Exhaustion and shock had turned my legs to rubber, and I lurched heavily from tree to tree. My left leg buckled several times, and I fell, pulled myself back up, and stumbled on. My hands and feet felt cold. And right at the bottom, just along the ravine bottom, I stepped on Bob John.

He'd been bleeding, and had rolled down the slope, collecting leaves as he went, and was now completely covered. I knelt beside him, raking the leaves off, exposing a thick bloody spot just under the left side of his vest. My fingers were too numb and cold to feel a pulse. I pulled off the nightscope, held my cheek down to his mouth, and felt a faint, wet pulsing warmth. The silence in my ears was being replaced gradually by a ringing. I wondered if I would hear the sirens when the locals came. Empty, I knelt beside Bob John and tried to force my tired mind to think. I looked back up the steep slope and then down at the pale face of my childhood friend.

If he stayed here—even if the locals arrived soon—he might well bleed to death before they found him. On the road, he would stand a chance. I knelt down and scooped him up in my arms, and slowly stood. His arms flapped uselessly, and I remembered the last time I'd carried someone like this. I raised my left leg slowly and planted it into the slope. As I shifted my weight, the leg gave way, and I dropped Bob John heavily into the matted leaves.

Cursing, I struggled up again and fell again, and again and again. The fourth time, Bob John rolled backward down the slope, and I lost my balance and tumbled backward, coming to rest on the bottom of the ravine with his deadweight on top of me. I wriggled out from under him and knelt, tears of frustration welling in my eyes.

I looked back up the slope, and still saw no lights. After all this, if I tried to summon help with my gun, would anyone come? Or would they just blast away down the slope? I looked back at Bob John. Clumsily I pushed the vest away to get to the wound. His walkie-talkie was in the way and I shoved it to the side. As I did, I felt it push up against his handcuffs. And got an idea.

I dropped my knapsack on the ground and tightened my belt to the last notch, then fumbled for the handcuffs. I clicked one onto

Bob John's wrist. Straddling him, I used his arms to pull him to a sitting position, then turned and pulled him up and over my back like a pack. I bent over so he rested on my back, and threaded the handcuff under my belt. I swayed, swinging his free dangling arm until I could catch it and snap it into the other cuff. Now Bob John rested on my back, his arms around my neck, fastened onto my belt with his own handcuffs. I stood a little straighter to test the weight, and the pull on my belt yanked my inseam right up into my groin. I gave a small, involuntary yelp of pain.

I struggled up the slope on hands and knees, pulling myself from sapling to sapling, trying not to rest, keeping my eye on the lighter patch that was the top of the ridge. Every small movement seemed to take forever. I found myself chanting, "One, two," over and over, for no apparent reason other than the sheer rhythm of it. Sometimes I would slip and slide back down a few feet, then I would have to kneel again, and once again struggle to all fours. As I climbed, I began hearing the rasp of my breath, and knew the effects of the explosion were wearing off.

When I finally reached the road, I dropped Bob John, loosened my belt, and slid out of his arms. I stood gasping. Suddenly—unexpectedly, he groaned and I grinned from ear to ear. I knelt, pulled off his walkie-talkie, and pressed the talk button. "This is Bob John," I gasped. "I'm hurt. We're clear. I'm walking down the road."

"Oh, Christ! I thought everyone was dead up there," a voice said. "Hurry!"

"Bob John?" the voice said.

I dropped the walkie-talkie, and turned to go. Then I remembered the handcuffs. There was no way to explain the handcuffs. Spinning back, I dropped down, frantically digging through Bob John's pockets. I heard the sound of an engine from below.

The key was in his right front pants pocket. I pulled it out. My fingers were cold and I dropped the key onto the bloody vest. The engine sound grew louder. I grabbed the now-bloody key, and it squirted out of my fingers and back onto the vest. I reached inside my jacket and pulling out the hem of the T-shirt, bent over and held the key in a fold of cloth. With the additional traction, I was able to twist the key and remove the cuffs. I stuffed them in my pockets to avoid having to worry about fingerprints, and rolled over the edge of the embankment, just as the headlights rounded the corner and spotlighted Bob John's body.

CHAPTER 53

I T TOOK ME HOURS TO GET TO MY TRUCK AND WEND MY WAY back through the back roads. I tumbled into bed, and slept until midmorning. There were eight messages from Gerald Morton, and he called a ninth time just as we walked into the office.

"I thought you'd want to know Bob John will be OK," he said coolly, no comment about the unreturned calls.

I dropped into the chair and grimaced. Benny mouthed, "What?" and I pointed to the extension, which he picked up. I reached over and turned up the volume. My ears still rang.

I said, "Benny's on the line" before he said anything. They exchanged hellos.

"What happened?" I asked. "How bad?"

"He had stakeouts on Danny and Menes. Followed Menes to the meet. Not clear if someone from the trailer took a shot, or if Menes and his crew just went in blazing. Apparently these guys were meth cookers. They kept their chemicals under that trailer. It must have stunk like crazy under there. At any rate, a bullet hit the stash and the whole thing went up in a fireball. Three dead inside—Ronnie Inman and Carl Lott, both nineteen, and Richard

Lott, 42—all with hard time. Found another one buried in a trench in the backyard, not yet identified."

"So how'd Bob John get hurt?"

"We couldn't move fast enough and get a team in place. When Menes came out, Bob John threw up a roadblock. We had two cars and four agents. They had three war wagons—huge Escalades—and tried to fight their way out. Menes or someone stitched Bob John with a semi."

"Did he have on a vest?" I asked.

"Yes, he wore a vest, but he caught one in the arm and one in the side. He lost a lot of blood, but he's stable now."

"Anybody else?"

"Menes and five more of his dead, two more hurt. We lost two. More of them than us."

"Did you get the money?"

"Sort of," he laughed. "There's green confetti all over the North Carolina woods. We found ten thousand in a Baggie inside the water tank of one of the commodes, but I suppose the rest is vaporized."

"Oh, man!" I said.

"It's a messy, messy crime scene up there," Morton said.

"I can imagine."

"That wouldn't surprise me. Although it would take some imagination to put all the pieces of this together. There's a spent magazine from an HK in the streambed. No HKs found in the wreckage. The only thing the techs can figure out is that maybe one or more of Menes's men escaped. And Bob John managed to climb a pretty steep slope and call for help on the walkie-talkie, but doctors can't quite figure out how he was conscious, amount of blood he lost. They have no idea how he made the climb," the man said.

"Pretty confusing," I agreed. Benny looked at me and ran his tongue along his front teeth under his lips. I avoided his eyes.

"No chance you know any more about this—is there, Top?"

"None at all. And I don't want to get drug into this business," I said.

"Danny says you set up the meet. I think you're already in it," he said.

"Danny's a liar," I said.

"Maybe I can keep you out of it."

"I'd be grateful," I said.

"How grateful?"

"Very grateful."

"Grateful enough to do bit of legwork down south?"

"Perhaps."

"That could be useful."

"I didn't set anyone up, Morton, God's honest truth," I lied.

"Truth doesn't matter much in my business. Just whether I can make someone believe it, and I think I can. OK, I'll take care of you," he said sincerely.

"Don't try to handle me," I said. "I'm not an informant, I'm an operative."

"I'm not handling you," he lied. "And I'll be in touch."

I started to hang up, then heard him say my name, "Top?"

"Yeah?"

"Don't worry about the phone you lost. Those things have GPS beacons in them. We found what was left of it this morning." He hung up.

"You think maybe this whole thing was a game to get you to work for those guys?" Benny asked. "Maybe they got you fired and tipped Menes that we were holding the money just to push you into doing this job?"

"Of course not. Why would you think that?" I answered, thinking that "of course not" was a bit strong, more likely it was "probably not." Or "maybe not."

"Do you smell that?" Benny wrinkled his nose.

"What?"

"Brimstone," he answered. I didn't say anything, just wound the blue spinner up and gave it a flick across the floor.

CHAPTER 54

W E SAT THERE FOR AN HOUR, ME SPINNING TOPS AND Benny listening to an avant-garde jazz CD. When it finished, he stood up and said he had friends coming over tonight, and wanted to set up the band room. I nodded and said I thought I'd go lift awhile. We agreed to meet up around five and have an early dinner.

But I didn't get up immediately. Instead, I took down the Confederate wooden top, which I rarely spun. I wound a string carefully around its cone, making sure there were no overlapping strands. I held it in my hand for a while, just feeling it, and then threw it onto the floor, mentally reminding myself, "Smooth, no jerks, just smooth." It landed, wobbled for just a second and then settled into a perfect spin, not even moving across the floor, just rotating around a single invisible point.

As I watched it, the telephone rang. I reached over and picked it up, without taking my eyes off the spinning top. "Look at ye fookin' security camera, the one on the outside south wall," the voice on the phone said. I didn't say anything, but quickly turned around and tapped the keyboard. The twelve views came up. In one of them were two figures. I double-clicked on that one.

Sid, Danny's bouncer, stood behind EJ, with his left arm around his neck. His right arm, which was in a sling, held an automatic jammed into EJ's side. He smiled up at the camera. EJ looked scared, and licked his lips. His body position was strained, as he automatically tried to hold his side away from the pistol.

"I see," I said.

"You and your little nigger come on out to the shed. Both of you, take off your clothes, every last fookin' stitch. That way I don't have to worry about that straight razor of Benny's. Make it snappy."

"Danny, are you sure you want to kill Elbert Day's son?"

"Arsehole, this line is probably bugged and you know it. Just come on out here, and no more of your shite. You've got ninety seconds—no more."

I called Benny, told him, then took off all my clothes and went outside into the chilly spring air. I walked carefully across the grass to the front of the shed, automatically holding my hands cupped over my genitals, and pushed open the door with one hand. It was dark inside and hard to see anything.

"Come on in, Top," Danny said. "Join our little party."

The shed was a small freestanding structure, about 9 by 12, with a concrete floor. On the bench lay various bicycle tools, and my bikes hung on hooks on two of the walls. The workbench held a bike stand, and assorted tools lay spread across it. Danny perched on the bench, and EJ lay on the floor, his hands cuffed behind his back. Sid stood in the farthest corner next to assorted bike fragments and a large, mostly empty drum. He used his good arm and the hand in the sling to hold a long-barreled shotgun pointed at Benny, who stood to my right and, like me, was completely naked.

"Well, well, here we are," Danny said cheerfully.

"What's all this about, Danny?" I said. "We were straight with you."

"Fookin' straight with me." He laughed. "Just like you were straight with Menes. I hear he's dead—that's how straight you were with him." Danny held his AR-15 loosely with just his right hand, and it rested on his leg, very casually. But his finger was on the trigger.

"I had nothing to do with that," I said.

"See, Sid, now that's how to tell a lie. Good eye contact, don't let the pitch of the voice rise or fall. Keep it short. You crack me up, Topper." He laughed mirthlessly. Sid nodded, but did not smile. Danny nodded toward the mangled frame on the wall. "A Waterford. Nice bicycle, Top." He pronounced it Wotterfoot, with a rolling "r."

"If you've come out here to talk about bicycles, you think maybe we could put some clothes on? I'm freezing my tail off, here," I said.

"The cold will slow you both down, make you easier to handle. I think we'll leave it that way for a while." He looked almost angelic, just a pudgy, friendly old man with snow white hair and ruddy cheeks, a broadly woven brown sweater and matching corduroys, sitting comfortably on the bench and swinging his short legs a few inches off the floor. But the assault rifle ruined the picture.

"I rode bicycles in Ireland, Top. Did everything in Ireland. I was a hell of an athlete. National age group boxing champion. Footballer. But I was a cyclist at heart. I rode with a local club, thought I might turn pro one day. 'Tis truth. But when I was sixteen, my legal troubles started, and that pretty much ended it. Bloody bastard

British wouldn't even let me travel to compete in races in Europe, left me stuck in Ireland." He said that last part with more than a little bitterness. Then he smiled and gave me a wink, and the warmth returned. "But I never had a Waterford frame—I'll tell you that. If I'd had a Waterford, maybe I would have ended up as a domestique in the Tour de France, carrying water bottles for boys like Lance Armstrong. Forget all this political shite, eh?"

"If you say so," I said, glancing at Benny out of the corner of my eye. He had an unusual expression on his face, holding his mouth funny. Perhaps it was the cold.

"Aye, I do say so, you fookin' arsehole. I do. Tell me now, were you a climber or a sprinter, Top? You're nothing now, I suppose, the way you limp around like a crip. Me, you see, I'm a climber. Most Irishmen are sprinters, but Ireland also produces some terrific climbers, even we don't have any mountains, not really. Still we produce climbers. Know why, Topper?"

"Wind training, probably."

"Exactly so. The wind's always blowing in Ireland, and always right in your face. Irish riders call the wind the 'hand of God,' because it feels just like someone has put a big fookin' hand right on your forehead and is pushing you backward. You ride against God in Ireland. You'd think that would be too sacrilegious for all us good Catholics, eh? But that's what we call it."

"Why are you here, Danny?" I asked. "What do you want?"

"Are ye in a hurry to die, lad? I'd think you'd love to live a little longer by listening to my reminisces." EJ rolled over and started to sit up. Without changing expression, Danny scooted down the bench a few inches and kicked him in the head. The old man was very fast, and I knew Benny had noticed it, too. EJ fell hard to the floor and lay there, apparently out cold.

"Good God, Danny! He's just a kid," I said.

"Just a fookin' nigger, Top. Their skulls are thicker than ours, fookin' scientific fact. You can't hurt a nigger by kicking him in the head, for goodness' sake." He shook his head at my ignorance. "Sid, cut off six foot or so of that rope. No, the brown hemp, not the yellow plastic stuff. Even like this, I think I want Mr. Culpepper tied up."

"We still don't know what you want, Danny," I said.

"I want my retirement money."

"Danny, we don't have the money. They found it in the trailer Menes blew up."

"They found *some* money in the trailer, aye. But I got to thinking, Top, when I heard about Menes and that mess up north. Goodness, that's tidy, I thought. Too tidy. I said to meself, 'Danny, lad, maybe old Top set us all up. Maybe he's sitting with that million and a half dollars, laughing his arse off right now.'"

"Why would I set Menes up?"

"Who knows, Top? For the money, or to settle a beef with the DEA, or because you got paid off by the CIA. Your old friend Soames and his outfit have been working hand in glove with those barstards forever. Maybe you're still on Shaw's payroll and they put you up to it. I don't know 'why,' but that doesn't matter much. It's the 'what' I'm concerned with." He shifted the AR-15 to both hands, a more natural firing position. Sid stood with his coil of rope, waiting for instructions.

"Maybe this is all some sort of trap by the Brits to get me back. They never fookin' forget. Maybe this is all some sort of game to get me crossways with the DEA or the Colombians, and Shaw's is setting me up. Who the fook knows?"

"You're sounding as paranoid as Dee Lane. Why would they go

to all the trouble to set a trap for an over-the-hill bartender?" I said. Benny shivered, and wrapped his arms around himself for warmth.

"Those Brits never fookin' forget, Top. I tell you, they never forget," he said. He shifted his attention to Benny.

"Uh-unnhh," Danny said. "Put those arms down, nigger." He shifted his eyes back to me. "But you see, I don't know if the trap is real, or if it's for me or for Menes or somebody, but I think the bait might be. My old bones tell me the million and a half is real."

"That's what you want to believe," I said.

"May be," he agreed.

"You've lost your mind, Danny. Half the cops in Georgia are watching this place," I said. EJ rolled over on his back, and began moaning softly.

"*Were* watching this place. They're all gone now. Sid and Ralphie sat on the ridge and spotted all sorts of cops in all sorts of hiding places, but we went up there today to take a look and found everyone gone, gone, gone. I think they said, 'Fook old Topper and his lawn boy.'"

He nodded at Sid. "Tie him up, but leave your guns behind in the corner. If you have a knife, leave that over there, too."

"I've got another man, Dice, who's waiting outside with a shotgun, and if we don't come out alive, you won't either," I said.

"Not according to this one," Danny said easily. "We had a wee chat with him before we called you. He says Dice is in town somewhere, probably doesn't even have his pager turned on."

Sid had waited and followed the exchange. Now he emptied his pockets onto the top of the fifty-five gallon drum, placed in the corner to hold used motor oil. He took the two steps over to Benny and said, "Put out your hands." Benny replied, but in too low a voice for me to hear him.

"What? I can't hear you," Sid said. "Hold your hands still." Benny shivered and leaned forward to whisper something to Sid. As his mouth neared Sid's ear, I saw his lips pull back and the shiny razor blade locked between his teeth. Benny leaned down and swung his head in a quick arc, and Sid sighed and dropped to his knees. His carotid artery pumped blood in a red fountain over Benny's knees. Benny stood calmly, the blade back inside his mouth.

Danny stared at Sid, unable from his angle to see the cut. "Sid, are ye all right?" He raised the rifle, and slid off the bench. As he stood, EJ pulled both his feet back quickly and kicked as hard as he could at Danny's ankles. The old man nimbly jumped up over EJ's legs, and swung the AR-15 down toward his head. "Who the fook do you think you're dealing with, you stupid sod?"

I'd started moving as soon as EJ had begun the kick, and before Danny could fire, I'd reached the bench, grabbed a fifteen-inch pedal wrench, and raised it. I brought it down as hard as I could on the back of his skull. As I swung, my foot slipped on the cold floor and the wrench twisted in my hand. As a result, I hit him with the side, not the flat, and it sank right through the skin, splitting through the bone like a machete through a coconut, and ending up sticking straight out of his skull like a shiny steel pigtail. Danny stood, swaying and Benny took a quick step over and plucked the AR-15 out of his hand. Benny turned and spat the razor blade out onto the floor.

"Better move, EJ," he said. EJ rolled out of the way and stood up.

"Better not stand there either," Benny said, and EJ stepped aside just as I vomited in the middle of the mess. One side of the kid's head was already swollen and beginning to discolor. Slowly Danny sank to his knees and pitched forward onto the floor. Benny felt the side of Danny's throat and said, "Dead."

EJ kicked the body as hard as he could. Benny and I didn't say anything. EJ said "Motherfucker!" and kicked him again.

"You OK?" I said.

"I don't know, he might have broken some bones with that kick," EJ said thickly.

"I'm going to get dressed," I said. "EJ, if you go to the hospital here, it's going to be a problem. We need to find their car. Benny can drive you to Atlanta in it. We'll give you some money to pay the emergency-room bill. I will clean up here."

Benny picked up a bottle of mineral spirits off the bench and unscrewed the top. He took some in his mouth, swished it around, and spit it out. "Yuck!" he said.

"Man, that's poison. Don't you see the label?" I asked.

"No telling what disease that guy might have had. It won't kill me if I don't swallow it," he said. He stepped outside and I heard the water tap running, and the sound of him spitting repeatedly. Then he came back inside.

"Man, this hurts!" EJ said. I ran my fingertips over the side of his face. "Busted orbit bone, maybe. I'll bring you some Tylenol 3. Do you have a problem with codeine? Try not to move. And don't talk," I said.

"Top?"

"Don't talk, EJ."

"Top, don't you think you forgetting something?" He held up his hands and showed us the handcuffs. I looked at him, then Benny, and we just started laughing, the three of us standing there, Benny and me barefoot in a pool of Sid's spreading blood. And we laughed, EJ wincing every time he smiled.

CHAPTER 55

I PACKED EJ AND BENNY OFF TO ATLANTA IN DANNY'S DIRTY brown Oldsmobile. Then I spread a bag of Oil-Dri around the shed to soak up the blood. I wrapped the bodies in heavy clear plastic and used a few wraps of duct tape to close the makeshift shrouds and stuffed the two bodies under the bench, throwing an old blanket over them.

I considered dumping the bodies along I-85 in Gwinnett County, where all the mob hits end up, but decided that the weapons involved, a bike wrench and a razor, might send too obvious a message. Instead, I decided to retrieve the bodies after nightfall and bury them under the floor in the basement of the school. Next week, we would burn the shed, tear up the concrete pad, and begin building a new workshop in its place. That done, I went inside and took a long shower, scrubbing my fingernails viciously.

I planned to fill the emptiness with good whiskey and spend the evening spinning tops and thinking about the people who had died in the last week, and what Soames would have to say about that and my inability to keep situations contained. But I didn't get to ponder very long.

Gillie and George showed up about dusk. She wore jeans and a thin sweater made of subtle olive and brown yarn. George wore a green Dickies work shirt and pants. I'd just opened a bottle of Jameson, with the full intention of drinking it. I offered the bottle to both of them and Gillie shook her head. They sat nervously on the edges of the two chairs in front of the desk. I sat on the floor with my back against the shelves, polishing my tops.

"You OK?" she asked.

"Fine. Dice will start moving the stuff back tomorrow. I put out an E-mail telling everyone to come back here day after," I said.

"I know," she said. "Are you sure it's safe?"

"Sure. Menes died in a shoot-out in north Georgia. It was on one of the news channels earlier," I answered. I picked up the remote and started flicking channels, but couldn't find anything.

"Great," she said. "It will be good to get back." Then, "Hey Top, you mind if I show George the auditorium? He hasn't seen it since we started on the ceiling."

"Nope, go ahead," I said, and then, as she and George jumped to their feet and scuttled to the door, "But it's not there."

"What?" she said disbelievingly.

"The laundry bag with one and a half mil that you had Dee Lane stuff in the ceiling, it's not there."

"I don't know what you mean." She sounded confused.

"OK, show George the auditorium."

She looked perplexed. George gave her away, though. He blushed deep red, right down to his balding, sandy-haired pate. She squinted back at me, her jaw working furiously. "Where is it, then?" Anger twisted her words into wire.

"By now, most of it is on a plane to the UK, where Shaw's is going to launder it and hand it out to various charities that work on schizophrenia. Probably make a large, anonymous donation to the Home," I said.

"You goddamned idiot! Do you have any idea what you've done?"

"Well, I didn't get Harlan killed. You did that."

"Oh, stop! Harlan was an unfortunate accident. We're not talking about Harlan, we're talking about a million dollars. Do you have any idea how hard it is to make ends meet these days? To get teeth straightened? To get the kids out of those public schools and into academies where they can get a real education?" she spat. "You goddamned loser!"

"To buy designer sweaters and tailored suits, and lattes all round," I said.

"Just because you don't want anything out of life except this dump doesn't mean the rest of us will settle for that, Top."

"You got a guy killed, Gillie—don't you get it?"

She shook her head violently. "No. Hell, no. I'll contact Shaw's, tell them to send it back or I'll expose them. I'll blow the whistle!" she snapped.

I put down my glass and stood up. "Gillie, please. I'm begging you now, please don't mess with Shaw's."

She stood and stared and stared at me for another moment, then bit her lip and stamped her foot. "Unnhhh," she grunted and looked upward. Tears began to well in her eyes, then to cascade down her face. George tried to drape his arm around her shoulders. She shook it off and he perched awkwardly behind her, arm raised.

"How long have you been playing me?"

"Not long. Only since I figured out that Dee Lane really *did* drop off the bag and I found the discrepancy in the phone logs. And of course it all makes sense now. This whole week has been like one of those stupid English plays where everyone's always in the wrong room at the wrong time. You and George wanted to retrieve the bag, but you couldn't get to it because someone was here all the time. We go to Atlanta, leave the place empty, and you come out and find Bob John and half the police in the state here. You come out Sunday, but you get here and find Bud debugging the place. And when was it, Tuesday? Maggie calls you and tells you I just showed up at the incubator, so you two have to turn around and race back. You've hidden a mil and a half and can't even get to it."

"That's enough," She reached in her purse, pulled out a small blue .32 automatic and handed it to George. He pointed it at me amateurishly.

"It's too late for that," I said. "The money's gone."

"Let's go outside, Top," Gillie said.

I laughed at her. "Well, George, for her plan to work, one of us had to buy it. I mean, Dee Lane knew he left the money, so unless she could claim somebody else stole it, he'd look for her to settle up. She had to figure he'd be back sooner or later."

"Shut up, smart-ass!" she said.

George stood up and pushed the gun at me clumsily. "You heard her, Top, get up or I'm going to use this." I didn't move. "I mean it," he said. "I'll shoot you."

"You should be shooting *her*. Did she tell you she's been sleeping with me, George? Talked about our future together? Want me to prove I'm telling the truth, tell you where her moles are? I don't want to be cruel here, buddy, but you're getting set up."

His jaw dropped open and he turned to stare at Gillie. Her head shook from side to side. "Gillie?" he said.

"George, the money is gone. All shooting me will do is leave your kids getting picked on at recess because their daddy's in Reidsville. It's over, man, it's over. Shooting me doesn't get you anything. Come on, think about it."

He raised the gun and tried to level it at me. His hand shook like the rattle on a snake.

"You ever killed a man, George?" I asked. "Even when you're used to it, it tears you up inside. Makes you sick."

"I can't do this, Gillie," he said finally. "I can't do it." He laid the gun carefully on one corner of my desk. Gillie stared at it, but didn't pick it up.

"Here," I said. I pulled a package from my back pocket and tossed her two hundred bills held together with a rubber band. She grabbed it. "There's twenty grand."

"What's this?"

"Severance."

She looked at me with narrowed eyes, waving the money to emphasize her words. "I'm going to use it to set up my own Poly-math. Clients like Kenzie Hamlin will come with me in a shot, you jerk. I'll run you two into the ground." She stuffed the money in her purse and whirled. "Come on, George!" He hesitated as if to say something, then turned and followed her out.

CHAPTER 56

BENNY LOOKED AT ME. "ARE YOU ALRIGHT?"

"Why do people keep asking me that?" I answered.

"It just seems appropriate a lot of the time," he said.

"No, I'm not OK. But I'll be OK."

"Do you want to shoot some hoops?" he said, changing the subject.

"Sure," I said.

"I'll meet you there in about fifteen minutes or so," he replied.

In the gym, we didn't say much, just shot and chased. At eight or so, Amanda came in. She walked across the floor in her low heels, and I saw tiny scuff marks on the shellac. She saw me staring, looked down, and quickly kicked off the shoes.

"Hi, fellows," she said.

Benny tossed her the ball. She put up a push shot that rolled around the rim and fell off.

"You're drunk," she said to me.

"Gently," I replied.

"I should be gentle because you're drunk?"

"No, I'm *gently* drunk. Not real drunk, but not hardly drunk, either. Just gently."

"I called her. I thought she might drive you to Atlanta to see Bob John. You're drunk and I can't drive you because some of the guys are coming over to practice." Benny said.

"Gently," she emphasized and looked at Benny.

"Gently," he confirmed.

"Come on, I'll drive you," she said.

"Promise not to smoke?" I asked.

"Absolutely not. It's my car."

"We'll take my truck," I said.

"Not if I can't smoke, we won't. Is that what this relationship is going to be like? Nagger, nagger, nagger?"

"I'll see you both later," Benny said and left.

"He left because you used the R word. Say, if we have a relationship, you want to go to bed now?" I motioned toward my bed, which sat at the other end of the court, tucked romantically against the Nautilus machine.

"Come on, let's go see Bob John. Now's not the time to make love."

"This time, like all times, is a great time if we but know what to do with it," I quoted.

"You're trying to talk me into the sack using Ralph Waldo Emerson?" she said, mildly incredulous. "Haven't you ever read any Browning?"

"I'm serious," I said.

"Guys always are. Pathetic, but serious."

"You didn't answer my question." I said.

"Maybe. I'll think about it on the trip." She turned and walked out.

I picked up my bottle of Jameson's and followed, one eye on her tight jeans and the other on the scuff marks. Tomorrow we'd need to get the floor buffer in here.

ACKNOWLEDGMENTS AND DISCLAIMERS

A friend of mine once stopped in a truck stop in Oklahoma where the only other patrons in the restaurant were a kid playing a guitar and a table of longhairs seated near the tiny stage. When the guitarist took a break and left the stage, one of the longhairs from the front walked back to the table where George and his friends were sitting. They looked up to see Willie Nelson, who said, *"I do wish ya'll would clap for that boy. You have no idea how soul-destroying it can be to be up there all alone."* Writing a book can be, at various times, a lonely, soul-destroying process.

My thanks to those people who helped make it less lonely, and who have helped make the final result better. Bill Loughner helped with the research for this book, as he has for my nonfiction work. His contributions range from finding out whether rattlesnakes have ears to helping me pace off the distance from Groovology to the Home. Michael and Michele Hill read very early drafts of this book and made valuable comments. Phil Grant, an old friend and a professional bookseller who specializes in first-edition mysteries, read both an early draft and the final. His comments were absolutely invaluable, and in particular his thoughtful questions shaped Benny's character and the relationship between him and Top. Editor Nanscy Neiman-Legette helped me with the pacing, structure, and character development. Christopher Ainsley critiqued a later draft. My wife Liz Upsall patiently read and critiqued uncounted rewrites.

Thanks to my superagent Philip Spitzer, and my publisher Otto Penzler for their help with this particular book, and to Philip for his sustained encouragement and support over the years.

In that same vein, let me offer a more general thanks. Barbara Martz, Russ Roberts, Joel Kurtzman, Steve Silver, Christine Fratturo, Ken Lambert, Helen Rees, and Brian Fischer all clapped for me at the right time, and I do appreciate it.

Finally, let me say that this book is a work of fiction. Except for Cool Papa Bell, none of the characters in the book exist. To the best of my knowledge, Mr. Bell had no illegitimate children. Athens, Winterville, Between, and Decatur are real places, but none of the people or businesses I have placed there are real. Arlene, the school, Shaw's Mercantile, Groovology, Stricklin's, the Busy Bee, Polymath, and Danny's exist only in our collective consciousness.

About the Author

Sam Hill has been a partner in a consulting firm and vice-chairman of one of the world's largest advertising agencies. He has written several nonfiction books, and his work has appeared in the *Wall Street Journal*, the *Los Angeles Times*, the *Financial Times, Fortune*, and the *Harvard Business Review*. He lives just outside Chicago.

Hill, Sam, 1953-
Buzz monkey.

$24.00

DATE			